Heartache. Betrayal. Forgi
to head back to Magdalena, 1
time with the people we love tc
to hate.

Gina Servetti was raised to believe she wasn't enough—not thin enough, not pretty enough, not clever enough. She's more comfortable with a spreadsheet than a conversation and doesn't trust easily, especially where men are concerned, most notably the good-looking, smooth-talking ones like Ben Reed.

When city boy Ben Reed arrives in Magdalena, he's not planning a long-term stay in a town filled with too many busybodies and too little excitement. He just needs things to settle down in Philly for a few months before he returns to his old life and his plan to win back his ex-wife. But once he gets to know the people in this town, he starts to care about them: one in particular—Gina Servetti. The longer he's around her, the more he realizes she's so much more than a woman with a scowl and a sharp tongue. She's real and honest, and as afraid of trusting as he is.

But can Ben and Gina open up and take a risk for a chance at real love? Well, if the rest of the town has anything to say about it, and they always do, this couple will take the big leap and end with an "I do"!

And would the story be complete without checking in on Harry Blacksworth's latest debacle...ahem...adventure? Harry's moved his brood to Magdalena and is taking advice but, thankfully, not fashion lessons from Pop Benito. That spells trouble on so many levels. Oh, but it's going to be interesting...

Join me as we peek into the lives of some of our favorites: Pop Benito, Lily, Nate and Christine Desantro, Harry and Greta Blacksworth, Mimi Pendergrass, Bree

Kinkaid...and many more.
See you in Magdalena!

Truth in Lies Series:
Book One: *A Family Affair*
Book Two: *A Family Affair: Spring*
Book Three: *A Family Affair: Summer*
Book Four: *A Family Affair: Fall*
Book Five: *A Family Affair: Christmas* (Nov 2014)
Book Six: *A Family Affair: Winter* (April 2015)
Book Seven: *A Family Affair:* ... (TBA)

NEW FEATURE: Magdalena's growing! People are getting married, having babies, and moving back to town, so I've decided to include a list of characters and their backgrounds—some new faces, some from previous books. You'll find *Who's Who in A Family Affair: Fall* located right after the dedication.

Print ISBN: 978-1-942158-10-3

A Family Affair: Fall

Truth in Lies, Book Four

by
Mary Campisi

Dedication:

To friends—that word for rare and precious people who
care about one another
Who cry together
Laugh together
Dream together
You live in my heart
Thank you, my friends!

Who's Who in A Family Affair: Fall

Ben Reed: *Policeman from Philadelphia, partnered with Cash, best man at Cash's wedding*
Naomi Reed: *Ben Reed's grandmother*
Paige Reed: *Ben Reed's cousin, lives in Philly, "dated" Cash, is a dancer*
Melissa Reed: *Ben Reed's ex-wife*
Kenneth Stone: *Assistant District Attorney in Philadelphia, fiancé to Melissa*

Gina Servetti: *Physical therapist, no-nonsense friend of Tess, Bree, and Christine, has weight and trust issues*
Natalie Servetti: *Magdalena's "sleep-around" woman, and Gina's cousin*
Carmen & Marie Servetti: *Gina's parents; they believe good looks trump intelligence and integrity*

Daniel "Cash" Casherdon: *Former policeman, married to Tess, works with Nate in furniture business and has camp with wife to help troubled kids*
Tess Casherdon: *Married to her true love, Cash, after years of separation due to tragedy. (He shot her kid brother while on duty.) Might not be able to have children; dog named Henry*
Ramona Casherdon: *Cash's aunt, raised him since he was eight, keeps to herself*
Will Carrick: *Former police chief, widower, uncle to Tess, mentor to Cash, in love with Olivia Carrick, his sister-in-law*
Olivia Carrick: *Widow, mother of Tess, lost son in*

shooting incident that tore Tess and Cash apart, hasn't seen oldest daughter in years, in love with Will Carrick, her brother-in-law

Nate Desantro: *Married to Christine Blacksworth, brother to Lily and son of Miriam. Runs ND Manufacturing, and has a furniture building business with Cash, stands for strength and principle.*

Christine Desantro: *Charles and Gloria Blacksworth's daughter, married to Nate Desantro, is a financial advisor, has daughter, Anna,*

Lily Desantro: *Daughter to Charles Blacksworth and Miriam Desantro, half-sister to Nate and Christine, has Down syndrome, is the "light" of Magdalena*

Miriam Desantro: *Charles Blacksworth's mistress, Nate and Lily's mother, artist/woodworker*

Jack Finnegan: *Plant manager at ND Manufacturing, works for Nate, worked for Nate's father*

Harry Blacksworth: *Former playboy turned husband and father, married to Greta, has two stepchildren and a baby (Jackson), he's Charles's brother and Christine's uncle (or is he?)*

Greta (Servensen) Blacksworth: *Married to Harry, former cook for Charles and Gloria Blacksworth, has three children*

AJ & Lizzy Servensen: *Greta's children, Harry's stepchildren*

Gloria Blacksworth: *Deceased widow of Charles Blacksworth, mother of Christine, and a woman bent on destroying her husband's "other" family...one way or another*

Pop Benito: *The Godfather of Magdalena, member of The Bleeding Hearts Society, town matchmaker, dispenser of wisdom and common sense; superb pizzelle maker*

Anthony Benito: *Pop and the late Lucy Benito's son, lives in California, has a daughter, Lucy*

Mimi Pendergrass: *Mayor of Magdalena, President of The Bleeding Hearts Society, proprietor of Heart Sent Bed and Breakfast, widow, lost a son, Paul and is estranged from daughter*

Bree Kinkaid: *Married to Brody, friends with Tess, Gina, and Christine. Lifelong goal is to be a wife and mother*

Brody Kinkaid: *Married to Bree, works for Bree's dad, more brawn than brains, on a mission to increase his "brood" and have a son*

Rex & Kathleen MacGregor: *Bree's parents, Rex owns MacGregor's Cabinets*

Rudy Dean: *Police Chief of Magdalena, father to Jeremy*

Jeremy Ross Dean: *Junior policeman in Magdalena*

Mrs. Olsteroff: *Dispatcher for police department, has dog named Marjorie*

Chapter 1

Ben Reed had spent most of his thirty-five years beating the odds. He'd never met his father, never even known the man's name, or if there was a definite name, or merely a list of possibilities. Despite a rough start, he'd found his path to the military, college, and later the Philly police force with the guidance, prayers, and help of the one person who had never given up on him—his grandmother.

But Naomi Reed was long gone and if Ben had any chance of beating the odds stacked on his chest right now, then he was in serious need of guidance, prayers, *and* help, not in any specific order.

"Kenneth has threatened to press charges."

The words squeezed his gut, made him wish he could rewind the last five years. Did every guy whose ex-wife was on the verge of getting remarried feel this way, or only the ones whose ex had a baby growing in her belly that wasn't his? *Damn.* He settled his gaze on Melissa's face, careful to avoid the evidence of another man's handiwork bulging beneath the maroon top she wore. That baby could have been his and—

"Ben? Did you hear me?" She sat on the tweed couch next to him, touched his forearm.

"I heard you." But hearing and understanding weren't the same. And accepting, well, that was a helluva different matter altogether.

"You think there's such a thing as a hospital interior designer?" He ran a hand along the back of the nubby fabric, zeroing in on the flecks of black amidst the rust pattern. If he stared hard enough, he could almost block out visions of Melissa and another man's baby. "I've spent a lot of time in hospital waiting rooms and damn, but the furniture all looks the same. Feels the same, too. And the pictures—"

"Stop it."

He glanced up, noticed the way her dark eyes narrowed in that "I'm really annoyed with you" look. "What? I was commenting on hospital couches and paintings. What's the harm in that?"

More eye narrowing, right down to a semi-slit. "Can you for once in your life deal with the real issue, head-on, instead of avoiding it?"

His gaze slipped to her belly, darted back to her face. He should have broken Kenneth's jaw instead of his nose. See if the jerk could make any more snide comments about how much he planned to enjoy Melissa's body. "I'm not avoiding anything. I told you, your boyfriend was talking trash about you and I wasn't going to let him get away with it." He paused, let the words sink in. "I had to defend your honor."

"Defend my honor? You broke his nose and gave him a black eye, and for what? Because he told you to stay away and start your own life?"

That damn liar. "That's not what he said and he knows it."

She blew out a breath and those pink lips he'd once known so well flattened. "Kenneth is in the emergency room right now because you still can't accept the fact that I'm going to marry him."

"The guy's a jerk."

"You think so?" She leaned toward him, eyes glittering, jaw tense. "I think the guy who won't talk about the pain of his past—the mother who left him, the father he never knew—that's the guy who's a jerk. He pretends it doesn't

2

matter, like life is one great big party and he's the host. No matter how hard the wife tries to break through the barrier, he won't let her in." Her voice dipped. "Until one day, she stops trying."

She was talking about him, about them. "I've changed." He clasped her hand, squeezed. "I'm a regular touchy-feely guy these days. I can share anything, just ask me."

Of course, that wasn't true and of course, she knew that, but he was desperate for one last chance to make things right.

His ex-wife eased her hand from his and stood, her expression more disappointed than annoyed. "You still don't get it, do you, Ben? I would have done anything for you. You were my life and all I wanted was the real Ben Reed, the one who was hurting inside, the one who needed to heal."

Why was she talking about him like he was a pathetic loser with personal issues? Just because he didn't want to puke out emotions that were buried deep inside did not mean he had issues. Or at least no more than any other guy. Especially guys who were cops.

"I get it." He forced his voice to remain even. It wouldn't do if she spotted *his* annoyance with the whole "You never opened up to me" spiel. "You want me to cry on your shoulder? Fine, I'll do it. I'll tell you what it feels like to know your mother didn't care enough about you to stick around and how you learned to make up elaborate tales about how your parents died rescuing you from a fire, or a capsized boat, or a would-be kidnapper, whatever the hell else signified unconditional love in the eyes of a kid. The bigger, the better, even though the other kids eventually figured out it was all a lie." He cleared his throat and continued, "I'll share it all if that's what you want."

"What I want is for you to accept that Kenneth and I are going to be married in two months and we're having a baby." She paused, gentled her words. "And you're not part of that. You're not part of anything in my life. Not anymore."

Those last words burned deeper and hotter than the bullet he'd taken in the thigh the first year on the force. Bad enough she was pregnant with Assistant District Attorney Asshole Kenneth Stone's baby and that she planned to marry him in sixty days or less, but to cut Ben out of her existence? He'd always believed he could win her back with time and hard work, maybe even a counseling session or two if she insisted. Apparently, he'd been wrong. "So now what? I just disappear and pretend we never knew each other?"

"You start over. Find someone and show her the real Ben Reed, because I guarantee he's someone she'll want to know. *But you have to move on,* and you have to do it now. Kenneth is in the emergency room getting treated for a broken nose and who knows what else? He will press charges," she paused, "unless…"

Oh, this would be good. The jerk wanted him to grovel at the foot of his throne and beg forgiveness for the punch in the nose and two in the gut. Right. Kenneth deserved a broken jaw for trash-talking Melissa. Why would somebody who supposedly loved her make a comment like that to the woman's ex-husband, unless the guy was a complete idiot? Stone might be arrogant, but he didn't lack intelligence. Actually, he was very clever and highly skilled, as evidenced in the string of court cases he'd won over the last several years. The guys on the force had dubbed him "Cagey Ken" for the way he used evidence and testimony to build a case…

The truth exploded in Ben's brain seconds before he jumped off the couch and towered over Melissa. "He set me up. Damn it, your boyfriend set me up."

"What are you talking about? Kenneth would never—"

"He *wanted* me to punch him and he knew exactly what to say to get me to do it."

Melissa shook her head and sighed, as though his assumption were impossible. "He's an honorable man and has been more than patient with you and your unhealthy obsession with me."

That pissed him off. "Unhealthy obsession? Because I care about what happens to you?"

Those dark eyes glittered with something close to disgust. "And why do you care so much, Ben? Why now when it's too late, or does the fact that I'm not yours anymore make me more appealing?" Her lips curled. "Kenneth didn't even want me talking with you. He said you'd be unreasonable, but I promised him you'd listen."

So they'd talked about him and how he should be handled? Now, he was really pissed. "And what was the message he wanted you to deliver? Apologize? Apologize and beg forgiveness? Or apologize—"

"Resign and leave town or he'll press charges." She didn't give him time to absorb the blow before she delivered a second, more deadly than the first. "You have seven days to leave Philly or he'll make it his personal mission to see you never carry a badge again."

***

"So Ben Reed just woke up one day and said, 'Screw city life, screw my job, I'm outta here? My heart belongs in Magdalena?'"

Cash looked up from the tabletop he'd been sanding and shrugged. "He put a little more polish on it than you just

5

did, but yeah, pretty much."

Nate ran a hand along the smoothness of the walnut tabletop. In the time they'd been working together, Cash had brought a luster and richness to Nate's work that, along with Tess's marketing abilities, had escalated the demand and the price of the furniture he made. Cash's return to Magdalena was a good idea and one the town had secretly hoped to see one day. But Ben Reed, a city boy hotshot who didn't know the difference between hardwood and particle board and definitely didn't appear enamored with small-town ways and attitudes, coming to Magdalena? It didn't add up. Yet. "Don't you think that's a bit odd?"

Cash lifted four unfinished table legs from the cart behind him and set them on the workstation. "It's strange, but Ben's like that. I didn't even know he was getting married until three weeks before the wedding, and I was his partner." Cash eyed Nate and said, "He's not big on sharing, kind of like somebody else I know."

Nate scowled and tossed him a rag. "I share." Pause. "With my wife."

"Well, Ben didn't share with anybody and that cost him his marriage. He had a screwed-up childhood. I only know bits and pieces of it from Paige."

Ah, Paige, the ex-girlfriend who wasn't a girlfriend. "Don't mention that around your wife. I don't think she'll want to hear that."

A dull red spread from Cash's neck to his cheeks. "Yeah, she won't hear it from me." He rubbed the rag over a table leg and said, "Anyway, I hadn't heard from him in over two months, then last week he called to tell me he'd turned in his badge, sublet his condo, and was thinking about heading to Magdalena. Even asked if we had something for him to do, or maybe if I thought he could join the crew doing the finishing work on Harry Blacksworth's house."

Nate shook his head and thought of the wood and stone structure spreading over three lots on the far side of town. "Does everybody on the East Coast know about the 'Mansion in Magdalena'?"

"When it's got eight bedrooms, ten bathrooms, a sauna, and a theater room? Yeah, I'd say probably so."

"Harry won't think all those extras were such a great idea when half the town lines up to try them out. Lily's been pestering him for weeks to get the pool finished." Nate sighed and recalled his sister's obsession with her uncle's pool and her insistence that the garden hose and a few good rains would fill it up. Lily always had a plan for any situation, usually involving people and relationships. Thankfully, this situation really was only about a structure and a hole in the ground.

"Something tells me Harry Blacksworth would hire a few lifeguards and a caterer or two and open his doors to anybody who showed up at his gate."

"Hmm. Maybe your buddy could be a lifeguard."

Cash laughed at that. "As much as the female population in this town would love it, I think he'll be busy filling the sergeant's position until Bud returns."

"You really think this is a good idea?" Nate still had his doubts. Cash had just admitted that while he and Ben were partners, there was a lot he didn't know about the man. And since his accident and return to Magdalena, Cash knew even less.

"Bud has another two months of rehab, if he doesn't have another complication or decide to retire. Why the guy thought he could bale hay and stack it with a bum knee and an extra twenty-five pounds around his middle is beyond me."

"Did anybody tell Ben about Chief Hard-ass?"

Cash shrugged and rubbed away at the edge of the table leg. "Rudy Dean might settle down once Ben gets to town. The man's never had the opportunity to work with real police before and this could change his whole attitude."

"You're kidding, right? Rudy never would have gotten that job if you hadn't left town." He paused, added, "And it didn't hurt that he married Mimi Pendergrass's niece."

"Yeah, well, Ben's a big boy. He'll figure it out."

"Oh, I can't wait to see Chief Hard-ass and Mr. Handsome go at it."

"Ben's a good guy. Very loyal."

"Sounds like your dog."

Cash ignored him, plowed on. "I think we were lucky to snatch Ben up before he changed his mind about city life."

That's what didn't sit well with Nate. Ben Reed hadn't acted like he wanted to hang out in Magdalena a half second longer than necessary. Not that several of the town's female population wouldn't welcome an opportunity to change his mind. They'd lined up and practically shoved each other out of the way in an attempt to dance with Cash's old partner. And when the slow dances started, well, that almost caused a stampede, but Ben stopped it when he took Gina Servetti's hand and forced her onto the dance floor. Not kicking and screaming, but certainly stalling and scowling. By the third slow dance, Gina had disappeared. "Wonder what Gina has to say about her dance partner coming to town?"

"Don't know but Tess isn't telling her; neither is Bree. They don't want her to start on another tirade of Ben Reed's invasion of her personal space. Damn, but she went on for weeks." Cash leaned over and inspected his work.

"Guess that leaves Christine, unless Pop gets a jump on the news and spills it at the garden club meeting."

"Hmm. Bet Pop beats Christine to it. The man loves a good drama." Nate shrugged and said, "Let's just be glad we're not part of the drama this time."

Nate was still thinking about drama and Ben Reed an hour later when he pulled into Gina Servetti's driveway. She lived on the north end of town in a white bungalow tucked among other bungalows and Cape Cods. Black shutters, red door, a giant oak, and a front yard that could be mowed in six swipes, maybe five depending on the sweep of the turn. Nice. Neat. Organized à la Gina Servetti style.

And then there were her flowers. Random. Vibrant. Explosive. Beds of them, popping with color and scent, a clump here, a cluster there, boasting a more expansive variety than The Bleeding Hearts Society's cumulative gardens. There were so many flowers Nate didn't know what to look at first. Lily did, though. She hopped out of the SUV and ran toward a tall, fluffy looking purple flower.

"Look, Nate! This is the one the little birds with the fast wings fly to sometimes. And the bees like it, too." She looked over her shoulder and smiled at him. "Gina said if we sit still and watch, we can learn all kinds of things."

That comment held true for a lot more than flower gardens. Nate eased out of the SUV and made his way toward his sister. "Let's see if Gina's ready for you."

"Gina said we're going to pick our flowers very carefully, and then we're going to lay them on a big piece of cardboard. And then, we'll put them in the flower press and if we run out of room, we'll use the big catalogs and put them between the pages."

"Right. In case you pick five hundred flowers and the

flower press is too small." He squeezed her hand and leaned forward to whisper, "Or maybe you'll pick six hundred and poor Gina won't have any flowers left." They'd been hearing about the special flower-pressing event for three days. Between that and Harry's waterless pool, Lily had filled up most of the conversations she'd had with their mother, Christine, Pop...pretty much half the town.

Lily rang the doorbell and glanced at Nate. He still didn't understand his sister's intrigue with Gina Servetti. It's not like the woman was the touchy-feely type who offered homemade cookies in boxes tied with bright ribbons like Bree Kinkaid did. As far as Nate knew, Gina didn't cook, unless it had to do with a microwave or a reheat setting. Christine said Lily's sudden interest in Gina had to do with the pressed-flower picture she delivered a few weeks ago. When Lily spotted it on the mantel next to Anna's Christmas photo, she'd made a beeline toward it, leaned so close her nose almost touched the glass of the frame, and said she wanted to make flower pictures, too.

And now here they were, waiting for Lily's teacher to open the door and begin instructing.

"Hi, Lily." They turned to find Gina walking toward them from the side of the house. She looked more relaxed than usual, but maybe it was the jeans and T-shirt, or the pink gloves and red clogs. Those last two were an interesting combination for a woman he'd never seen in anything brighter than navy, with the exception of the bridesmaid gown she'd worn at Tess's wedding last year. Gina nodded at Nate and said, "How about I drop her off in a few hours at your mom's?"

"Sure."

Lily ran down the steps and gave her a quick hug.

"We're going to pick flowers and make pictures, like artists, aren't we?"

Gina Servetti looked about as comfortable with that hug as a vegetarian at a pig roast. She met Lily's gaze and said, "We'll pick the flowers today but we have to dry them before we can glue them onto paper or they'll ruin, remember?"

"Uh-huh." Lily eased her hold on Gina and stepped back. "We have to suck the water out of the flowers so they don't lose their color. If we don't, they get all rotten and brown." She scrunched her nose and made a face. "And very wrinkly and ugly and nobody will want them." She giggled. "We'll make our pictures beautiful because everybody wants a beautiful picture, right?"

Something in Lily's words bleached out the tan on Gina's face. What was it? Nate replayed the last few seconds, stopped when he got to the "beautiful" part, which was when the color eked out of her face. Christine told him Gina had a lot of issues with her looks and he'd bet that last comment had gotten to her. So the woman wasn't a toothpick or a beauty queen? Who cared? Then again, the Servetti clan prided themselves on appearances first, intelligence and integrity second, or maybe tenth. Gina's cousin, Natalie, certainly hadn't been interested in integrity or anything other than trapping a man with her good looks and sensuality. She'd tried to trap him and when she'd failed, she'd joined up with Gloria Blacksworth in a blackmail attempt to destroy Nate's marriage. If he never heard the Servetti name again, it would be too soon. Gina was the exception because she didn't fit into the family "screw you" mold.

And that had caused her years of misery and mockery—from her own family. He guessed it would be a nightmare to possess an overabundance of intelligence and integrity in a family like that. Kind of like being orphaned by your parents because you had the wrong hair color.

"Bye, Nate. See you later." Lily waved at him, her pink-sneakered feet fidgeting her impatience for him to leave.

He hesitated, glanced at Gina. "Are you sure this isn't too much for you?" Christine had assured him that Gina had a soft side even if she didn't show it often. And she must possess a fair amount of patience or she wouldn't be a physical therapist. And hadn't she worked with Cash when he first got back to Magdalena and refused to act like a human being? And—

"We'll be fine, Nate." Gina actually gentled her usually serious tone. "I appreciate the vote of confidence."

Was that sarcasm or sincerity? That was the thing about Gina Servetti; you just never knew. Maybe that's why he'd never seen her with a guy, never even heard about a guy. They wouldn't like the uncertainty and guesswork involved in the mating ritual, especially early on in the game. They'd pass her up for someone more transparent. Like her cousin. With Natalie, everything was on display and for sale, from the tight shirts and painted-on jeans to the short skirts and backless tops. But Natalie was more short-term parking than an extended stay, and no matter how hard she tried to entice her men to hang around, it wasn't happening. His right temple pinched just thinking about the grief that woman had caused him. Once Ben Reed hit town, he'd be fresh meat and Natalie would be on the hunt. Somebody better warn the guy, but that somebody wasn't going to be him. This husband knew the scent of danger, even if it presented in the form of stilettos, cleavage, and a killer smile. Maybe a woman should warn Ben Reed. He hopped in his SUV and glanced at the lawn where Gina and Lily stood. And maybe Gina Servetti was that woman.

Chapter 2

Lily Blacksworth might possess childlike innocence and naïve curiosity, but the girl saw things others didn't, maybe because they weren't looking or maybe because they simply weren't interested. Lily was looking *and* interested, which made a lethal combination for someone like Gina who preferred to remain in the background with her own thoughts and opinions.

But Lily seemed intent on dragging Gina into the open with observations and questions even Tess, Christine, and Bree didn't dare mention. Like why wasn't Gina married and did she have a boyfriend. And if that wasn't horrible enough, she wanted to know why Gina only wore "sad" colors instead of "happy" ones, like orange, yellow, and purple.

What on earth to say to that? They'd been working in the backyard for over an hour. Gina identified each flower, helped Lily snip the blooms and place them on a large piece of cardboard covered with paper towel. There were pansies, cosmos, dahlias, bee balm, and alyssum, in purple, pink, fuchsia, and yellow. Roses, butterfly bush, black-eyed Susans, and phlox. When the cardboard was full, they placed it on the deck and transferred the flowers to the flower press Christine had given her for her birthday, compliments of her husband's woodworking skills. Old department store catalogs had served as presses long after their listings had grown outdated, and Gina still relied on stacks of the two-inch books when she encountered a season with an overabundance of blooms.

They'd placed three layers of flowers in the press and

started on the fourth as Lily chatted on about the velvety softness of a rose petal that reminded her of her niece's skin after a warm bath, and the lavender phlox that was the same color as her Sunday shirt. She was full of stories and observations and as long as she kept her inquisitiveness aimed at the task, Gina could almost relax. But she should have known Lily would expand her questions before the afternoon was over, and those questions would include Gina.

"You should get a dog."

Gina looked up from the white alyssum she held. "A dog?" *A dog?*

"Yup." Lily stretched out on the deck and leaned back on her elbows. "A black one." She flashed a smile and added, "Or maybe spotted."

Gina placed the alyssum on the cardboard, careful not to touch the other flowers, and clamped the press shut. Something was going on in Lily's head and it was about more than a black or spotted dog. The real question was, did Gina want to know what that "something" was? Absolutely not, but it didn't matter because in the short period of time she'd spent with Lily, she'd learned the child said what was on her mind. So, she took a deep breath and asked, "Why do I need a dog?"

The smile grew, split open until Lily said with great matter-of-factness, "Because you don't have a boyfriend."

"How do you know I don't have a boyfriend?" Okay, she didn't have a boyfriend, hadn't had one in years, eleven to be exact, but how did Lily know that?

Lily reached for the glass of lemonade Gina had fixed for her, sipped through the pink straw, and set it aside. "Pop said you don't."

"Pop Benito?" Why was he discussing her love life with

Lily? And who else had he told? Was he blabbering about it at The Bleeding Hearts Society meetings? She'd missed the last two meetings…maybe that's when Pop tossed in the boyfriend comment. But wouldn't Bree have told her? Gina couldn't say for sure because Bree's response often depended on the state of her hormonal level and her pregnant versus nonpregnant state. Of course, after what happened to her four months ago, it was hard to tell.

Lily took another sip of lemonade and studied Gina. "He said if you can't get a boyfriend, you should get a dog because they'll keep you warm and keep you company." She giggled. "And they don't leave their socks and underwear around the house." Another giggle. "Dogs don't wear socks and underwear."

Wait until she saw Pop again. She knew his game, knew he was aware Lily was coming to visit her and would eventually share what he'd told her. Exactly as he planned it. This all had to do with what happened at Tess and Cash's wedding and that fake sprained ankle stint he tried to pull so she'd dance with Ben Reed. She should have reminded him she'd seen her share of sprained ankles in her line of work and his wasn't one of them. But she'd opted for politeness and, truthfully, she'd been so flustered when Ben Reed pulled her into his arms that she couldn't formulate a response. And that had bothered her as much as it annoyed her. Of course, Ben Reed hadn't been similarly affected; he had enough alcohol and arrogance in him that night to carry on a conversation while clutching her against him. Way too close. The memory was not a welcome or pleasant one.

"So, are you going to get a dog?"

"No. I am not going to get a dog." *Or a boyfriend.* She grabbed her lemonade and took a healthy swallow. "And

I'll have a thought of two for Pop on that subject."

"He says he thinks you're going to end up with a dog and a boyfriend." Lily tilted her head to the side as if considering this. "What kind of dog will you get?" Before Gina had a chance to tell her there would be no two or four-legged creatures walking into her life, the child pushed on with the imagination of a great fiction writer. "How about a beagle? They have a funny bark. Mr. Finnegan has two and he says they can sniff out a lie while it's still in the person's mouth." She scratched her jaw, her eyes bright behind her glasses. "I want a beagle but Nate says you don't get a dog for the tricks other people say he can do. And he says lies can sneak past anybody if they look enough like the truth." She frowned and glanced at Gina. "You think that's true?"

Nate Desantro might not put a lot of polish on his words but he knew what he was talking about. "Your brother's right." She'd once believed lies that slid past her defenses with the smoothness of a milk chocolate truffle. Honest. Sincere. Heartfelt. And they had been none of those. By the time she realized the truth in the lie, it was much too late. She'd lost her confidence, her self-esteem, her belief that a man would want her for herself. The only way to get past the destruction of the betrayal had been to avoid relationships with men. And while there were pockets of loneliness and "what ifs," they were bearable as long as she remembered the lies she'd once believed and the pain they'd caused.

"Gina?" Lily's curiosity sifted past Gina's thoughts and pulled her back. "Pop says if you find the right man, he'll be more loyal than ten Labrador retrievers." She giggled. "Maybe you should find a boyfriend first and then you can both pick out a dog."

Maybe Gina should drop Lily at her mother's and head

straight to Pop Benito's where she'd set him straight on dogs, boyfriends, and why he should stay out of her personal life. Just because she'd asked him for suggestions on the best way to cultivate her soil did not mean she wanted his assistance cultivating a male-female relationship. It was one thing to rally the town to get Cash and Tess back together, and yes, Pop had been successful in his matchmaking ventures, so much so that people now dubbed him "The Matchmaker of Magdalena" as well as the "Godfather of Magdalena". But the man had no business intruding on her affairs and she planned to tell him that.

"What about Ben Reed?"

Ben Reed? She ignored the sharp twinge in her gut and said, "What about him?"

"He's moving to Magdalena." Lily sat up, a smile stretching across her face. "He could be your boyfriend."

Hardly. Even if she were remotely interested, which she wasn't, and even if she considered the man slightly intriguing, which she didn't, and even if she were willing to risk heartbreak again, which she definitely wasn't, it wouldn't matter. She bet Ben Reed dated women with long hair, skinny waists, and skinnier IQ's. The man was all about appearances and flash. Anybody could tell that from a two-second look and that's all Gina had needed: the tan, the muscles, the blue eyes and soft voice all shouted *player* and *dangerous*. The first time she saw him had been in Lina's Café, the afternoon he rode into town with his cousin, the "maybe" girlfriend Cash hadn't told Tess about. There'd been an arrogant sense of self-assurance in the man's voice and the way he held himself, as though he weren't used to being questioned. Well, they had questioned him and at the wedding, when he'd tried to make small talk with Gina, she'd shut him down so fast, those blue eyes sparked with what looked a lot like annoyance. Why did people ask things they really didn't care about? What did it matter where she'd gone to college or what she did for a living? It didn't and it was not his business and she was tired of being polite, so she'd done what she thought Tess, Christine, and even Bree might do in a similar situation. She'd made up a story, a good one, too, according to Cash who said his buddy wasn't pleased to learn the woman he'd been paired up with in the bridal party was not an aeronautical engineer with a patent pending but a physical therapist who worked in the local hospital.

The man really did need to learn the difference between a truth and a....nontruth. While Gina had never been one to read people or relationships, she'd bet her new rototiller that was the reason Ben Reed had clung to her during the dance at the wedding. Payback. A man like that would be able to read a woman's body language and he'd know she'd rather throw up than have him touch her—which was exactly why he pulled her against him, planted his hand at the small of her back, trailed his breath along her neck. And what he'd done when the music ended—the kiss—had reeked of payback. Only it hadn't tasted like payback for the four seconds (or had it been six?) when Ben Reed's lips moved over hers, firm and persuasive, coaxing her mouth open, eliciting a sigh from her that sounded an awful lot like desire, even to an unskilled woman like herself.

Remembering his boldness made her all jittery, and if she could relive that dance, she'd have kicked him in the knee, stomped on his foot, and made her escape. But he'd caught her off guard and she'd had no time to prepare. With a swarm of females after him, why would she think he'd zero in on her? Had she been part of a bet from her cousin, Gino? Kiss Gina and win a six-pack? Or maybe Pop Benito had offered a tray of pizzelles if the man could coax a dance from her? Whatever the reason, it wasn't a good one and she'd been relieved the next morning to hear he was gone.

She'd hoped that meant gone for good. As in permanently. Months had passed and there'd only been the occasional mention of his name, usually associated with danger. Ben was involved in a drug bust. Ben foiled a robbery attempt. Ben chased a car down the highway at 90 miles an hour. Ben tackled a guy who had a gun aimed at his girlfriend...Did the man do anything that didn't involve an adrenaline rush and danger? Like normal people in a normal life?

"Gina? So what about Ben? Don't you think he's cute?"

Cute? She tightened the clamp on the flower press, avoiding Lily's curious gaze. There was nothing cute about the man. The muscles, the eyes, the look he gave women? No, that would not be *cute*. Dangerous, that's what it was and that's what he was, too.

"I think he's reckless, Lily, and I think he likes danger."

"Oh." She wrinkled her nose and considered this. "But don't you think he's cute?"

This was where Lily Desantro was the dangerous one. She saw inside people to the places that made them uncomfortable and asked questions that made people's heads and hearts ache. The only protection from Lily's inquisitiveness was to sidestep the questions and try to distract her. The tactic wouldn't last long and might not work at all, but at least it would give Gina time to formulate an answer, even if it were bloated and noncommittal.

Gina leaned forward, met Lily's gaze, and said in a

quiet voice, "I think *you* think he's cute." When the child blushed, Gina smiled. "You do, don't you?"

"Kinda." Lily giggled. "He's like a hero in a movie. You know, big and strong and not afraid of anything. He breaks down doors to save the girl." She slid a smile Gina's way and added, "And you can be the girl."

***

When strangers rolled into a place like Magdalena, people noticed. The different license plates were giveaways but a person could ride a bicycle into town and be labeled a stranger. Most of the residents were familiar with one another through church, work, marriage, or blood. Those who weren't related by blood or bond were still recognizable by the very fact that they were what some called "antisocial". Take the owner of Rusty's Bed and Breakfast on the edge of town. Word had it he hadn't housed a guest in over three years, not since the night a raccoon ran through the guest's bedroom and hopped out the window. That was bad enough, but the sight of Rusty in his long johns, firing a shotgun and a string of cuss words at the departing animal, was too much for the out-of-towners. They packed up and left that night—in their pajamas!

There was no socializing or civilizing with Rusty Clemens, a bearded former logger who had yet to connect with soap and running water on a daily basis. Even so, the town accepted him as a bit off but still one of theirs. That belonging bred tolerance and loyalty. Now a stranger, no matter how appealing, was another animal altogether and one to be closely studied. When Ben Reed drove into Magdalena in his fancy black sports car and impressive police credentials, the young women stared a second too long, their breath hitched, eyes bright. The rest of town, the

21

ones not affected by flashy cars and handsome men, considered the story behind the man's sudden arrival a bit suspicious. Was the tale that he was tired of city life and longed for a small-town place fact or fiction? Time would indeed tell.

Mimi Pendergrass had more than a question or two on the subject but she preferred to observe the man and draw her own conclusions. And she'd have plenty of time to observe seeing as he'd taken a room at Heart Sent. *Indefinite*, is what he'd told her when she'd asked him his plans. That could mean anything from *None of your business* to *I'm making Magdalena my home*. One thing was quite clear: Ben Reed did not plan to expand on that statement. Well, that was fine because she'd never let a closed door stop her from entering before. Ben Reed was the kind of policeman this town needed: experienced, capable, determined, the perfect role model for the junior officers, namely Jeremy Dean, Rudy's son. After Will Carrick and Cash Casherdon vouched for Ben, Mimi did her own bit of persuading and talked Rudy into offering him the sergeant job while Bud Zeller recovered.

"Miss Pendergrass?" Ben Reed stood at the entrance of Heart Sent, a duffle in one hand and a small suitcase in the other. "Nice to see you again."

Oh, but he reminded her of her son, Paul. The chestnut hair, the blue eyes, the ready smile. The air of recklessness, the latter gleaned from the stories she'd heard of his professional and personal life. Again, like Paul. She mourned the boy still, even though he'd been dead longer than he'd been alive. Friends had tried to comfort her and cursed Elderberry Road, saying if it had been widened as the town had requested years ago, the accident might have been prevented. But Mimi knew the sad truth. There would have been another Elderberry Road, or if not that, some equally dangerous situation and Paul would have been right in the middle of it.

"Welcome, my boy." Mimi rushed toward him, arms outstretched, ball earrings jingling with each step. He dropped his bags and she pulled him into a big hug, then stepped back and gazed up at him. He was a good foot taller than she was, maybe more, with broad arms, a thick neck, and the bluest eyes. Like Paul's. "So, tell me, how was the trip?"

A smile slid across his tanned face. "Great. Perfect day." He glanced outside. "Hard to believe I'm here."

Had she detected a hint of sarcasm? Hmm. "I do find it a bit odd you've chosen our town when I'm sure you could have gone anywhere." She pinned him with the no-nonsense stare that had gotten her pegged as a woman who meant business; perfect for her mayoral campaign.

The smile faltered for a split second, then spread. "My old partner's here and according to Cash, there's no place like Magdalena."

Mimi grinned and waved a hand. "Shoo, those are the words of a boy in love. He could be living in a 2x2 pen and have the same sentiments."

That made him laugh. "True."

"So, have you come for friendship," she paused, "or are you looking for something a little deeper, like love?"

Ben Reed coughed. Cleared his throat. "I think I'll settle for the friendship."

"Of course, you will, but you never know what might be waiting for you around the corner. It's not every day a fine young man comes waltzing into town with a face like yours and a smile to boot." She tsk-tsked and grabbed his suitcase. "Follow me and I'll show you your room. You're the only guest at the moment, so you'll get the primo package."

"That's not necessary, Miss—"

"Mimi. Name's Mimi. And of course it's necessary. Didn't Cash tell you my great-great-grandfather and grandmother were founding members of this town and I'm the mayor?" She toted the bag to the top of the steps and turned right, stopping when she'd reached the second door. Two bags did not sound like an indefinite stay. Hmm.

"He did say you were the mayor and the head of some garden club."

Mimi threw him a look and fitted the key in the lock. "It's not a garden club, young man. It's called The Bleeding Hearts Society, and we do a whole lot more than grow plants and fix landscaping issues. We mend hearts, listen to problems, help with relationships. We're about being there for people, lending a hand, and hope." She stepped inside the room and flicked on the light. "It's a privilege to belong and I'm honored to be the head of it." She set the suitcase next to the bed and fluffed one of the pillows. "Maybe it's karma that laid Bud out and created a spot in the police department. Heaven knows, Rudy could use a man like you. Just be patient with him; if you can look past the gruffness, you'll see a decent man."

"Huh. Cash didn't mention those requirements."

"Don't worry, you'll get along fine. Now don't go thinking we're a rowdy town, but we have our moments. If Skeet Gunther tips one too many at O'Reilly's and creates a ruckus, you'll get a call and he'll get a personal escort home. And Sissy Maystock will no doubt visit you at least once a week with one complaint or another." She laughed and shook her head. "She's got a thing for a man in a uniform. At seventy-four, I don't know what to tell you. Of course, you'll have the occasional dumped garbage can and graffiti-marked window. You'll be able to track down the scoundrels before dinner if you talk to the neighbors." She picked up the afghan from the foot of the bed and refolded it. "In this town, someone's always seen something. It's just a matter of asking the right questions, and most times, you don't even have to ask. They'll offer up the information."

Ben Reed cleared his throat. "Miss Pendergrass, I mean, Mimi, can I ask you something?"

"Sure."

He met her gaze, his blue eyes filled with what looked an awful lot like dread. "Are there any real threats in Magdalena? Robberies? Assaults?" A faint pink crept up his neck, spread to his cheeks. "You know. Something more substantial, like real police work?"

***

What the hell had he gotten himself into? Ben tucked in his shirt and fastened his belt. In less than a half hour, he'd find his way to Bree and Brody Kinkaid's for the welcome cookout they'd planned for him. Cash and Tess would be there, and Nate Desantro and his wife. What about Gina Servetti? Just thinking about another encounter with that woman and her opinions pinged his right temple with the beginnings of a headache.

He'd been in Magdalena less than two days and already people were descending upon him with questions and looks that suggested they found him more intriguing than a whodunit movie. Maybe he should have rethought his decision to come here and wait out his "sentence" so he could return to Philly. Of course, that jerk assistant DA boyfriend of Melissa's hadn't offered a return date. He'd wanted Ben's departure to be permanent. To hell with that.

No man, no matter what his threats, was going to keep Ben from the city he loved, and certainly not from the woman he loved. Actually, he'd almost ignored the man's damn ultimatum, but something in Melissa's eyes told him her boyfriend would make good on his threat to destroy him. People in power could do that.

So here he was, staying at the Heart Sent bed and breakfast, owned and operated by Mimi Pendergrass, businesswoman, mayor, straight shooter. She reminded him of his grandmother in her younger days: strong, dependable, trustworthy. Everybody needed someone like that in his life and he'd needed Naomi Reed. She'd be disappointed with him right now. If she were still alive, she'd have a thing or two to say about his current situation. *Benjamin*, she'd say, *you have so much goodness in you, why can't you let it out? Let people see what's inside, instead of that rough-and-tumble boy you pretend to be.* And then, *Trust is the key. And if you can't learn to trust, you'll end up all alone.*

Naomi always thought he was better than he really was, but he guessed that's because she loved him and believed in him more than he believed in himself. She had a point about the trust, though, and he'd finally understood it, even though it hadn't come until after the divorce. But understanding and implementing were not the same, at least not for him. Cash and Tess had that kind of trust and he was glad for them. That was one of the reasons he'd declined Cash's offer to stay with them a few weeks until he found a place to rent. He might not know a lot about relationships, but a relative of an ex-girlfriend wasn't usually a welcome houseguest. And then there was the other reason. He could only pretend to want to be in this backward town so many hours a day.

It was time to head to the Kinkaids and act as if life couldn't be better than settling into a place with backyard barbecues, country roads, and town halls. He wished he had his Harley, but he couldn't put a hitch on the back of a sports car and once winter set in, he'd have to deal with storing it. Besides, this was a short-term stay. The less he brought with him, the better. Ben grabbed the bottle of wine he'd purchased at Sal's Market, turned out the light, and closed the door.

When he pulled into Brody and Bree Kinkaid's driveway a short while later and spotted the tricycle, softball bats, jump ropes, and bucket of chalk strewn about the front lawn of the old farmhouse, he seriously questioned the wisdom of accepting an invitation to a kid-friendly event. What did he know about kids other than they'd trapped more than one man and sucked the life out of too many women? Christine Desantro was an exception and he'd guess Bree Kinkaid might be one, too.

But when Bree opened the front door, Ben had to revise his earlier assumption about his host. When he'd seen her at Cash's wedding, she'd been a beautiful, pregnant strawberry blond with a wide smile and a golden tan. This Bree Kinkaid was thin, sunburned, and looked like she needed three weeks of sleep.

"Bree." He grinned and held out the bottle of wine. "You look wonderful." Maybe the compliment would help her *feel* wonderful.

Her lips twisted into a sad smile and she hugged him. "Thank you, Ben. You're a sweetheart." She pulled away and took his hand. "Come on; everyone is out back." He followed her through a maze that might have once been a dining room but now served as a giant laundry bin with piles of bright-colored clothes stacked on a long oak table.

This room led to the kitchen that boasted another long table, white with a highchair in the corner and a deacon's bench against the wall. Two bowls rested on the floor beneath a mat stamped with black paw prints that read *chow time*.

Ben blinked to adjust his eyes to stacks of paper products on the counter, dishes in the drain board and sink, some dirty, some not, drawings and reminders plastered on the white fridge, a flip-top garbage can stuck in the open position by a cereal box. And shoes. Lots of shoes: sneakers, flip-flops, boots, big, small, red, brown, polka-dot, heaped in a corner and spilling over each other.

Bree caught him staring at the shoe pile and managed a small laugh. "I threatened to make them all go barefoot if they didn't straighten up their clutter." She nodded toward the shoes. "They found every last one and I do not even want to tell you who the worst offender was." She paused and offered up her husband's name. "It was Brody."

Cash once told him the guy had more muscles than brains. Maybe he could have used some of those muscles to do a dish or two. Ben smiled at Bree and shrugged. "Never would have guessed."

***

Gina spotted Ben Reed the second he walked onto the deck. He looked pretty much the same as he did the last time she saw him, with the exception of his tux, which he'd swapped out for jeans and a T-shirt. Still too good-looking, still too self-assured. His deep laughter spilled from the deck to the circle of chairs near the fire pit where Gina sat with Tess and Christine. She'd considered turning down the invitation to tonight's cookout with a made-up excuse, but when Bree called to invite her, she'd sounded almost happy, a word that hadn't been associated with her in months. Besides, there was something Gina needed to talk to Ben Reed about and the sooner, the better.

"Poor Ben," Tess murmured as he approached them with a wide smile and wave of his large hand. "By tomorrow morning, he'll have every available female in this town hunting him."

Christine laughed. "Oh, I think the man can handle himself."

Gina frowned. "I think he's the one who will be doing the hunting."

"Hi, ladies." Ben Reed's blue gaze scanned the circle, easing from Tess to Christine and settling on Gina. The gaze narrowed, sparked, and smoothed. "How's my dancing partner?"

Gina's frown morphed into a scowl. "Hello, Ben. Still insinuating yourself on unsuspecting victims?"

That comment actually made him laugh. "Victim? That's not usually a term women use when they're talking about me." He scratched his jaw, crossed his big arms over his chest, and studied her. "Are you referring to yourself? If so, I'm not remembering you looking or sounding like a victim. Now, granted I'd had a drink or two, but I do recall the dance and then there was the after." His eyes narrowed, held her. "Is that what you mean? The after part?"

She bit the inside of her cheek, waiting until her breathing evened and she could control her voice. Oh, but Tess and Christine would have a million questions about that comment. She could hear them now. *What exactly did he mean by that comment? What happened? Tell us.* "Actually, that's exactly what I wanted to talk to you about." Her forced smile turned real when she spotted a split second of confusion flash across that handsome face. Gina stood and nodded at Tess and Christine who made no attempt to hide their curiosity. "If you'll excuse us? This won't take long." She turned to Ben and said, "We can head to the kitchen and cut up the watermelon while we talk. The kids like wedges."

"Uh, sure."

Gina hid a smile as they walked toward the house. There was nothing sure about the tone in the man's voice. What did he think she wanted to talk to him about? Did he even remember or had he merely been goading her? She imagined too many drinks and an "every woman wants me" attitude could muddy the clearest memory. Well, too many months had passed with unanswered questions. She wanted the truth and darn it all, he was the only one who could tell her.

The kitchen was a jumble of clutter, paper products, and crockpots, but Gina found an open space on the kitchen counter and plopped the watermelon on a cutting board. It would be easier to work and talk; that way she wouldn't have to look him in the eye. How many lectures had she received growing up about the correlation between direct eye contact and the truth? *Look someone in the eye*, her mother had said. *It makes you appear trustworthy. Dart those eyes around the room like a fly refusing to land and that's a sure sign of dishonesty.* Her mother had been wrong about that, but she'd been wrong about a lot of things. People could look you right in the eye and lie to you, even people who said they loved you. She grabbed a knife from the drawer but Ben Reed held out his hand and said, "I'll cut the watermelon. You talk."

Maybe he didn't like the idea of eye-to-eye contact either. She handed him the knife and positioned a large plastic bowl decorated with sunflowers next to the cutting board. "Cut it into wedges."

"I know." He whacked into the melon and split it in half on the first try. "Because that's how the kids like them."

"Right." His hands moved with grace and precision as he cut, sliced, and created wedges out of the juicy melon. Gina arranged the pieces in the bowl, eyeballing the shape of the wedges, betting each one was within a quarter inch of the others. He certainly had an eye for measurement.

"So, what did you want to talk about?" He continued to slice the melon, his gaze intent on his work.

"What happened at the reception?"

His lips twitched. "You mean the after part, right?"

"Yes. Did Gino put you up to it?"

"What?" He stopped slicing and turned to her.

He looked like he had no idea what she was talking about, but men lied all the time, and she'd bet Ben Reed had a bag of lies for every occasion, especially when it came to women. Well, she wasn't playing his game, or any game. She wanted the truth and one way or another she'd get it from him. "Did my cousin Gino put you up to the kiss?"

Those blue eyes narrowed on her. "No." And then, "Why would he do that?"

She ignored the question and pushed on. "Anthony then? He's Gino's younger brother. Did he do it?" Before he could answer, she said, "He likes to wager six-packs. Is that what he did? Bet a six-pack on me?"

The left side of Ben Reed's jaw twitched and his lips flattened. "I didn't bet anything."

She studied his face, tried to pick out the sincerity of his words. She'd never possessed the ability to read a person's expression or body language, and they had better say what they meant, because she was what people called a "literal" person. No making statements like *It'll be a year before I figure this out* if it wasn't really going to be a year.

"Then why'd you kiss me?"

Even with her less-than-acute interpretive skills, she could tell by his expression that he thought she was a bit crazy. "What kind of question is that?"

Now they were getting into her comfort zone. "I think it's a very logical one and I've spent quite a bit of time trying to analyze the reason behind your actions. I really thought my cousins were somehow involved, though they didn't act with the normal excitement they use after such tricks."

"They've bet on you before?"

She settled her gaze on his hands and tried to ignore the heat creeping from her neck to her cheeks. Strong hands. Capable hands. Hands covered in sticky, watermelon sweetness. "A time or two."

"I don't play those kinds of games."

There was an air of quiet anger in his voice. *That,* she heard *and* interpreted. "Well, unfortunately, they do." She glanced at him and shrugged. "And since they haven't, I'm left to conclude you were attempting to punish me for telling you I was an aeronautical engineer."

Those eyes sparked a second before his mouth worked into a slow smile. "You were very convincing. I pictured you working on a jet, even asked Cash about it. I'll admit, I was ticked when I learned you'd made a fool of me, but that wasn't why I kissed you."

"Of course it was. It had to be."

"Gina?" His voice gentled, smoothed out. "A kiss really can be just a kiss. It doesn't have to be analyzed and put under a microscope. It doesn't mean we should be picking out china patterns or matching monogrammed towels. It could mean just what it was—a simple kiss."

Maybe that would be true if she were someone else, but nobody just kissed her for no reason. There was always a reason, and usually not a good one, and never for the pure sake of wanting to kiss her. That had ended years ago with the man who had broken her heart. "Did Tess or Bree put you up to it?"

He shook his head. "No. My brain and too many bourbons put me up to it."

"That is a horrible excuse."

He grinned at her. "Sorry, it's the truth. One minute we're catching a breath from the heat inside and the next, I'm looking at your lips. The moonlight hit them a certain way and I don't know; for a minute I forgot how much sarcasm spilled from them like a gusher, and thought about how soft and kissable they looked." He shrugged. "Like I said, my brain wasn't working and the booze got me."

"Obviously." If she erased bits and pieces of those last sentences, having to do with sarcasm and booze, she might actually find a compliment in there.

Ben Reed's grin faded. "Some guy really did you wrong, didn't he?"

"Why do you say that?" The words spilled out too quickly, with too much emotion. She tried again, this time stretching her syllables and scrubbing the emotion from them. "Why do you say that?"

"Because you can't take a compliment. Because you aren't comfortable with the opposite sex. Because when we danced at the reception, all you could talk about was personal space. Because you are hell-bent on insisting that if I kissed you, it had to be tied into a sick wager or a punishment. Because—"

"Okay, okay. I get it." She hefted a sigh and looked away. "And I don't want to talk about it."

"Code for some guy did you wrong."

"I could say the same about you, couldn't I? You walk around like you're a gift to every breathing female. You say all the right things, but you don't really say anything. Do you actually have more than a ten-line playbook?"

Darn if he didn't laugh. "I have fifteen or twenty lines and they haven't failed me yet." He studied her and said, "But something tells me they wouldn't work on you, not even if I had fifteen hundred lines."

She smiled. "The man possesses intuitive capabilities."

He nodded. "And he even knows how to use them on occasion."

Her smile spread. He was actually half human and somewhat entertaining when he forgot to be so full of himself. Ben Reed turned back to the task of watermelon cutting and for the next few minutes, Gina watched him and listened to tales of how he grew a nineteen-pound watermelon when he was ten.

"I wanted to enter it in the fair, but my grandmother didn't want me to look like a braggart, so we cut it open and shared it with the neighbors." He shrugged. "I could have won that darn ribbon."

"No doubt, but maybe your grandma was trying to teach you a lesson in humility."

"Yeah, maybe." He tossed the last piece of watermelon in the bowl and slid her a smile. "I'd say she failed; what do you think?"

Chapter 3

If anyone had told Harry Blacksworth that he'd find himself sipping coffee from a two-story deck connected to a gigantic house in the middle of Nowhere, USA, with a couple of kids and a wife, he'd have saluted them with his scotch and laughed. Not happening, as in *ever*. But, here he was, stretched out on a patio chair with *The Wall Street Journal* folded at his side and the *Magdalena Press* open on his lap. And the kids? They were inside, probably trying to teach the baby some new trick, like the kid was a wind-up toy. And the wife? She'd be whipping up a batch of his favorite pancakes: banana walnut smothered in real maple syrup. Any minute now, she'd bring him a plate, perch on the edge of his chair, and if he were real lucky, feed him the first bite, followed by a nice, long kiss.

He sighed and glanced at the expanse of land that stretched three lots and included a swing set, treehouse, mini putting green, enough flowers and bushes for a greenhouse, and, of course, the biggest story in town—the big-ass pool with four lanes and a diving board. All that was missing now was the damn water. The building inspector cancelled on him twice: once because his wife went into labor with their sixth kid, and then last week, when his mother-in-law tripped over one of the kids' toys and twisted her ankle. What a mess. Harry had been two steps away from calling the guy's supervisor but Greta pitched a fit and told him he'd better find some compassion in that heart of his, because a man without compassion was not one bit attractive.

Ah, hell, he'd backed down and not only that, he'd

invited the inspector and his brood to swim in the pool, if and when the friggin' thing ever got inspected. He'd left that last part out, because Greta would not have appreciated the side comment, and what she thought of him mattered a helluva lot more than he liked to admit.

"Harry?"

The screen door slid open and Greta stepped onto the deck carrying a plate of pancakes and a carafe of coffee. When she smiled at him, he forgot how much he didn't deserve her and thanked the good Lord for the second chance He'd given him with Greta. She'd taught him how to love, not only her, but himself. After too many years of denial, he could finally accept the battered, bruised, and far-less-than-perfect excuse for a human being he was, and sometimes, he even liked the guy. Today was one of those days. Greta and the kids thought he was some kind of hero and who was he to argue with that? In fact, it made him want to do better, made him want to *be* better. For them. Maybe even for himself. Harry eyed the plate, heaped with three pancakes slathered in maple syrup and served beside two slices of Canadian bacon. He grinned at Greta and said, "You're the sexiest cook I've ever met. Even in a T-shirt and shorts—" he planted a kiss on her lips "—but I wouldn't mind seeing you in one of those little French maid outfits. What do you think? Maybe you can model it for me next Saturday when the kids stay at Christine's."

She blushed and set the plate in front of him. "Oh, Harry. You are the silliest man." She shook her head and golden curls tumbled over her shoulders. "I am not a young woman anymore. I have carried three babies and worked hard for many years. This body tells its own story and it is not a sexy one."

"Oh, you're sexy, Greta. You'll be sexy at eighty, trust

me on that." He'd caught the landscapers staring after her last week when she brought them lemonade. And when the crew installed the pool, hadn't they glanced up every time she stepped onto the deck? Hell yes, they had. Harry had seen them, but he couldn't blame them for admiring a beautiful woman, even if the woman was his wife.

"Lily called this morning," Greta said, sliding into the chair next to him. "She wants to know if you talked to the building inspector yet."

Maybe he should give Lily the man's number and she could talk to him herself. If anybody could persuade a person to get the job done, it was Lily Desantro. "What did you tell her?"

Greta's voice dipped with humor. "The same thing I tell her every morning. That if all goes well, she'll be swimming in the pool before school starts."

Harry laughed at that. "Did she ask for specifics? I can't imagine Lily accepting an answer as vague as that."

"She wanted to talk to you about the building inspector. Apparently, she thinks if the man had help with his expanding family, he could concentrate on his job." Greta paused and laid a hand on his forearm. "She offered to dust and help babysit the kids so the man could get his work done."

"You don't say?" Harry forked another piece of pancake. The kid was a born salesperson. "What did Miriam say to that?"

"She thinks Pop Benito is behind the idea and she said he better stop filling her head or she was going to call his son in California and tell him Pop was still driving even when he promised not to, and she knows he's not locking his door when he goes to the garden club meetings because Christine told her."

Harry set down his fork and settled back in his chair. This town was like a regular soap opera; you could tune in to the shenanigans of this person or that one and it was always entertaining. He knew what Pop was doing because they were buddies, but damn it, the man promised he wouldn't drive until his eye checkup. "And how in the hell does Christine know?"

"She gives him a ride home most times, and she said he walks right up the steps, turns the knob, and in he goes. No pauses to pull out a key." She shook her head and sighed. "Christine said she thought he lost it, but when she asked him about it, he marched inside and returned with *two* keys. He said nobody's going to steal from him because he doesn't have anything worth stealing except for his pizzelle maker and the new T-shirt his son sent him."

"Huh." He'd met Pop the first week they hit Magdalena. The old man was power-walking down the road wearing a designer jogging outfit, red high-top sneakers, and a Yankees baseball cap, and looking like an advertisement for athletic wear. Harry had slowed down to get a better look at the man and when Pop spotted him, he yanked out his earbuds, grinned, made his way to the car, and thrust out a bony hand, welcoming Harry to town. Apparently Pop Benito knew Harry, even if Harry didn't know him. Later, he would learn that Lily had been the one to enlighten Pop about her "uncle" and from the raised brows and close-lipped comments, Lily had told him everything she knew, maybe more than she should.

That encounter began an interesting friendship between Harry and Pop that included Wednesday morning pancakes and eggs at Lina's Café. At 8:00 A.M. every Wednesday, Harry picked up Pop from his house on the other side of town and drove to the café. Pop had insisted on driving the second time, but after running a stop sign and hitting a curb while parking, Harry flat-out told him that until he got his eyes *and* the car checked, nobody was going anywhere in the Crown Victoria, including Pop. The old man hadn't argued, but he hadn't looked like he agreed either. So, had he been driving again or not?

"Maybe we should invite Pop to dinner. What do you think, Harry? I could fix him penne pasta with spinach and garbanzo beans. And a tomato and cucumber salad with basil. Christine said he's very proud of his basil, and it's larger than anyone else's in town." Her lips twitched. "He says it's because of a special secret that many think has to do with his wife, Lucy."

Harry shot her a look. "Lucy. Right. The dead woman he talks to every day?"

"She might not be walking this earth, but she's not dead, Harry." Her voice dipped, gentled. "She lives in his heart." Greta clutched his hand, placed it on her heart. "Just as you live in mine."

Greta could say Harry lived in the tip of her toe and if it made her happy, he'd agree with her. Who would have thought he'd go so "New Age philosophical" since marrying Greta and taking on the role of husband and father? Sure as hell not him, but here he was, relaxed, happy, committed. In love. With one woman. How about that? This town and these people were good for them; he could feel it, even though they'd only been here a few months. No wonder Charlie couldn't wait to get back here. Four days a month wouldn't be enough; he could see that now. You'd just get comfortable and it would be time to pack up and head back to that other life, those other responsibilities, that other person, the one who sucked the heart from you, who despised you but would never in this lifetime, or any other, let you go.

Thank God Gloria Blacksworth was relegated to an urn in a locked storage unit in a Chicago suburb. Thank God indeed. The family home was gone, sold to a big insurance executive, who offered for the "contents of the dwelling," which proved damn convenient for all parties concerned. Chrissie hadn't been interested in many keepsakes, but she had wanted the photos and photo albums, as well as the urn housing her mother's pulverized remains. And there had been the odds and ends of memorabilia she couldn't quite part with—the desk where she'd first done her homework assignments, the chair in her father's study where he'd spent hours of quiet reading time and that Harry had dubbed "the escape chair," and the dining room set, though why in hell she'd want a reminder of those tormented dinners, he couldn't even guess. The must-haves also included a few special glasses, dishes, and plaques; hardly big monetary catches in comparison to what she left behind. But Chrissie wasn't interested in the money, hadn't ever been interested in it. The things she took were about remembering a past she could tell her kids about. Or maybe if that past proved too painful, she'd re-create one. People did it all the time. Harry had even done it a time or three, before Greta walked into his miserable existence and made sense of it. He'd never been one to think much past his next pleasure, but life was different since Greta and the kids, richer, deeper, *significant*. Harry Blacksworth had a life that was significant. Think of that? Who knew what the next days and years would bring? He sure as hell didn't, and right now he'd be happy with a pool full of water so Lily would stop squawking at him. But here's what he did know: with Greta at his side, he could conquer anything, even a less-than-respectable past, and that's exactly what he planned to do.

***

The inside of the Magdalena Police Department was straight out of an old movie: the cement-gray uniform, the dated police cruiser, the clunky two-way radio, and, of course, the bumbling and inept junior police officer. Ben could forgive the uniform and the lack of updated electronics because they were creature comforts and not necessities. And while he wasn't thrilled with the cruiser, he doubted he'd encounter a high-speed chase where he'd need the speed. But, an inept junior police officer was a problem, a big one.

Jeremy Ross Dean looked about twenty-two, an inch or so shorter than Ben, twenty or twenty-five pounds lighter, with chestnut hair that stood two inches high and made Ben wonder if his hat fit him or if the hair got in the way. Cash had told him Jeremy was the police chief's son and it was his father's obsession with the law that steered Jeremy to the police academy and a position on the Magdalena police force. But ten minutes with the boy and Ben knew he didn't belong anywhere near law enforcement. There was no spark when he spoke of police work; his voice didn't resonate with conviction or passion, and his angular shoulders actually slouched. Where was the excitement, the interest, the intellect? Even if the boy couldn't feel it for a deadpan, backward town like Magdalena, he should at least act like his pulse doubled when Ben told him about the work he and Cash used to do: the busts, the chases, the stakeouts. But nope, the boy's expression remained blank, with a pinch of interest, not a bucket, like normal police would show.

So, what the hell was this kid's story? And why hadn't Cash filled him in? And where the hell was the police chief? Ben had been so determined to convince his buddy he wanted out of city life and into Magdalena life that he'd never once stopped to consider Cash might have been doing his own share of "selling". Well, apparently that's exactly what had been going on.

"Where's the dispatcher?" He'd been so busy trying to get a bead on Jeremy Dean that he didn't notice the absence of a dispatcher.

The boy fidgeted with the notepad in his hand and turned a dull red. "Mrs. Olsteroff had to take her dog to the vet this morning, so I told her I'd fill in. She's having ACL surgery."

"Who? The dog or Mrs. Olsteroff?"

The red crept from his neck to his cheeks. "Marjorie. That's Mrs. Olsteroff's Lab."

"Ah." People took over shifts and fill-ins so their co-workers could do all kinds of things for their family: weddings, funerals, births, surgeries. But a dog? Now he knew he wasn't in Philly anymore. Ben pinned Jeremy with a "you've got to be kidding" look and sighed.

The boy cleared his throat. "Mr. Reed?"

Mr. Reed sounded like an old man or a father and Ben was neither. "The name's Ben."

"Ben." He spit the name out, repeated, "Ben."

"Yup. Now how about you tell me who's who around this place and why the roster says we have eight and it's just you and me?"

Jeremy tried to explain the internal workings and setup of the Magdalena Police Department, but everything ended with *That's how the police chief likes it* and *It's just our way*. Didn't anybody in this place ever hear of chain of command and protocol? This lackadaisical attitude toward rules, regs, and the boss would never fly in Philly. Hell, the violations would hit so hard and fast, they'd earn the offender a suspension, maybe even two.

But this wasn't Philly; it was a long way from Philly, like a universe away.

"Where's the police chief?"

Jeremy cleared his throat twice, settled his hands on his utility belt, and said, "The chief heads to a wholesale store in Renova every third Monday of the month. Buys what we need for the office: paper products, cleaning supplies, soft drinks, maybe a pizza or two."

The police chief went grocery shopping every third Monday of the month and that's why he wasn't here to welcome his new hire? Was this for real? Ben couldn't resist pressing a bit more. "What kind of paper products?" Copy paper, envelopes, file folders? Wouldn't the chief in Philly get a kick out of this?

The junior policeman lifted a lanky shoulder. "Paper plates, cups." Long pause. "Toilet paper."

Ben stared at him. "You have got to be kidding." *Toilet paper?*

Jeremy slid a glance in Ben's direction. "Chief says it's more economical this way, even with the extra nineteen miles to Renova."

"Huh." Ben rubbed his jaw, trying to make sense of what the boy had just said. Who knew that police work in small towns involved grocery shopping at warehouses, and toilet paper was the pick of the day. Not only would his old chief not believe this; no one would.

"Chief says we got to start taking turns." Jeremy rubbed his jaw. "Wonder if he'll put your name on the rotation."

"Yeah, I wonder." Great. "Jeremy? Do you call the chief Dad at home or does he like to be called Chief there, too."

Tinges of red spurted on the boy's cheeks. "Chief.

We've always called him that; me, my Mom, my sisters. Everybody."

Ben gave up asking questions somewhere between the time Mrs. Olsteroff entered with a smile and a handshake, and the discovery that the shoebox-sized room these people called a cafeteria because of the ancient fridge, sink, and microwave also served as an interrogation and interview room. This last revelation came when a woman stormed in and demanded to speak with someone about the drunk-and-disorderly occurrence outside her bedroom window last night....the suspect was one Virgil Bensen, the woman's husband.

It was almost noon and Ben had just finished taking the woman's report when Rudy Dean, police chief of Magdalena, sauntered in carrying a six-pack of paper towels in one arm and toilet paper in the other. He spotted Ben, frowned, and tossed the paper products on Jeremy's workstation.

"Ben Reed." He said Ben's name with a mix of annoyance and hesitation. "Thought you were starting next Monday."

Ben shook the man's extended hand, noting the strong grip, the sausage-sized fingers, the muscled forearm. "Sir."

Rudy Dean was a bruiser of a man, looked to be in his mid-fifties, tall, broad-shouldered, square-faced, with a crew cut and a slash for a smile. "So, you're the city boy they've all been talking about. Said you're worth your stuff." His pale gray eyes sifted over Ben, came back to his face. "We'll see soon enough, won't we?"

"Yes, sir." Ben waited for the man to say more, but he merely nodded, picked up his paper towels and toilet paper, and headed toward the lunchroom. By the time Ben clocked out that afternoon, he had the beginnings of a real headache. If he were home, he'd de-stress in the weight room, but seeing as he had no idea if there was a gym within 50 miles of this place, he decided on a run. Magdalena did seem to have decent roads and lots of scenery, and he wouldn't have to worry about getting run over by excessive traffic. Yup, that last one wouldn't be a worry at all.

He stopped at Heart Sent to change clothes and let Mimi know he'd be back around 6:00 for dinner. It had been several years since he had to check in with anyone; probably the last time he'd let a woman keep tabs on him had been his grandmother. Naomi Reed had rules and expectations and he'd known better than to challenge her. But mostly, he'd honored her straightforward requests because she never gave up on him, even when he questioned his own abilities. Of course, he'd never let anyone else see his insecurities, especially not a woman. That's why he kept a wall up, why he'd never been able to let anyone get too close, not even Melissa. She learned early on in their relationship that he didn't need or want a mother, and the more she tried to plan his time and rework his schedule, the more he fought it. Why couldn't he have given in a little? So, she wanted to know when he'd be home or where he'd gone after work? So what? Would it have been that difficult to share that information, maybe adjust it to please her? He'd fought that question since the night she packed up and left, even told himself he could and would change.

But he knew he wouldn't, not unless he dealt with a whole lot of messed-up issues that started and ended with the mother who'd left him and the father he never knew. He pushed past thoughts of the couple who'd created and discarded him like a used napkin and thought of Melissa as he jogged from Heart Sent to the road that led out of town. The late summer wind lifted the leaves on the trees: maple, oak, birch. Soon, they would turn red, yellow, and orange, drift to the ground, leaving the trees naked and exposed. Winter would follow with snow, ice, and harsh winds, and if he were lucky, he'd be back in Philly by then. Closer to Melissa.

Paige would call next week with an update on his ex-wife. His cousin thought he was on an out-of-town undercover assignment with the force because that's what he'd told her, but if she stopped to consider that he'd never done this before and it made absolutely no sense unless he were in a movie, she'd realize he wasn't telling the truth. But Paige wouldn't question him. She believed everyone always told the truth, even when she had no reason to believe that. Hell, had she never wondered why Cash didn't care where she was traveling for her dancing or when she'd return? Cash hadn't wanted anything to happen to her, but if she'd told him she was moving to Alaska, Ben guessed he would have just hugged her and wished her well. Not the actions of a man in love, certainly not the same man Ben witnessed with Tess, before or after the wedding. The man couldn't seem to stop looking at his wife, or touching her, and he sure seemed unable to wipe that silly lovestruck smile from his face.

Who would have ever guessed? Not Paige, which made her the perfect accomplice in Ben's attempts to keep tabs on his ex-wife. She still believed Ben belonged with Melissa and pooh-poohed the fact that they were divorced and she was pregnant with another man's baby. She called these *mere inconveniences*, not insurmountable tasks, and insisted the uncoupling of Ben and Melissa was two-sided. He'd let Paige think he was a prince if it helped get information on his ex-wife while he was in Magdalena. And Paige knew just how to do it; she knew where Melissa lived, where she worked, where she grocery-shopped. She'd vowed to do whatever was necessary to get Ben and Melissa together again.

When he rounded a curve, he stopped and snatched the towel from his neck, dragged it over his face, and breathed in the mountain air. He'd spotted no more than a handful of cars and a truck or two in the past hour. This road would be treacherous in winter and guardrails wouldn't keep a car from going over the edge. How many had landed in the wooded area below, the passengers injured or killed? He was used to the dangers of city driving: the speed, the traffic, the highways. But country driving posed its own problems: winding, narrow, less-traveled roads, animals, ice and snow. When he reached another mile marker and turned back toward town, he decided that maybe the truck he'd spotted in the back of the police department parking lot this morning wasn't such a bad idea after all.

Ben miscalculated his run by almost an hour and when he headed up the driveway of Heart Sent, Mimi Pendergrass sprang from her wicker rocker and rushed toward him in a swirl of blue and magenta stripes, her ball earrings swinging. "Lordy, where have you been? I was just about to hop in my truck and come looking for you."

He pictured Mimi Pendergrass in a pickup truck and stifled a smile. "I didn't mean to worry you. I guess I lost track of time." He wiped the sweat from his face and neck and let his smile slip out. She had his grandmother's eyes, soft and blue.

"Next time you up and decide to take off, you'd better keep track of your time." She crossed her arms over the striped top and said, "We have bear in this area and all manner of animals that a city boy like you knows nothing about."

And the woman had his grandmother's no-nonsense attitude, too. "Yes, ma'am."

She nodded her salt-and-pepper head and clasped his arm, leading him toward the porch. "Now, come on inside and get a quick shower so I can feed you." Her voice softened and the stern tone evaporated in the early evening air. "There's fried chicken, potato salad, and a special zucchini-tomato blend that gets the whole town talking. They want the recipe and they've tried to copy it, but I won't give it to them. Not yet." She opened the screen door, looked up at him, and grinned. "We have to have some secrets so they keep guessing now, don't we?"

That last comment stayed with him through a shower, two helpings of the tastiest potato salad he'd ever sampled, more than his share of fried chicken, and a big bowl of Mimi's zucchini-tomato blend. Had she been referring to more than her recipe? There'd been something in the way she looked at him that made him wonder if she knew he was keeping a secret or two of his own, starting with his reason for being in Magdalena.

"Well?" Mimi eyed him over the frosted rim of her lemonade. "How about a piece of strawberry pie? I can guarantee you're gonna love it."

Ben stuffed the last bite of potato salad in his mouth and chewed. If he kept eating like this, he'd be two sizes larger by the time he left this place. Then again, he hadn't had strawberry pie since Naomi made it for him, right before he headed into the service. "Sure," he said, caught up in the nostalgia of his grandmother. "I'd love a piece." He pushed back his plate and patted his belly. "But I'm going to need to double my run tomorrow if I want to fit into my clothes."

She laughed and waved a hand at him. "Oh, pooh. Anybody can see you're a specimen of fitness—" Mimi eyed him from shoulders to chest to arms to belly "—and anybody can see you aren't going to lose it with a few extra helpings. This town's growing some fine-looking men. First, there was Nate Desantro, and then Cash came back to us, and now you. Before we know it, someone will be contacting us about getting you boys to pose for a calendar."

Now that would be interesting, and not going to happen. "I'm not exactly a calendar guy." Neither was Cash, and Nate Desantro sure as hell wasn't.

Mimi grinned and shrugged. "You'd be surprised how many people start out saying they'd never do this or that, and the next thing you know, they're doing it." She threw him a sly look and said, "And I can be very persuasive; do not doubt that for one single second."

"Oh, I don't doubt that, not at all." He could see why she was mayor, why Jeremy and Mrs. Olsteroff spoke about her as if she were the president.

"I like having you here, Ben." Her eyes grew bright, her expression solemn. "You make this place feel alive." He didn't miss the sadness in her voice or the catch in her throat when she spoke. Had something happened in her past to take the life from this place? Maybe she'd lost someone close to her, a husband? He wanted to ask her about it but hesitated a second too long.

Before Ben could formulate a question, Mimi pushed back her chair and stood. "Now give me a second and I'll get you that pie." She disappeared into the kitchen and a few seconds later called out, "Coffee? Splash of whiskey?"

Mimi Pendergrass was one interesting woman and she was certainly full of surprises, but the sadness he'd just witnessed reminded him too much of his grandmother's face when someone asked about her absent daughter. Raw pain. He wanted to ask Mimi about it, but not at the risk of causing her more grief, or worse, having her tell him to mind his own damn business. Somebody in this town knew the story behind that sadness. He'd hoped to ask Mimi for a mini "playbook" of the town's residents, but now he wasn't so sure he should bother her with it. Still, he had to gather some halfway intelligent information on the residents of this town before he took another misstep like he'd done today when he asked Mrs. Olsteroff about her husband. Yeah, the husband who took off two years ago with the organist in his church—right after Christmas Eve services.

Ben couldn't make such an error again, but who could he ask for help? Cash was too caught up with his new wife and his mission to save kids, one would-be delinquent at a time, and Nate Desantro was the kind of guy who wouldn't tell him even if he did know. Besides, Ben didn't like the way Desantro watched him, as though he knew Ben wasn't being 100 percent straight with his reason for being in Magdalena. Best to avoid him as much as possible and that meant avoiding his wife, too.

Bree Kinkaid didn't seem like the kind of person who could peel layers of a story away to get to the truth so she was out. Actually, she probably really did believe the truth was whatever anybody said it was. And no to Bree's testosterone-buzzed, baby-producing husband, Brody Kinkaid. The man did not project the intellect to decipher people or issues, perceived or otherwise. If he did, would he continue to impregnate his poor wife when she was obviously overworked and worn out? There was always the waitress at Lina's Café. Phyllis. Or was it Lois? Hell, he couldn't ask her for a rundown on the town personalities if he didn't even know her first name.

What about Gina Servetti? The second he thought of her, a dull ache pinged his left temple. She was logical, no nonsense, analytical, and she wouldn't sugarcoat the information or leave out important details. Still, did he really want to ask the woman and give her an opportunity to say no? And not just no, but maybe a big "hell no"? And if she agreed, then he'd be indebted to her, wouldn't he? Just the thought of that last one double-pinged his temple. Damn Cash for going and falling in love and getting all gooey on him. Ben liked him better when he was a restless guy's guy—like him. Now there was a wife, a sense of belonging, hell, a purpose.

So, Gina Servetti it was. Ben sucked in a deep breath, massaged his left temple, and headed out the door.

Chapter 4

Gina sat in a rocker on the back deck, feet propped up on the table, glass of red wine in her hands. She loved to sit in the dark with the sounds of night soothing her: crickets, owls, the wind. In a few months, the cold would set in, strip the trees of their color, lay down blankets of snow, and force the animals to seek shelter. The cold wouldn't keep Gina inside. She'd stuff her feet into boots, her arms into a down coat, fit a hat on her head and mittens on her hands. The briskness of the night would steal her breath, but it would be worth it for a few minutes of pure quiet. Bliss, that's what it was. Nobody bothered her here, maybe because they didn't want to venture out in the heat and risk bug bites or the cold and worry over a chill. Or maybe they simply didn't care where she was or what she was doing.

She sipped her wine and acknowledged the last possibility was perhaps the truest. What did it matter? Her life had always been about being forgotten, neglected, left out. Even the one time she'd thought she mattered to someone had ended in disaster and betrayal. She didn't mind being alone, would rather spend time with herself than fabricating niceties to get through a dinner or an occasion with a stranger she neither liked nor cared about. She had her work, her books, her flowers, her friends. There was no point adding family in that last thought because they weren't there for her, had never been there for her, not even when she was a lonely child, struggling with self-doubt and weight issues. In fact, a therapist would probably pin them as being responsible for the self-doubt and the weight. What child wanted to hear she wasn't cute enough, thin enough, clever enough? What child wanted her mother to say she wished she could be more like her cousin, the one the whole town knew was a slut?

The Servetti clan did not value intelligence, loyalty, or integrity. They were interested in shiny things that drew attention—people's good looks, flashy personalities, and cleverness, even if those attributes fizzled in the bleariness of daylight. As for their only daughter, Carmen and Marie Servetti were only interested in her when they needed money or a signature on a loan. She hadn't seen them in six weeks, even though Carmen Servetti worked at the auto body shop five minutes from Gina's job at Magdalena General Hospital. It had stopped mattering so much a long time ago.

"Gina?"

She jumped at the sound of the male voice, splashing wine on her shorts. "Damn. Who's out there?"

"Ben Reed." The voice grew closer. "I thought I'd stop by and say hello."

"What?" She stood and swiped a hand across the wet spots on her shorts. "How did you find me?"

He moved up the steps, his large frame illuminated by scraps of moon. "I'm on the police force, remember? I can find anybody in this town."

"I do not appreciate the fact that you used the benefits of your job to gain personal access to private information." What possible reason could Ben Reed have for waltzing into her backyard, invading her privacy, peeking into her life?

"Consider it a shortcut. You're in the phone book and searchable online. If you'd been unlisted or unsearchable, I might have reconsidered coming here." He paused, held out a bottle of wine. "Vintage merlot, the best Sal's Market had to offer."

"I already have wine."

"Oh. Well, maybe you can show me the kitchen and I'll uncork this one so we'll both have a glass."

She didn't miss the half second of awkwardness filtering through his words. Bet that was a first. "Look, I don't know why you're here but it's late and I was relaxing, so…" Surely he could figure out the rest. *Leave, leave now.*

"I need your help."

Ah. So this wasn't about saying hello or sharing a glass of wine. This was about Ben Reed needing something. Now *that* made a lot more sense. She should ignore the comment and send him on his way, but curiosity and manners won out. "How could I possibly help you?"

"How about wine first, questions later?"

She tried to control her annoyance but the man knew how to agitate her without even trying. "When a person barges in on another person, he usually forfeits the right to make demands and suggestions."

His voice dipped, filled with humor. "Unless the other person takes pity on the intruder's parched lips and grants him one last wish. Come on, Gina, what's one glass of wine?"

She should have known better than to trust the man. He didn't talk about the real reason for his visit until he'd almost finished his entire glass of wine and poured another. Sitting at the kitchen table. In her house. It was a stretch to say he'd been invited but he didn't seem to notice her reticence toward him, or her annoyance. If she'd had her way, he'd have remained on the deck while she retrieved a glass and a wine opener, but he'd pulled a folded piece of paper from his back jeans pocket and told her he needed light to read his notes, and that meant inside her house unless she handed him a flashlight, which she considered.

Why did people think they had a right to invade another person's life? Gina preferred her own company and her own thoughts, unless she was with her friends. Tess, Christine, and she guessed even Bree provided a welcome diversion and a safe place to talk about things that mattered. Bree tended to go off kilter, but lately she'd been less "cotton-candy sweet" and more subdued. Who wouldn't be subdued after what she'd been through? Damn that Brody Kinkaid.

Ben Reed set his wine glass on the table, retrieved the paper from his back pocket, and scanned the contents.

"What's that?"

He glanced up and threw her a smile that she was sure was meant to be charming. It might have worked if she'd been one to succumb to such antics. But she wasn't. And the hitch in her breath had more to do with the pepper she'd eaten at dinner and less to do with a good-looking man and his smile. "Let's call it a cheat sheet for the residents of Magdalena." He ran a hand through his hair and sighed. "In the city, you don't have to know people's names, much less their dogs' names. By the way, Mrs. Olsteroff's Lab, Marjorie, had ACL surgery this morning and is recovering quite nicely."

Gina stifled a smile. "Mrs. Olsteroff is very attached to Marjorie. She found her two years ago, right after her husband took off. The dog was all bones with her ribs sticking out, an eye infection, and a bad gash on her shoulder. Scared of everything, even birthday candles."

"Do I dare ask how you know that?"

"Birthday party."

"I see."

He said it like he didn't see at all. "Marjorie is like Mrs.

Olsteroff's child. She never had any of her own, so it all worked out."

"Sure did. The old man takes off and the dog gets the kingdom."

Gina shook her head. "Not exactly, but animals can help people in more ways than the obvious. Marjorie gave Mrs. Olsteroff purpose."

"Purpose." He rolled the word around on his tongue as though it were foreign and sour.

"Yes. *Purpose.*" She tried to glance at the words on the paper but she was too far away. "So, now you know about Mrs. Olsteroff and Marjorie."

He reached for a pen and marked the paper. "Checking off Mrs. Olsteroff. How about Jeremy Dean? What's his story?"

"What do you mean?" Jeremy was a nice boy who had no business near a gun or a desk. He belonged in a kitchen, creating recipes and filling bellies. If she told Ben Reed the boy only signed up to please his father, he might hold it against the boy.

"Jeremy belongs in a police department about as much as Mrs. Olsteroff's dog does."

Gina toyed with the base of her wine glass, pretending great interest in it. "Why do you say that?"

"It's obvious. The kid's not interested. I picked that up within five minutes of meeting him."

"Maybe." She would not tell him he was dead on, or that Jeremy snuck away to Lina's Café a few times a week to try out new recipes on her customers. Most of the town knew about it—except for Jeremy's father—but they wouldn't dare breathe a world about it. A secret was a secret until the owner chose to reveal it.

"If he doesn't like it, he should quit and find something

else."

She sipped her wine and said, "Have you ever risked going against your parents to do something you knew they wouldn't like?" She'd done it when she headed to college and later, when she returned and bought her own house and refused her mother's matchmaking attempts. Marie Servetti believed the worst cross in life was to be alone.

"My parents are dead."

"Oh." A spurt of sympathy trickled through her. "I'm sorry."

He shrugged. "Don't be."

She thought he might say more, but he didn't. The brackets around his mouth and the coldness in his voice did, however, say quite a bit. Even to someone like herself, who was not good at reading people or their emotions, his reaction said he had issues with his dead parents.

"What about Mimi Pendergrass?"

"What about Mimi?" She didn't feel right talking about these people as though they were being prepped for dissection. It was one thing to grow up here and know the good and bad of the town, but for an outsider to come in and attempt to pick apart their lives, well, that didn't sit well.

"I'd like to know more about her. She's one strong woman, but there's a sadness about her that creeps in every once in a while and I'm trying to figure that out."

"Why?" Of course there was a sadness about the poor woman. She'd lost a teenage son in an auto accident, buried a husband and a brother, and mourned the loss of a daughter she hadn't seen or heard from in years. No one knew the details about that last one and no one dared ask. Still, Mimi never complained. Some said they spotted her at her son's gravesite every Sunday, on her knees, head bent in prayer. It wasn't Gina's place to tell him any of this, especially the part about the gravesite or the estranged daughter.

Ben sighed his annoyance. "I like the woman. I just want to know her backstory."

"I don't think so. If Mimi wants to tell you, she will."

"Come on, Gina, help me out here. You could make this transition a lot smoother if you gave me the inside scoop on these people."

"Maybe. But it feels like gossip, and I don't gossip."

"Oh, for the love of…" He shook his head and uncorked the wine bottle. "Can't you consider it information sharing?"

Was the man serious? "Not when I'm doing all the sharing and you're doing all the gathering."

That made him smile. He was probably used to women giving him anything he asked for; maybe he didn't even have to ask, maybe they just gave it away: information, secrets, their bodies. She coughed and almost spewed her wine on that last thought.

"You okay?" He stood and moved toward her, but she held up a hand to stop him.

"Fine." It fell out like a croak, but two coughs later, she cleared her throat and repeated, "Fine."

He refilled her glass, then his own, choosing to lean against the sink, a few feet away. The man didn't fit in her kitchen; he was too big and the kitchen was too small, but he didn't seem uncomfortable. No, she was the one who was uncomfortable. When was the last time a man was in her kitchen? It didn't take long to remember: three months ago when Herb Carey fixed her garbage disposal.

"How about we come to an agreement? You give me as much information about the people in this town as you're comfortable with, and if I ask something you can't or don't want to answer, you simply say *pass*."

That was the most one-sided agreement she'd ever heard. Ben Reed had laid it all out for her with his "stay in your comfort zone" spiel, but what was he offering *her?* She was the one doing him a favor, and a big one. If he didn't want answers so much, he'd never have come to her. "Why didn't you go to Cash with your questions? He's your friend and I'd think he'd give you what you want."

He cleared his throat and shook his head. "Cash can't see much past his new wife, and besides, I don't think Tess much likes me."

"Oh?" Gina lifted a brow and let that single word sink in his brain. "Do you think it has anything to do with the fact that you brought your cousin here? A woman Tess knew nothing about?"

He pinned her with his blue eyes. "I never even knew Tess existed, and I doubt my cousin did either. Cash and I didn't talk about the past," he paused, "or our women."

Women, as in more than one. That was not a welcome visual and one she'd just as soon erase. She stared back at him, let her voice mirror her distaste. "You almost cost him the woman he loved."

His gaze narrowed, zeroed in on hers in a flash of emotion. Anger? Despair? Sadness? And then the look was gone. "Yeah," he said, his voice a mix of calm and resignation. "Lucky for everyone things worked out."

Did he really mean that? Did he know anything about relationships, especially ones between a man and a woman that involved commitment, maybe even love? Doubtful. She'd peg him for more of a short-term parking kind of guy, the kind she found absolutely disgusting.

"So, do we have an agreement? I ask questions, you

answer when you want or say *pass* when you don't."

"You're a crafty one, Ben Reed." She crossed her arms over her chest, wishing she weren't wearing a ten-year-old T-shirt with paint stains on the shoulder. "What am I getting out of this, other than indigestion at the thought of your questions?"

He laughed and slid her a smile. "My company isn't enough?"

"No, definitely not." Though she could see where some women might disagree. Okay, most women would disagree. But not her. Thank goodness she was composed of sturdy, practical DNA and was not about to succumb to a handsome face and a nice set of biceps.

"Fine." He straightened and made his way to the fridge, opened it, and peered inside. "I'll cook you dinner." He closed the fridge and sighed. "You can't live on Greek yogurt and chocolate-covered pretzels."

"I'm not living on—" she stopped, glared at him "—how did you know about the pretzels?" She kept them in the freezer, behind the packages of kale and spinach. "Were you looking in my freezer?" She'd gone to the bathroom and had hesitated leaving him unattended but hadn't really thought he'd go snooping around her kitchen.

He shrugged and pretended great interest in the napkin holder resting on her counter. "I wanted an ice cube for my wine and I spotted the bag of pretzels."

The man was ridiculous and he was a liar. Well, she was having none of it. Gina closed the distance between them in three seconds. "You spotted them buried behind the kale and spinach? Hardly."

When he looked at her, she thought she saw remorse, but whether it was because he'd offended her or merely because he'd been caught was hard to say. "I'm sorry. I was just curious."

"Curious? About me? Why?" She didn't want him to be curious about her; she didn't want him to think of her at all.

"Damned if I know." He shoved his hands in his pockets and said, "I guess I find you intriguing, like a puzzle."

"You need to leave."

His gaze darkened. "I really am sorry. I was out of line." He held out a hand and said, "Can we start over? Ben Reed, nice to meet you."

Gina ignored him and his outstretched hand. "You came to my house, uninvited, I might add, asked for information on the residents of this town, some of whom might not be thrilled to have their life stories shared, and then, when I leave the room for two minutes, you rifle through my freezer? And lie about it?"

The outstretched hand slipped back into his pocket. "Look, I said I'm sorry, and I am. I shouldn't have done that and I shouldn't have lied about it."

She looked up at him, narrowed her gaze on his. "But you did. And now I'd like you to leave." She snatched the paper from the table and handed it to him. "Here. Find someone else to spit out information for you because I'm not doing it."

**

The roses arrived the next day. Twelve of them. Blood red. Forgive-me-red. I-really-am-sorry-red.

No one had ever sent Gina flowers, unless she counted the bouquet a twelve-year-old patient brought from his mother's garden. The note accompanying the roses was bold and direct, like the man who'd sent them.

I'm sorry. It won't happen again.

Did he mean the snooping or the lying? Or both? She could send a response to him at the Heart Sent with a comment that read, *You're right, it won't happen again. Good-bye, Ben Reed.* That's what she should do. That's what she'd intended to do from the second Mick Hastings stepped out of the delivery truck and handed her the box. But once she opened it and smelled the delicious scent of roses, her brain clogged and she *couldn't* send them back.

No one had ever sent her roses before and for just a little while, she wanted to enjoy them, pretend they came from someone who truly cared about her; someone who loved her, and not a man she barely knew.

***

Harry stepped out of his Jaguar and headed toward Lina's Café. One day soon, he expected Greta might gently "suggest" a more kid-friendly vehicle, one that didn't require special maintenance, with a sound system that cost more than her old car. And maybe he'd cave and buy something more practical. Hell, he'd done a lot of caving these past several months, starting with the move to Magdalena, though he'd already been half in before she began hard-selling him on the idea. He missed Chrissie and liked the idea of seeing her more than once every four months. A place like this was good for kids, too, and now that they'd factored into his life, he had to consider more than just what he wanted. Gone were the days of glass and chrome and uniformed doormen. They'd been replaced by hardwood, extra bedrooms, and land. He sucked in a fresh breath of mountain air and let it fill his lungs. Magdalena wasn't Chicago, but it was growing on him. And the people? Well, they belonged in a family drama, categorized under Interesting Characters.

He opened the door to Lina's and fell back twenty years.

The Formica tabletops, the red vinyl booths, the pastries in a glass case, even Phyllis, the head waitress with her up-do and gum snapping. Harry grinned at her and said, "Did you save any of that peach pie for me?"

She pointed to a dish covered in tin foil behind the counter. "All ready for you, Harry. Just needs a few secs in the microwave and a dollop or two of ice cream."

He winked at her and laughed. "If I weren't meeting my niece for lunch, I'd skip the meal and go straight to the dessert."

"You wouldn't be the first, and you won't be the last."

Harry laughed and made his way toward the back of the café where Christine sat, head bent, reading the *Magdalena Press*. "How's my favorite niece?"

She looked up and smiled. "You'd better not let Lily hear you say that or you'll have a lot of explaining to do."

He laughed and gave her a hug and a peck on the cheek before he slid into the booth opposite her. "Lily knows you're both my favorites, and if I forget, she'll set me straight."

"You know she's got her bathing suit and towel packed and ready for the second you give word the pool's ready."

He sighed and grabbed a menu. "I know, I know. Who would have thought I'd be bothered so much by disappointing a bunch of kids? This whole pool business is downright annoying. If I were in Chicago, we would have been swimming three weeks ago."

Christine shot him a look that said he was full of it and he knew it. "If you were in Chicago, you wouldn't even have a pool."

"That's beside the point. This town is growing on me, but damn, can things not move any faster? The inspector is supposed to call me later today and he'd better, or I'm heading over to his house and he's not going to like what I have to say."

"Mr. Abernathy? Be nice to him; his wife just had a baby."

Harry blew out a disgusted sigh. "So if a person has a life issue, like a baby, a marriage, or hell, a divorce, he's allowed to be incompetent?" What the hell kind of place permitted that?

"No." Her voice gentled. "He's allowed to be human."

"I'd like to see that husband of yours putting up with this. I'll bet he wouldn't tolerate a man telling him he couldn't get his work done because he had to stay home and change diapers."

"Uncle Harry, be nice."

"I just don't want to keep disappointing the kids. It bothers me. And then there's Lily. She's so excited about this pool, even told me she had a list of friends to invite. If you had told me two years ago that I'd be worried about a pool and kids, I'd have said you belonged in an institution. But here I am, in the middle of no-man's land and actually not minding it."

"That's because you're with the woman you love, and the kids you love. If you'd told me *that* two years ago, I would have put you in an institution."

He laughed. "Yeah, well, I guess crazier things have happened."

Christine was the best part of his old life, the one person before Greta who'd kept him from becoming a totally worthless human being. She'd loved him despite his many failings, even the one he'd thought she'd never forgive. He pushed that memory away, back into the dark corners of his brain, where he could almost forget it existed. He'd do anything for Christine, had forced himself to put up with her mother's ridiculous monthly dinners and complaints over her bad back and every other friggin' ailment she could conjure up. Gloria had been a real piece of work, but lucky for all of them, she was long gone and incapable of causing them further pain.

"So, what's going on with that husband of yours?" Harry bit into the ham and Swiss he'd ordered and decided Greta really would like this place, even if it weren't Harry's Folly, and even if they didn't serve penne with spinach and garbanzo beans.

"Nate's fine. Busy." She forked a strawberry from her fruit cup and said, "He and Cash just got an order for a bedroom set from a woman in Connecticut. How cool is that? Tess is thinking about expanding the marketing even further, maybe eventually as far as the West Coast. And Nate is talking about bringing on another person—" she paused and met his gaze with a half smile "—but you know my husband is very picky about who he lets into his inner circle."

"Huh." That was like saying a beer connoisseur was picky about his beer. "The man doesn't trust easily, but once you've got him, you've got him for life." He leaned toward her and lowered his voice. "I like to think I'm part of that inner circle, but with that guy, you just never know."

That comment made her laugh. "He likes you, Uncle Harry. A lot. And I know he'll never admit it, but he's glad you're here."

Harry sipped his ice tea and shrugged. "Probably about as glad as a cook without a kitchen. Every time he visits, he starts on me about why I think I need a place that takes up three lots and could house five families. The only thing he does seem to like is the fact that building the place gave a lot of people jobs." He paused, grinned, and added, "And my liquor. He's learned not to refuse the good stuff when I offer it to him."

"Don't spoil him."

"Not likely."

Her voice dipped. "And don't try to change him. I love him exactly as he is, with an occasional adjustment here and there."

"An adjustment? You mean like teaching him to pretend he likes someone, or can at least tolerate the person, when he can't stand to breathe the same air? Or to keep his mouth clamped and his expression blank when he disagrees? In the name of social etiquette and political correctness?"

"Uncle Harry. Nate is not that bad." When he raised a brow and stared at her, she plowed on in an attempt to make him see how "social" her husband really was. "He's much calmer than he was when I first met him. And more forgiving."

"Right. Tell that to anybody who's ever crossed him."

"He's big on loyalty, and telling the truth. I wish more people had that kind of integrity."

Harry almost heaved his ham and Swiss sandwich. Was she talking about him? Hell, he'd never been one for telling the truth, and loyalty? To what? A brand of scotch or a style of clothing? He certainly hadn't been loyal in the women department, except when it came to protecting Chrissie. But then he met Greta and she'd changed everything, including the part about telling the truth. Now he pretty much spit it out like projectile vomit, because the not telling ate a hole in the center of his gut, and fear of losing her over a lie ate at his soul.

And then there was integrity. No one had ever strung that word and Harry's name in the same sentence—until his wife. Damn, but the woman expected a lot out of him, and damn if he wouldn't do anything not to disappoint her.

"Nate's becoming more tolerant, too."

"Yeah, I'm sure." Harry bit into his sandwich. See if he'd give Nate Desantro any more of his top-shelf liquor. A saint shouldn't drink, should he? Nope. Harry chewed and pictured his next encounter with the man, when Harry would tell Nate he was too good, too loyal, with too much integrity to hang around with Harry and his booze. Desantro would laugh at him and pour them both doubles. Nate was a good guy and Chrissie was lucky she married him and not that worm, Connor Pendleton.

"He really is becoming more tolerant."

She was not going to let it go. "Fine. The man's more tolerant."

Her lips twitched. "I said he was *becoming* more tolerant. There's a difference. But, I was very proud of him for not hunting down the new police sergeant and interrogating him."

"Why would your husband interrogate the policeman? Isn't it usually the policeman who interrogates the civilian?"

"Unless the new police sergeant is Ben Reed, Cash's old partner in Philly. Do you remember him from Tess's wedding? Tall, big muscles, dark hair, blue eyes?"

"Sure you aren't talking about me?" Harry grinned. "Is he the guy all the women were swarming around?"

She nodded. "That's the one."

"Hmm. He did seem to have a way with the ladies; kind of reminded me of myself in my younger days."

That made her smile. "I'm sure. He's very friendly, but Nate says a guy who acted like Magdalena was made up of a bunch of lumberjacks and hillbillies would not suddenly up and leave a city to move here."

"Your husband's got a point." Maybe this Ben Reed guy found a woman here. Or maybe he'd been run out of town and was in hiding. Or maybe he'd gotten a woman pregnant and high-tailed it out of the city as soon as the pregnancy test read positive. Or maybe—

"The only reason Nate didn't pursue it was because Cash vouched for him."

"Well, that should mean something, shouldn't it?" And weren't cops part of a brotherhood? They wouldn't screw each other, not with the whole brotherhood-partnership deal in their skulls.

"It does, and that's why Nate's not hunting the man down with a notebook of questions. But he's got an eye on him."

"He's got an eye on everybody, doesn't he?"

Harry had meant it as a joke, but he didn't miss the pain flitting across her face or the sadness in her voice when she spoke. "Nate's had his share of hurt from outsiders and he wants to protect this town and the people he cares about from them." She paused, added, "In case they aren't who they say they are."

Chapter 5

Word of Gina Servetti's roses spread through town faster than Cash's lightning abilities at a shooting range. If only the news were as accurate as Cash's shots. Some said the roses were the result of a lover's quarrel from the boyfriend the town had yet to meet. Others said they were from a secret admirer, perhaps married or simply too shy to own up to the attraction. And then there were those who insisted the bouquet had come from one of Gina's relatives in an attempt to stir up interest among the unmarried men in the community.

Ben blew out a sigh and glanced through the police blotter. Runaway dog, runaway cat, runaway hamster. Hamster? He slammed the blotter shut and considered his predicament. According to Jeremy, who filled him in on the rose rumors, the first round of possibilities had swirled around an hour or so ago, when This Flower's For You delivered a box of long-stemmed roses to Gina Servetti's address. The delivery man could have ended the speculation by offering the name of the sender, but maybe it was his way of drawing out the tale, providing snippets of possibilities like a guessing game. Ben figured his name would surface before sundown, but how and in what capacity was anybody's guess. Maybe they'd toss him and Gina in the middle of a lover's spat with Ben begging forgiveness. How ridiculous was that?

He'd sent the damn roses because he was out of line and she'd called him on it, something not many women did, probably because they'd take any attention he offered. Not Gina, though. She'd just as soon boot him out the door as have a conversation with him. Her indifference was intriguing and damn perplexing. Most women got all soft and gooey when he slid a smile their way or lowered his voice a few decibels to what they perceived was an intimate and "for their ears only" conversation. Gina hadn't been interested in his words, his smile, or his voice. But he wasn't giving up on her because she was the key to making the people in this town believe he really wanted to be here and the more he knew about them, the easier his stay in Magdalena would be. A few months of cooldown was all he needed before he could contact Melissa and if he had to, that jerk assistant DA boyfriend of hers, to see about coming back to Philly.

All Gina had to do was give him that information and he'd figure out how to use it. It's not like he was asking her to divulge dark secrets; he only wanted what most of the town already knew, but in a workable format minus the emotion and guessing. What he knew about Gina Servetti so far was that the woman could give a dispassionate account of people, relationships, and backstory.

"Hear you sent Gina Servetti roses."

There it was, dropped in the middle of his day by a kid who still couldn't grow more than three whiskers on his chin. Ben glanced up from his papers and narrowed his gaze on the junior officer. "Who'd you hear that from, Jeremy?" *Play it cool and see what the boy knows.*

"Is it true?" The boy's face lit up. "Did you really send twelve long ones to *Gina Servetti?"*

Ben picked up his pen, turned it end over end, and said in a casual voice, "Maybe. And why do you say her name like it's crud from the bottom of your shoe?"

"Not crud." Jeremy pulled up a chair and leaned forward, lowering his voice. "More like a jalapeño pepper.

You don't go near them unless you're ready to get burned, and that woman will burn you with that tongue of hers." His voice dipped lower. "She's a viper."

What would Gina think of that description? A jalapeño pepper and a viper. Hmm. "Are you saying she's burned you or bitten you?"

"Nah, not me." He shook his head so hard, his flat top shook. "But no guy will go near her. She's not bad to look at, a little too curvy for my taste, but she's deadly. If you look at her a second too long, even if you didn't mean anything by it, she'll come after you."

Ben tried to picture Gina going after the male population of Magdalena. He doubted she "went after" men like Nate Desantro or Cash. Maybe she only went after the ones who tormented her, but why would they torment her? Now *that* was the question. "There's nothing wrong with a woman who has curves." He smiled. "Especially if they're in the right places." Gina had curves, nice ones, and they were definitely in the right places. He could see where somebody like Jeremy might find a waif-type more attractive, but what did a twenty-two-year-old kid know about women?

"So, why'd you send her flowers? Are you and Gina together?"

"No. She's my friend." *Or she will be once I talk her into it.*

The boy's face scrunched up and he scratched his jaw. "Friend?" And then, *"Friend?"* he repeated, this time with a hint of something that sounded like doubt. "Gina doesn't have guy friends."

Ben shrugged. "Well, she does now." He shut down the conversation after that, certain there would be looks and backward comments from the residents once news of the roses spread through town. Cash might have a thing or two to say about it, and Mimi Pendergrass would no doubt bring up the subject. And there was probably no escaping Nate Desantro, if the man chose to comment.

The real question was what made Gina burn men like a jalapeño pepper and bite like a viper? Ben had no idea, but he intended to find out.

***

"The pesto is excellent. Did you make it yourself?" Ben twirled a forkful of pasta, plunked it in his mouth, and savored the taste of basil, garlic, and Romano cheese. This was his second helping and he'd already eaten three slices of bread, a salad, and a cup of wedding soup. He'd need to run to Philly and back if he kept eating like this, but damn, Mimi could cook.

"Actually, no." She hesitated, cleared her throat, as though uncertain of her response. In the short time he'd known Mimi Pendergrass, the woman hadn't hesitated over anything—not her words, actions, or expressions. She had an opinion and she put it out there with confidence, no dancing around issues or feelings. So why now, over a dish of pasta?

"This isn't my recipe, though it is my basil." She dabbed her mouth with a paper napkin and gestured toward the table. "But the rest, the wedding soup, balsamic vinaigrette on the salad, even the garlic bread, are all the handiwork of a very talented young man."

"I'm impressed." Ben enjoyed cooking, knew good food, and this was the real deal. "I'd like to meet this guy." He'd bet the pasta was homemade, too, and not purchased in the refrigerator section of Sal's. Okay, now he really wanted to meet the guy. Any person who made his own pasta was a worthy opponent in the culinary arena.

Mimi's cheeks turned a dull rose that had nothing to do with the empty wine glass in her hand. "I'm sorry, Ben, but that's not possible. You see, while he may be talented, he doesn't possess the confidence to tell his father about his passion. He hides it and works in a career that's not suited for him."

"That's crazy."

Her voice dipped in sadness. "He can't disappoint his father."

That was something Ben didn't understand, but then he'd never had a parent to disappoint. "I've never understood people who gave up their happiness to fulfill another person's expectations."

"It happens. And sometimes the other party doesn't even realize they're making unfair demands until it's too late. The relationship is fractured, sometimes even irreparable."

Was she talking about the boy or a page from her own life? A husband? Child? Friend? It wasn't his business, but he liked Mimi and didn't want to think about her torn apart by a past misstep. He refilled her wine glass and said, "Would you be speaking from personal experience or observation?"

No hesitation this time. "Both."

The set of her jaw and coolness in her blue gaze told him that was as much as he was going to get. "I'm sorry."

She forced a smile and shrugged. "It's done and there's no changing it. All that's left after a grave mistake is the choice to curl up and stop breathing or stand tall and take the next step, and then the next, until you feel almost alive again."

There was pure pain dripping in those words. "I really am sorry," he said again. "Do you think you can convince this boy to tell his father?"

"I have no idea. He's old school, a pillar in the community. Young men in Magdalena work in factories, drive trucks, or build things. They do not work in a kitchen and create the perfect Bolognese sauce."

Ben ripped a hunk of bread from his plate and dipped it in the olive oil mixture. "Then it's time for this town to change." He popped the bread in his mouth, savored the flavor of garlic and oil. "Say the word and I'll vouch for the kid's culinary skills. It's as good as anything in Philly."

Mimi smiled, a real smile this time, and said, "That's very kind of you, Ben, but it's a bit more involved than that, and," again the hesitation, "his father isn't going to value the opinion of an outsider."

"Oh." Well, that put him in his place.

"People make their own choices, good or bad, and they have to live with those choices." She cocked her head to the side and studied him. "So, what's this about you sending Gina Servetti roses?"

"Does the whole town know about that?" He'd sent the damn things three days ago. Bad enough everybody was talking about it except the one person who should be talking about it, the one who hadn't answered his phone calls or his visit last night. Gina Servetti was avoiding him, but sooner or later, he'd catch up with her and find out why. And damn it, she was going to tell him.

"This is Magdalena," Mimi said. "If it has to do with a relationship, a fight, or a baby, this town wants to know about it. And, the fact that the recipient of those flowers is Gina Servetti has everyone's interest piqued."

"Why?" Because according to Jeremy, the men in town thought of her as a jalapeño pepper and a viper?

"Gina is a lovely girl—intelligent, nice to look at,

loyal—but she's wearing armor that's stronger than an armadillo's. The girl's petrified of getting hurt and she's not going to let any man close enough to do that."

That sounded like the Gina he knew. "Did some guy hurt her?" He didn't like to think about that, but it would explain a lot.

"Not that I know of, but it's hard to tell. When you're raised in a house where looks and fitting into a size 2 are held in higher regard than brains and compassion, it can mess with a young girl's head, not to mention her self-esteem. By the time that poor girl headed to college, she'd buried her unhappiness with food and an attitude that said, 'I don't give a darn what you think about me,' even when she cared very much what people thought." Her voice softened. "She wanted to be accepted for who she was and that darn family of hers just would not do it."

"What about the cousin? Natalie? Did Gina's family accept her?"

Mimi's lips pulled into a serious frown. "Stay away from that girl. She's nothing but trouble and she's caused her share of it."

Ben set his napkin on the table and leaned in. "I'm guessing man trouble."

"Oh, you guessed right." Her gaze narrowed. "Almost broke up Nate and Christine. Horrible mess."

"Nate and Christine Desantro?" *Mr. and Mrs. Perfect?*

Mimi nodded her salt-and-pepper head. "The very ones. Could have had a tragic ending if the town hadn't gotten involved." She tapped her chin and said, "Pop Benito led the crusade to get them back together. And poor Christine was pregnant...and to think her own mother was behind it all." She sighed and made a quick sign of the cross. "I know it's not right to speak of the dead, but that woman was pure evil."

"Are you saying her mother tried to keep them apart?"

"Keep them apart? The woman paid Natalie Servetti to drug Nate and pretend to seduce him. Even hired a man to take pictures and had Natalie deliver them to Christine. Can you imagine?"

No, he really couldn't. Nate Desantro, pillar of the community, caught up in a scandal involving photos, seduction, and his *mother-in-law?* This was worse than the mess with Melissa. "What did the mother-in-law have against him?" The man might act like a tough guy but his own mother-in-law plotting to do him in was like a bad soap opera.

"Ohhhh." Mimi lowered her voice, glanced toward the closed door that led to the hallway and kitchen. "That is another story altogether. Nate's one of the finest men I've ever known, but there was a time a few years back when he was angry, resentful, and pure miserable." She stopped, spread her hands on the table, and leaned forward. "You do know Christine was a Blacksworth, don't you?"

"You mean she's related to the guy in the mansion?"

Mimi nodded. "That's Harry. Came from Chicago. Christine's from there, too."

"I didn't think she was from around here." There'd been something about Christine Desantro that breathed class, which made the fact that she was married to Nate Desantro very interesting.

"She came here when her father died. Bad accident. It was all so tragic." Mimi cleared her throat and met him with a head-on, no-nonsense gaze. "He had a secret life here with Nate's mother. Visited them four days every month, and he'd been doing it for fourteen years. They even had a daughter together."

"Lily." The girl with Down syndrome.

"Yes, Lily. The light of this entire town. When Christine first came here, Nate wanted to boot her out, tried to do it, too, but in the end, well, he realized he wanted her at his side."

Ben rubbed a hand along his jaw. "Mimi, that is seriously messed up."

"I only told you so you know that no matter how you start out, it's how you end up that counts."

"Meaning?"

She smiled and he swore she winked at him. "Meaning, you and Gina. She's a diamond in disguise and just needs the right man to unearth that sparkle."

"Me? No. *No*. We're just friends. Sort of." *Or would be if she stopped avoiding me.*

"Friendship is important in a lasting relationship." Damn, she did wink this time.

Ben pulled at the collar of his button-down shirt. It was too hot in here, almost roasting. "Mimi, you've got it all wrong. There's nothing romantic going on between me and Gina."

She threw him a knowing look and said, "Yet."

"No. Ever." He opened his mouth to tell her about the ex-wife he couldn't forget, but the words fizzled on his tongue. She didn't notice because she was too busy smiling and nodding.

"Don't worry, I won't say a word. Not one word. Besides," the smile spread, "the roses said it all."

***

The grand opening of the Blacksworth pool occurred on a hot Saturday afternoon, two weeks before school started. As promised, Lily was first in line, dressed in a pink-and-blue-striped two piece and pink flip-flops with Lizzie and

AJ right behind her.

Harry had hired four lifeguards from a neighboring town, a catering service to grill hot dogs, hamburgers, sausage, and serve soft pretzels, salads, cotton candy, and funnel cakes. A real belly upset, but what the hell. The kids had helped with the menu and they'd been so excited to add their picks to the list, he couldn't say no. Greta had shaken her head and tsk-tsked him, but he didn't miss the smile slipping past her lips. She was pleased. He'd build two pools to see that look on her face every day.

"Mr. Blacksworth, I mean, Harry, thank you for inviting us. The children and I are very excited to try out the new pool."

Harry turned to find Haywood Abernathy, the building inspector, and five of his six kids. The man was half Harry's size with thinning hair, glasses, and hands that were smaller than Greta's. Six children? How did he keep them all straight? He shook the man's small hand and threw a smile at the Abernathy clan, trying to calculate the age differences, but gave up and settled on "too exhaustingly close."

"It's a thing of beauty, isn't it?" Abernathy said. "Well worth the wait."

No sense debating the fact that if not for the man's personal situations, the pool would have been ready weeks ago. If Harry opened his mouth, Greta would be all over him, and an angry Greta was worse than three-days of heartburn. "Sure is."

"Five minutes until pool time!"

Harry glanced at the lifeguard with the megaphone. There was a limit to the number of people allowed in the pool at one time, and those who had to wait stood behind a thick, corded rope, drinking slushies and eating soft pretzels. "Come with me," Harry said. "I'll move you to the head of the line." Haywood Abernathy beamed and motioned for his clan to follow.

When Harry had them situated, he made his way to the drinks and grabbed an ice tea. In another life, he'd have splashed vodka in it, or more likely he'd have splashed tea in his vodka. Not now; now things were different. He had to stay alert and with three kids running around and a wife who looked like Greta, he needed all the energy he could muster.

"Harry?" He turned to find his wife smiling up at him, dressed in a white sundress splattered with poppies. "This is lovely. Everyone is so happy, and you made this possible. Thank you." She leaned on tiptoe and kissed him softly on the mouth.

He stroked her cheek, cupped her chin, and kissed her again. "Anything for you, Mrs. Blacksworth, anything at all."

When the whistle blew signaling pool time, children jumped into the crystal blue water, shouting and laughing as they splashed about. A disc jockey with a Hawaiian shirt and sunglasses blared beach music from his setup under a giant oak tree. Smart man to pick the coolest location aside from the air-conditioned house. Harry slung an arm around Greta, pulled her against him, and watched the late-summer festivities. There would be a pack of kids heading home with sunburns and upset bellies. Greta had left sunscreen at all the lifeguard stations but Harry knew it was a wasted effort. Same with the signs she'd insisted placing at the food stations that read *Eat responsibly* and *Don't overeat*. Kids were going to eat until they exploded and refuse anything that said *protection*. He should know; he'd done the same thing at that age. Hell, he'd done the same thing at fifty—before he met Greta.

"Well, if it isn't Mr. Swimsuit himself."

Greta shielded her eyes and looked toward the gate. "Pop came." Her voice filled with delight and excitement. "Lily will be so pleased."

"No doubt that's all we'll hear about for the next three weeks." He clasped her hand and said, "Let's go greet our guest."

He wouldn't tell Greta that Pop almost hadn't come and wouldn't have if Harry hadn't taken him out for pastrami on rye at Lina's Café and convinced the man to come. Turns out the day of the pool party was also his deceased wife's birthday. She'd been gone almost three years, but Pop still spent the day with her, talking, sharing memories and photographs. Before Greta, Harry would have said a revelation like that was the first step toward certifiable insanity. Talking to a dead wife? Most of the men he knew didn't talk to their wives and they were alive. But since Greta, he got how losing someone like that would leave you empty, desperate, scrambling for a reconnection, anything to keep them close. And if it meant hanging a gigantic portrait of that person in the living room, chatting away as though she were seated next to him and engaged in the conversation, then so what? Harry noticed how Pop referred to Lucy in present tense; *my Lucy loves truffles,* or *my Lucy loves summer.* Who cared? They could learn a lesson or two on love, marriage, and relationships from Angelo Benito, and Harry would be first in line for the lessons.

"Hey, Pop, glad to see you here." Harry thrust out his hand and grinned at his friend who wore a Hawaiian shirt and swim trunks more suited to a California surfer than a senior citizen. Harry had paid one of the caterers to pick him up, telling Pop it was a good idea, in case he wanted to drink. Right. They both knew that wasn't the real reason, but this was about pride and saving face. It must be hell to live in a seventy-something-year-old body when your brain tells you that you're still thirty-five.

"I had to come and see what all the ruckus was about." He smiled at Greta and gave her a peck on the cheek. "How are you, my dear? This man treating you okay? Because if he isn't, you let Pop know and I'll give him a talking-to he won't forget."

Harry shook his head. "Yeah, yeah, you'll suffocate me with all of your sayings is more like it."

Greta laughed. "Thank you for asking, but you have no worries. My husband treats me like a queen." She clasped Harry's hand and smiled up at him as if he were a king, and damn if he didn't feel like one when she looked at him that way.

Pop winked at her and said, "Glad to hear it." He turned to Harry and pointed to his shirt and swim trunks. "So, what do you think? Pretty snazzy, huh? Tony says this is what the surfers wear."

Tony was the son in California, the one who hadn't returned to Magdalena since he left, except for his mother's funeral. Something was definitely up there. Maybe the guy eased his guilt by sending his father designer sporting wear, and maybe Pop let himself believe these gifts actually replaced a visit.

"Well? What do you think?"

Harry blinked. What a thought that was. Neon orange trunks and a matching floral shirt with green flip-flops on a seventy-something-year-old man was just wrong. "You plan to light up the place tonight, Pop?"

"Nah." He tapped his sandaled feet in a quick dance step

and said, "Just trying to keep up with the latest fashion. Age doesn't mean you have to hand in your style sense." He scratched his jaw and adjusted his glasses, squinting at Harry. "I think you'd look good in blue trunks and a matching shirt. Match your eyes."

That was not just no, but hell no. "Thanks, Pop, but I'm all set."

"Suit yourself. And let me know if you want to borrow any of my music for your workouts. I don't loan out Frank and Dean to just anybody, but I'm making an exception for you."

"I told you, Pop, Frank Sinatra and Dean Martin are not going to get my blood pumping. I can't believe you can power-walk to them."

Pop hoisted up his trunks and thrust his hands on his bony hips. "And why not? Who doesn't love Frank and Dean? Huh?" He turned to Greta, his lips pinched. "What about you, Greta? You love Frank Sinatra and Dean Martin, don't you?"

She nodded her blond head, a bit too fast. Did she even know who these men were? He doubted it, probably never heard of the Rat Pack either. "Okay, Pop. Bring the CDs to breakfast this week and I'll try them out, but only if you check out my exercise room." He and Greta had transformed part of the basement into a full gym, complete with weights, exercise equipment, a sauna, even a juice bar. "I'll put you on a machine that's a helluva lot easier on your knees than the pavement."

Pop scratched his head and eyed Harry. "I'll try out the equipment if you try out the T-shirt and shorts Anthony sent me last week." He grinned. "Neon blue with white stripes."

Chapter 6

Harry's life as he knew it ended six days after the grand pool opening. There'd been no warning, no sirens, nothing but the parched lawn crackling under his feet and the dry air sucking the moisture from his lungs as he made his way to the deck and his wife. The sprinkler system hadn't worked in six days and it would be six more before the repairmen came. Life in the country had its drawbacks, but there were a lot of bonuses, too: early morning coffee on the deck with Greta, afternoon playtime with Lizzie on the jungle gym, helping AJ practice his golf swing, napping with Jackson crooked in his arm. Even sitting in the dark, listening to night sounds. Saying absolutely nothing. And peace. Pure, perfect peace, the kind he'd never known before. Hard to say if Greta and the kids were one hundred percent responsible for this newfound peace or if it was a combination of his new family and the move to Magdalena.

He didn't know and he wasn't about to analyze the hell out of it. What he did know was that he'd never slept better or felt healthier or happier in his life. And that was saying a lot for a man who had made a career of pursuing pleasure and personal satisfaction.

Harry fixed his gaze on his wife and bounded up the stairs, anxious to fill her in on his breakfast with Pop. The man had a bag of stories and Italian folklore to fit every occasion. This morning he'd told him about his granddaughter, Lucy, and how being a grandparent was so much different from being a parent. Less stressful. More joyful. And then he'd slid him a grin and said again, "Definitely less stressful."

"How's my bride?" She always blushed the palest pink when he called her that, but she wasn't blushing now. As a matter of fact, she looked white, ghost-white, if he had to peg it. "You okay?" He placed a hand on her forehead and leaned close to get a better look. Greta didn't get sick often and the thought of her in any kind of pain made him anxious and queasy.

"Stop." She batted his hand away with her right hand and eased out of the chair to stand several feet away.

"What's the matter?" He glanced at the envelope in her left hand. "What's that?"

The question bleached out the color on her neck and shoulders and leached its way down her arms. "This?" She held up the envelope, glanced at it as though she couldn't quite remember what it was. But when she thrust it at him, her gaze seared him with fury, telling him she knew exactly what the envelope was about, and *it had to do with him.*

Slivers of panic climbed from his gut to his chest and inched up his throat, threatening to spill the pancakes and Canadian bacon he'd had for breakfast. "Greta?" She reminded him of a rabid animal, nostrils flaring, mouth clamped shut, eyes glazed. "Talk to me."

"Talk to you." Those perfect, full lips pulled into a scowl. "Talk to you," she repeated, disgust dripping from each word. "Why don't I show you what arrived in the mail today and then maybe you can talk to *me?"* She advanced on him, thrust the envelope at his chest, and stepped back before he could touch her.

Harry sucked in a deep breath and worked a hand through his hair. Whatever was in this envelope had to be bad. Was it a letter from Bridgett or a woman from his past informing him he was a father? Oh God, no. Please, not that. He'd been so careful for so many years, had always taken precautions, actually, until Greta... The more likely case was some woman claiming he'd fathered her child. He'd have to find an attorney, take a paternity test, head back to Chicago...

"Read the letter." He glanced up. Greta stared at him, lips pinched, eyes narrowed. "Read it."

The envelope was addressed to Greta Blacksworth and had a return address of Thurman Jacobs, Esquire. Why the hell was Charlie's attorney sending Greta a letter? He opened the envelope and pulled out a single sheet of paper.

Dear Greta:

By now you will have settled into your new life. I imagine your husband has charmed you with his words and his wealth. When he puts his not-often-used brain to the task, he can be lethal. I should know; I once succumbed to that gilded tongue. During a dark and lonely period of my life, Harry persuaded me to believe my husband didn't love me and that his trips to London were of a more personal than business nature. I didn't want to believe the man I loved more than my own breath would betray me, but Harry insisted it was true, and I had no reason to doubt my husband's brother and confidante. Surely, he would never lie about his own brother. But that is exactly what he did.

By the time I learned of his duplicity, it was already too late. Harry Blacksworth, the man you married, seduced me and ruined my life. And do you know why? Jealousy. He was jealous of his brother, the man who had always protected and defended him.

But there is more—painfully, much more. Charles discovered I'd had an affair, but he didn't know the man's name. I could not destroy my husband with the truth, so I remained silent. When I learned I was pregnant, I didn't know which brother was the father. When Christine was born with Blacksworth eyes, Charles was convinced she was his. But is she? Who knows?

Your husband turned me into a woman filled with bitterness and disappointment. I took my last breaths in the care of a paid companion—a stranger. Harry Blacksworth has walked this earth for too many years without a care for others. He stole my marriage and my happiness. He stole my life. Had I not been seduced by him, Charles would have remained faithful to me—his wife. Please get out while you can. Don't let that man steal your life.

Sincerely,

Gloria Blacksworth

When he finished reading, he folded the letter and placed it back in the envelope as though that might relegate the contents to their previously unread state. Gloria was a liar bent on destroying everyone around her, true to the end. He looked at his wife and opened his heart, willing her to see the pain inside. "I'm so sorry." He took a step toward her, careful, cautious, and let the grief pour out. "Forgive me. Please." And then again, "I'm so sorry."

"Your own brother?" The words spilled out in a whisper of sound. "He loved you."

Harry hung his head, wished he could have spared Greta the disgust of knowing.

"How could you take advantage of Gloria when she was struggling and vulnerable?"

His head snapped up. "That's bullshit. Gloria was never vulnerable a day in her life and I did not seduce her." He paused, pushed out the truth. "She was more than willing."

Greta gasped. Was that a sound of disbelief, or pure disgust? Probably both. "Why did you do it? You could have had any woman you wanted. Why your brother's wife?"

He thought of lying, but he couldn't do it. "I was always the second brother, the playboy. The joke. Charlie was always first, always the best. I resented the hell out of that and wanted to take something that belonged to him." He fell back to the days of the affair, the bedroom, the years of self-disgust. "So I slept with Gloria, but I never said Charlie had other women and I sure as hell never forced her. She had her own reasons for doing what she did, reasons that were centered on feeling neglected and unwanted."

There. He'd told her the truth.

"You betrayed your brother." She swiped a hand across her face to stop the tears. "Will you betray me, too?"

"No. No!" *How could she even think that?*

"Does Christine know?"

He nodded. "I told her. I had to. Gloria wouldn't stop pressuring Christine to give up the trips to Magdalena and settle down with that asshole, Connor Pendleton. Can you picture her with that guy? He was more interested in her portfolio and her society ties, nothing like Nate. But Gloria wouldn't give it up, no matter how many times I threatened to tell Chrissie about us. Finally, I saw what I had to do and I did it; I told Chrissie about the affair and the pregnancy. That broke the hold Gloria had on her, gave her the courage to leave. But it also killed their relationship and that made my dear sister-in-law hate me more than she already did." He held up the envelope. "That's why she sent this; to destroy me by getting to you."

She turned away, hugged her arms across her middle,

setting up a shield from his words. From him. "Greta, look at me." Harry counted the seconds until finally, she inched her gaze to meet his. The betrayal smeared on her face stabbed his soul. He'd done this to her and now he had to find a way to make her understand how much he regretted what had happened, but mostly, how damn much he needed her forgiveness. He sucked in a breath and said, "I've regretted what happened for years. Hell, I hated what I'd done, hated myself. It's one of the reasons I was bent on self-destruction and excess—" he paused, his voice dipped "—until you came along. You gave me hope, made me believe I wasn't such a worthless piece of nothingness."

Greta, the only woman he'd ever truly given his heart to, opened her beautiful lips and whispered, "Maybe I was wrong."

Harry shut down after that, curling up until there was nothing left but four simple words that pierced his brain, his heart, his soul, and marked his destiny. There were more words, spoken in a voice that held no anger, no passion, nothing. He heard them, would later recall each syllable, but now, in the moment of such pain, he could not grasp their meaning, or perhaps he refused to do so.

I need time.

I think you should move to the guest room until I can sort this out.

Maybe I was wrong.

How could you?

How will I ever trust you again?

Your own brother?

Will you betray me, too?

Maybe I was wrong...

Harry spent that night and the next in the guest room, only leaving long enough to grab a few bottles of water and a package of crackers. Who could eat when he'd been ripped apart, guts, heart, lungs, and left to rot in his own stench of misdeeds? He hadn't showered, hadn't changed from the slacks and polo he'd worn on that fatal day; hell, he hadn't even combed his hair. Had he brushed his teeth? He couldn't remember. He'd stayed in this room, telling the kids they couldn't come near him because he had the flu. Highly contagious. Yeah, he'd bet Greta wanted him to stay as far away from the kids as possible so his depravity didn't infect them.

What if Greta couldn't forgive him? What would he do? He sat on the edge of the bed, dragged both hands over his face and sighed. *What the hell would he do?* Hadn't he avoided real relationships with women because he knew they could end up like this, with him on the edge of losing the person who mattered most? But what he'd shared with Greta—hell, why was he thinking past tense—*what he shared with Greta* had been worth risking his damn heart and his independence; it had been worth risking everything and he was not going to let Gloria Blacksworth destroy that.

But how was he going to stop her? Even dead, the woman was lethal. Harry closed his eyes and bent his head. He'd never much believed in prayer, but right now he had a feeling it would take a miracle to save his marriage, and so he prayed.

The next morning, Harry woke, showered, shaved, put on a clean pair of slacks and a polo, and left the house before anyone was awake. He stopped at Lina's Café and picked up two coffees to go and two pecan sweet rolls. As Phyllis fixed the coffees, he even managed a smile and a bit of idle chit-chat. Almost normal, if a person didn't know him.

But Harry couldn't fool Pop Benito. The second the old man opened the door, his smile flattened and his bushy brows pulled into a straight line. "Harry? What's wrong?"

It all fell out then, the sordid truth about how he betrayed his brother when he slept with his sister-in-law, a woman he didn't even like. Harry had kept this secret inside for so many years that speaking about it so soon after telling Greta made him hoarse. And then, the other part, even worse than betraying Charlie, was the possibility that Christine could be Harry's. What if he'd stripped Charlie of the one person who had really mattered in his brother's life?

"I'll say you're in a pickle." Pop scratched his head, stared at the vegetable garden he called his "playground," and added, "Yup, it's a doozy."

"I know." Harry sat back in the rocker and blew out a long breath. They were sitting on the back deck with a garden surrounded by chicken wire, tin pans, and a fake owl, and for some crazy reason, the sight relaxed him. Maybe because Pop found comfort there...or maybe because it was simple. Or maybe, because Harry had no place else to go.

"And Nate doesn't know that Christine might be your child?"

Harry shook his head. "No. And Christine doesn't know about her mother's letter."

Pop rubbed his jaw and popped the last piece of pecan sweet roll in his mouth. "This is getting more complicated than unwinding a clematis vine from a fence." He eyed Harry, shook his head again. "Nate's not one for doubletalk or hiding the truth, especially if it involves his wife. He's a different man since he married Christine, more trusting and empathetic than he used to be, but don't cross him, or it'll be wiped out faster than an ant in a tub of water. Gone. Not coming back."

There was a lesson tucked between Pop's stories and if Harry picked out the vine and the ant, he understood what Pop meant. "Okay, so Nate's going to be pissed at Christine for not telling him. I don't want that on my head. What can I do to help them?"

"That's an easy one. As soon as you leave here, head straight over to Christine's and tell her about the letter so she can tell Nate before people start talking."

"Why would people start talking?" Harry paled and tasted bits of pecan sweet roll in the back of his throat. "The town isn't going to find out about this." Pause. "Are they?"

"Nah. Not the particulars, but these people are smart. They watch movement and patterns. You're at Lina's this morning before 9:30 A.M.—" he pinched a piece of pecan sweet roll from Harry's plate and popped it in his mouth "—and they start to suspect. Do it three days in a row and they're wanting to piece the details together. Where did you go after Lina's? How long did you stay? And by the way, has anyone seen your wife? If so, how did she look? Happy? Sad? Mad?" He snagged another piece of pecan sweet roll. "Seemingly insignificant details, when pieced together, can make up a story worth reading, or interpreting."

Harry handed Pop his plate with the half-eaten roll. "You think the town is paying that close attention?"

Pop smiled and nodded. "They're always watching. Always thinking. It's not really nosiness, but more what I like to call interest. And they usually tell me, so I'll keep my ears open and my eyes on any suspicious activity."

"Like?" Despite Harry's forlorn and hopeless state of

mind, the man had him curious.

"Like, are two busybodies talking to one another? Like, are questions being asked by people who have no business asking? You need to stick to your routine. Don't change a thing."

Harry cleared his throat, tried to ignore the heat creeping from his neck to his cheeks. "I've been sleeping in the guest room."

"Huh?" And then, "Oh. Well, kids tell stories, can't help that."

"I told them I had the flu and had to stay away."

"That should buy you another day, tops. Nothing you can do but pray they don't land on that subject and start chirping like a robin in spring." He shook his head. "I remember when my son, Anthony, came home and told my Lucy I'd been holding hands with Ruby Vincina. When I got home, Lucy was waiting for me with a wooden spoon and a tongue that was sharper than two-year-old New York cheddar. She went on past lunchtime, but I had to wait until she finished her tirade before I could tell her I was helping Ruby get a rose thorn out of her finger, and the reason she had it there in the first place was because she was giving the bush to Lucy, seeing as Ruby wanted to thin out her border and Lucy loved roses."

"Huh. How about that?" If only Harry's situation were as simple as a rose bush and a thorn.

Pop's expression softened and his voice dipped in memory. "My Lucy said she wasn't having another woman touching me, not even for twenty rose bushes."

"So you worked it out?"

"Eventually." He scowled. "I had to sleep on the couch for a week; she said Ruby Vincina had stolen three men from their families and I wasn't going to be the fourth. Oh, but I had to do some penance and some promising." He scratched his chin and nodded. "No more homemade pasta from Dolly Regati. No slices of salami from Nesta Tagliona. And absolutely nothing, not even a smile, from Ruby Vincina."

Harry pulled himself out of his situation long enough to ask, "Were you a ladies' man?"

Pop turned and pinned Harry with eyes that sparkled beneath his glasses, followed by a grin that covered half his face. "I had a way with the ladies. Polite, smooth, sharp dresser." He tapped his sneakered feet together. "Back in the day, I didn't go out of the house unless I was in my Sunday best, hair slicked back, hat in my hand, shoes shined. The key to the ladies is taking the time to make them feel special, pay a compliment or two. Not a lie, but an embellishment. Doesn't hurt anyone and it makes them feel like a beauty queen."

"No kidding?" So Pop *had* been a ladies' man. And he was giving Harry lessons. If his heart weren't broken, he might actually laugh.

"But that all stopped the day my Lucy came to Magdalena. She was visiting her aunt for the summer. I sat three pews behind her in church and stared at that beautiful red hair and when she turned I caught a glimpse of pale skin. Didn't hear a lick of the sermon, but when she walked out of Mass, I was waiting for her, hat in hand, smile on my face, and a line of sweet words all wound up and waiting." He swiped his eyes and chuckled. "I didn't get four words out before she glared at me and said she didn't like syrup on her pancakes and that's exactly what I was. Sticky and bellyache sweet." He shrugged. "She came around." A spark of mischief flashed in his eyes. "Ended up loving syrup, on her pancakes, French toast, rolls, just about everything."

***

When the police chief handed Ben the call of suspicious activity at a house on Bayberry Street, he recognized the street number as Gina's. Was she home? If so, did she know she could be in danger? He raced to the cruiser, hopped in, and tore down the road. Within minutes, he was outside of Gina's house. He pulled in the drive, drew his gun, and began to check the perimeter. He'd made it inside the gate leading to the backyard when he heard the noise. Part whimper, part moan. He made his way toward the sound, and when he reached the deck, he spotted a woman curled in a ball on a lawn chair, head bent, shoulders shaking, feet bare.

Ben holstered his weapon and approached the woman, stopping when he was a few feet away. "Ma'am. Are you all right?" The whimper-moans stopped and the woman lifted her head. Her face was streaked with mascara, her eyes and nose swollen and puffy. "Bree?"

Bree Kinkaid stared back at him, confusion clouding her face. "Ben? What are you doing here?" She swiped both hands across her face and made a valiant effort to pull herself together, but it was useless. The woman was too disheveled and in too much misery.

He pulled a chair toward her and sat down, noting the scrapes, blisters, and ground-in dirt on her bare feet. "I got a call that someone was trying to break in, so I came to check it out."

A small laugh escaped her lips and for a second, she sounded like the woman he'd met at Cash and Tess's wedding. "That's silly. I wasn't trying to break in. Gina leaves a key in a box under the hydrangea in the front bed, and she said I can come over whenever I need a break."

Another laugh, this one stronger. "But I couldn't get the darn key to work." She paused, fished in her shorts pocket, and pulled out the key. "Do you want to try it?"

"Sure." He took the key from her and held out his hand. "Why don't we try it together?" He wasn't leaving her alone, not in her current state of mind, which was at best, unstable.

"Okay." She took his hand and unfolded herself from the chair to stand. He noticed again how thin she was, how un-Breelike, her hair, a tangle of strawberry blond, her shirt stained, her feet blistered and dirty. Had she walked here from her house? Why? And where were her children? Were they responsible for running their mother into the ground, or was there another reason for the exhausted appearance and lackluster attitude?

Ben took the key and led Bree to the front of the house, noting her unsteady gait, the pressure of her hand on his arm, the quiet sniffs. When they reached the red door, he fitted the key in the lock and turned it. No hassle, no problem. He opened the door and said, "Why don't you go sit down and I'll get you something to drink."

She glanced at her feet and said, "Gina won't like it if I walk on her carpet with dirty feet. I'll stay in the kitchen."

The woman looked like she was about to topple over and sitting on a wooden chair with no cushion was not going to help. "Why don't we get you cleaned up and then you can curl up on that cozy-looking couch?"

Her lips pulled into a semblance of a smile. "It is cozy; I've fallen asleep on it lots of times." Her brows pinched together and she looked at him. "Have you ever fallen asleep on Gina's couch?"

"What? No, I haven't." Why would she ask him that?

"Just wondered." She nodded, pushing a tangle of hair

off her neck. "You'd make a good couple." More nodding. "I've thought so since the wedding." Her voice drifted as she made her way to the kitchen chair. "Something about the way you were watching her, with this intense expression on your face." A trickle of laughter slipped from her lips. "And she was definitely watching you, probably trying to dissect your brain. That's Gina, only trusts what she can see on a spreadsheet with supporting documentation." She sighed and eased onto the chair. "Maybe I should have been more like Gina instead of trusting my heart and my messed-up brain to guide me."

What to say to that and what to say to her assessment regarding his attraction to Gina Servetti and Gina's interest in him? Of course, Bree was way off. Hadn't she just admitted to a messed-up brain? He guessed Bree tended to romanticize people and situations, even when there was absolutely nothing to romanticize—as in whatever she thought she saw or felt with him and Gina.

Ben found a metal pot in a bottom drawer, filled it with warm water, and grabbed the dish soap. Gina would probably have a fit that he was using her kitchen as a clean-up facility, but he didn't have much choice. Besides, he planned to have Bree cleaned up and resting before Gina got home. "Is Gina working?" He knelt on the floor and bathed Bree's right foot, careful not to scrub too hard and open any cuts.

"Uh-huh. What time is it?"

"Almost five." He lifted her foot out of the water and wrapped it in a dish towel. "Other foot."

Bree placed her left foot in the pot, wincing when it touched the water. "Ouch." She lifted her foot from the water and examined her baby toe. "Yuck."

The underside of her toe was raw and swollen. "Let's

get you fixed up." Ben took extra care cleaning the area and when he was done, wrapped her foot in a matching dish towel. "There you go." He leaned back on his heels and smiled.

"My own personal foot-care specialist." When Bree smiled this time, the smile reached her eyes. She lifted both dishcloth-clad feet in the air and said, "Wouldn't Gina have a fit if she saw us?"

Yeah, he imagined she would. "I'm sure she'd have a thing or two to say about it." He paused, added, "More like an hour's worth of how I invaded her privacy and her personal space."

Her smile spread. "You're absolutely right. See, I knew you two were perfect for each other."

"Bree—"

"No, really." She held up a hand. "You figured out how she would react and it didn't stop you; you did it anyway. Most men wouldn't even try. They'd consider Gina too much work, too odd, and definitely too standoffish." Her voice dipped, softened to a whisper coated in sadness. "New love is so special. There's nothing like it."

Okay, he'd let her think whatever odd-conceived notion she wanted about him and Gina if it got her to tell him what was really going on. "Bree." He kept his voice low and even. "What's the matter?"

Her lips quivered and she shook her head. "Have you seen the honeymoon suite at the Heart Sent? It's so beautiful and Mimi scatters rose petals on the bed." She paused, and he had to lean closer to hear the rest. "Lots of them. So very beautiful." Her eyes glistened when she looked at him. "You'll see. Gina doesn't like the idea of making love on rose petals, but she'll change her mind with you."

"Bree."

"I know it's early, but it's going to happen." A tear spilled down her cheek, slipped to her chin. "I always know about these things. That's my gift. I knew Cash and Tess were going to get back together…and Will and Olivia Carrick. I can see it and feel it, just by watching other people. There's this energy between the couple; it's like they're shooting laser beams, even before they realize they're attracted to each other. But—" her voice wobbled, fell "—it only works on other people, not me." More tears. "Why isn't it like that with Brody? He's my whole heart; shouldn't I be able to see those laser beams?"

What the hell was she talking about? Ben's right temple pinched and he wished Gina would hurry up and get home. She'd find a way to put a stop to Bree's chatter about sorting couples via laser beams and whatever else she thought she sensed. Somewhere between all this jabber was the reason for today. He picked on the point where the tears ramped up. Talk of her husband and a lack of connection? Was that what she meant? Were they having problems? This was way out of his comfort zone and certainly his area of expertise. Ask him about motorcycles or cars and he was all over it, but relationships and how they happened? Nope. Melissa was a casualty of his inability to open up, talk about feelings, and all of that other nonsense.

"I'm not very good with relationships, but you and Brody seem like a good couple." What did he know about what made a good couple? He'd pick Nate and Christine Desantro and Cash and Tess over Bree and Brody, but what else was he going to say? He couldn't tell her he hadn't liked the way her husband summoned her the afternoon of the barbecue, sitting on the deck in a cushioned recliner, asking for a beer, telling her to look after the kids. Wasn't there supposed to be a sharing of duties and respect for the other person? He might not know much, but Ben did remember that.

Bree sighed. "He wants another baby."

There it was. That's what this was all about. He'd bet his Harley on it. "A boy?" Calculated guess.

Another sigh, this one longer, deeper. "Uh-huh."

"And you don't." Guessing again, but with a sigh like that, he'd bet he wasn't far off.

She shrugged. "I don't know." She sniffed and wiped her eyes. "I still haven't gotten over losing Samantha."

"You had a miscarriage?"

"Four months ago."

"Weren't you pregnant at the wedding?" She'd been ready to pop at the wedding and that hadn't even been a year ago. So, she'd gotten pregnant *again*?

"I was carrying Scarlett. She'll be one in December. Brody wanted to keep trying for that boy, and, of course, I understand that, but I needed some time to recover. I was just plain worn out." She swiped at her eyes. "But he said our children were gifts and it was our duty to bring them into our lives while we were able to, no matter the work or sacrifice involved. He said every father wants a boy, kind of like a legacy passed down. Girls are important, too, he said, but we need a boy. Brody provided the legacy for his daddy, but I guess my daddy didn't get his legacy, seeing as I was an only child, and a girl at that." Sadness coated her words, slipped a few octaves. "Daddy wouldn't even let me work in the family business, said manufacturing was a man's job and when the time came, he'd turn things over to Brody. My husband can't even balance a checkbook; how's he going to run a business?" She swiped both hands across her face but the tears kept coming. "Doesn't matter. My job is babies and providing a legacy." She sniffed. "I'm not smart like Gina and Tess. I never went to college and I never had a job except cashiering at Sal's part-time. I understand my responsibility to my family and I love them more than anything." She squeezed her eyes shut and whimpered. "But I am pure exhausted right now."

"Bree." He didn't like the way she talked down about herself. It wasn't healthy for her body or her mind, but she'd probably been hearing how inadequate and disappointing she was her whole life. Why wouldn't she think these opinions were true? He knew what cruel and hurtful words could do to a young brain, how they could make the person believe they were no good, would never be any good, and deserved the misfortune that came their way. Ben laid a hand on her arm. "It'll be okay. You don't have to have more children if you don't want to. And whoever says a man needs a boy to fulfill some legacy is just plain wrong." He rubbed her back, spoke in a soft voice. "You're worn out, mind and body, and you need a recharge. I don't know anything about having babies but your body's telling you it needs a rest."

What kind of jerk would demand his wife keep spitting out babies until he got a boy? What the hell was wrong with Brody Kinkaid? And why did Bree put up with it? He had a long list of questions for Gina, if she ever got home, starting and ending with the backstory on Brody Kinkaid.

Chapter 7

The first thing Gina noticed when she walked in the door was the smell. She sniffed, sniffed again. Was that a man's cologne? She couldn't identify the scent and after a few more sniffs wasn't sure if it was cologne or the scented garbage bag in the trash can. She made her way to the kitchen and had almost convinced herself she'd been imagining things when she noticed the kitchen chair was askew. Not only that, but two dish towels, folded in half, rested on the back of the other chair. And someone had used her pasta pot and set it in the drain board.

Someone had definitely invaded her home, used her chairs, her dish towels, and maybe helped themselves to a bowl of pasta. But who would do that? Bree had been stopping over lately, supposedly for a breather, but the visits had grown more frequent as Bree became more forlorn. Soon, Gina had to tell someone else, maybe Tess and Christine, and then maybe they could all talk to Bree about getting professional help to deal with the loss of her baby. Nobody wanted to talk about it, especially that oaf, Brody. He wanted to move on as though Bree hadn't carried a child inside of her, as though the baby didn't matter. One look at Bree and anyone with half a brain cell could tell she was grieving the loss of her baby and needed time and closure. What she did not need was another pregnancy.

If Bree stopped over when Gina wasn't here, she always left a note on the dry erase board in the kitchen, telling her what she'd done: taken a nap, a shower, painted her nails, cooked ham and eggs. Gina glanced at the board and sure enough, there was writing on it. She moved closer but the bold scrawl didn't mention a shower, a nap, and certainly not painted nails.

We need to talk. See you at 7:00. I'll bring dinner. You're low on dish soap. Ben

How had that man gotten into the house? She ran outside, knelt down, and looked at the base of the hydrangea bush for the small box where she kept a key. She spotted the box, grabbed it, and flipped it open. Empty. How could he possibly have known she hid a key outside, let alone under a gigantic bush? This was all about those damn roses he sent and the phone calls she'd ignored. Did the man really not understand that maybe she just didn't want to see him, that maybe she had nothing to say?

If he thought a meal and roses could get her to spill her guts on the town's who's who, he could think again. Why on earth had he selected *her?* She wasn't good at reading people, had never understood the subtle nuances that marked a person upset or merely annoyed. The ability to differentiate wasn't in her DNA.

Of course, he'd be used to women tripping over themselves to thank him—for a smile, a kind gesture, a dozen roses. She wasn't interested in a conversation where he would apologize and then try to weasel information from her. And what had he been cooking in her kitchen, and why were two dish towels neatly folded on the back of her kitchen chair? And the comment about needing more dish soap? What on earth was that about?

Ben Reed had broken the law and waltzed into her house and should be glad she wasn't going to press charges. How would it look if the new police sergeant were charged with breaking and entering? The whole town would read about it in the *Magdalena Press*, and if they had doubts about the pretty city boy and his intentions before, those doubts would disappear. They'd probably want to get rid of him, maybe beg Bud to return, despite the bad knee and weeks of physical therapy ahead.

Gina changed into jeans and a navy top, glanced at her watch, and realized she still had twenty minutes before he arrived. When he pulled in the driveway, she should tell him to go home and take his dinner with him. No man had ever brought her dinner and she certainly didn't need one to start now. She could fend for herself, which included preparing meals that, while not exactly gourmet, were palatable and filling.

As for the twelve breathtakingly beautiful long-stemmed roses, well, she should box them up as well and hand them back. She glanced at the cut glass vase and knew she couldn't do it. The roses were too beautiful, the gesture too rare.

Gina planned her interrogation down to the way she'd hold her head and the tone of her voice. But when she opened the door and saw the look on his face, she forgot the anger and arsenal of accusations. "What's wrong?"

"It's Bree." He stepped inside, carrying two bags. As he passed, she smelled the same scent that had filtered through the house earlier: Ben Reed's cologne.

"Bree?" She followed him into the kitchen, stared at his back as he removed containers from one of the bags. "What about her? Is she all right?"

He turned to face her. "Not really. A phone call came in this afternoon of suspicious activity outside your house."

"Here?"

"I took the call. When I got here, I found Bree on your

deck. She was in bad shape."

Poor Bree. She could not get past her loss. "Did she talk to you?" Did Bree tell him about the baby she'd lost? Or that Brody wanted more, a son to be exact? Or that even if he got his son, he'd want another one? And what about the fact that Bree's heart was breaking with sadness over the child who had died in her womb. She could barely talk to her friends about it, and certainly hadn't mentioned it to her parents or Brody's.

"As a matter of fact, she did." He glanced around the kitchen and asked, "Where are the plates and utensils?"

Gina made her way to the cupboard and pulled out two plates, opened the silverware drawer and removed forks, knives, spoons, and placed them on the table. "What did she say?"

He ignored the question as he filled their plates with chicken, brown rice, and asparagus. "We need napkins and something to drink. Water's fine. The chicken breasts were marinated in balsamic vinaigrette with garlic and rosemary. Mimi said you liked rosemary." He placed each plate on a Gerbera daisy placemat and sank into a chair. "I guessed on the asparagus."

Gina handed him water and a napkin and sat down. "You guessed right." She studied the food on her plate, a reasonable portion size with protein, fiber, and a healthy green. "Did you cook all of this?"

He shrugged and a tiny swirl of red crept up his neck. "I did. Mimi let me use her kitchen. She offered to send over chicken parmesan, but I wanted to cook."

"Oh. Thank you." No man had ever cooked a meal for her before. She took a few bites of chicken and rice, then forked an asparagus. "This is delicious, but you really didn't need to do this."

His gaze pulled her in. "Yes, I did. I owed you an apology."

"But the roses—" she stopped, cleared her throat "—they're beautiful, but again, not necessary. We can just agree that we were at odds on that particular subject and move on."

"Right." He studied her a few seconds too long, as though seeing more than she wanted him to see.

"Tell me about Bree."

He shook his head, sighed. "That whole situation is one big train wreck waiting to happen. Has she been like this since she lost the baby?"

"She told you about that? I'm surprised because Bree doesn't really talk about it, though it's not like we can't tell she's struggling. Anyone who knows her can see the sadness in everything she does: her voice, her actions, her smile."

"She said you leave a key for her in case she stops over and wants to rest a bit or needs a break. I didn't ask what she needed the break from because I figured it had to do with the kids, but now I'm wondering if it's her husband."

Gina clamped her mouth shut, trying to keep her personal feelings for Brody Kinkaid inside. The man was an idiot, bursting with testosterone and the desire to procreate. She chewed her food and let the seconds tick away. Maybe Ben Reed would continue speculating and she wouldn't need to say anything.

"Actually, I'm pretty sure the husband is a big part of the problem."

Bingo. "That man is the main problem. Bree isn't allowed to be a person. She can be a mother and a wife, but not Bree Kinkaid, *person*." The words spilled out before she remembered that she wasn't going to say a word.

He toyed with his fork and said, "I'm not much on analyzing marital relationships, but she seemed happy last year."

"Oh, you mean at the wedding? Bree is always happy when she's pregnant." She tried to yank the words back but they kept coming. "That's the only time she *is* happy, and she wants everyone to have babies, even those who don't want them."

Those blue eyes pierced her. "Like you?"

"What? I'm not looking to have a baby."

"Now. Or ever?"

"That's a very inappropriate question," she blurted out. "And my personal life has nothing to do with Bree's issues. We've tried to get her to counseling, alone or with Brody, but she refuses. We even told her we'd find a therapist in another town, but she didn't want to hear about it."

"Who's the we?"

Gina eyed him, trying to decide whether she should divulge that information.

"I don't even have to take an educated guess and I'm fairly certain I'll get the names right."

Which meant he already knew. "Tess and Christine."

"Do their husbands know?"

"You mean did they give their wives permission to help a friend?"

"No. I meant exactly what I said, because I'm guessing Cash and Nate Desantro would not sit by and do nothing if they thought a woman was in distress."

He was right. Nate would have a face-to-face with Brody and demand he grow up and learn to respect his wife. Cash wouldn't be so diplomatic; he'd probably try for a quick left hook to the jaw, followed by a right. Brody might be a mass of muscles, but he didn't have the fight in him that Cash did.

"Well? Do they know their wives are trying to help with a domestic situation that could get ugly?"

She shook her head. "Brody might be a lot of things, but he'd never hurt her."

"Do you have any idea how many times I've heard that? Usually right before the guy hurts her."

Brody wouldn't hurt Bree. He wouldn't. "Bree just kind of lost it after the miscarriage. Some days she doesn't shower and that is so not Bree. She used to put on makeup and a nice outfit to go to the mailbox. Her house was spotless, not a smudge or paper out of order. Now?" She shook her head and sighed. "You saw her house at the cookout. That's not normal. And the way she forgets to—" Gina stopped. She'd said too much. Way too much.

"The way she forgets to what?" he prodded.

"Nothing. We'll take care of it. I'll call Tess and Christine tomorrow and we'll talk to Bree again. Please don't say anything to Nate and Cash. Let us try to work it out. If they get involved it's going to get messy."

He stared at her. "I don't like it."

"Please." Her voice dipped, softened. "We'll talk to her."

Several seconds passed before he spoke. "Only if you keep me informed." When she frowned and opened her mouth to protest, he held up a hand to stop her. "Those are my terms. If it were my wife getting involved in a domestic dispute, I wouldn't like it, but I'd sure as hell want to know."

"Okay. I'll keep you posted."

"Daily reports." She rolled her eyes. "And be careful."

Gina sighed. "Yes. Daily reports and I'll be careful. Now, are you going to tell me what you were doing with my pasta pot and dish towels?"

He shrugged and smiled. "Making pasta?"

***

Nate found Christine in the backyard pushing Anna on the swing set he'd built this spring. If anyone had told him a few years ago he'd have a swing set in his backyard and plans to build a fort in his notebook, he'd have said that was a sick joke. But everything had changed when Christine walked into his life, and though they had a rough start—okay, impossible start—he thanked God every day for bringing her to him. Christine was his light, and Anna was their joy.

She hadn't spotted him yet and he took this time to watch his wife and daughter, unobserved. Anna looked more like a Blacksworth with each passing season, her black curls rich and lustrous like her mother's, her eyes an unforgettable blue. They'd talked about another baby, had actually done a bit more than talking, and if they were lucky, there would be news to share in a month or two. That would thrill Lily who loved being an aunt and told them at least once a month that she needed more nieces and a nephew or two.

Nate made his way down the deck steps, smiling at the sound of his daughter's laughter. Maybe they'd have another girl, with black curls like her sister's. Or a boy. It didn't matter. What mattered was that they were a family and would build a solid foundation for their children to learn, and love, and grow.

"Hey." He was a few feet away, a step or two from touching distance. "How are my girls?" When Christine turned, the first thing he noticed were the puffy eyes, the swollen nose. "What's wrong?" He glanced at Anna, who squealed and waved her hands at him, a smile covering her face. "Is it Anna?" Their baby looked perfect and happy, but children could be taken away in a few breaths. Nate unfastened his daughter from the swing, lifted her into his arms. Her eyes were bright, her skin pink, her tiny fingers strong as they patted his face. "Christine?" He didn't like the near panic in his voice or the ache in his chest, but he'd realized long ago that loving and fear were intertwined. "Tell me what's going on."

She tried for a smile, but her lips quivered and flattened. "Oh, Nate." Her eyes glistened with tears. "I don't even know where to begin."

He stiffened. Comments like that put him on alert. They signaled a warning of impending disaster on some level, personal or professional, most of the time involving relationships. Was Christine unhappy with him? Did she think their relationship was in trouble? He breathed faster, harder, but he couldn't get enough air. She loved him; they were solid. She was nothing like his first wife; their relationship was nothing like what he'd shared with Patrice either, if you could call it sharing. He'd never shared with anyone but Christine, but Patrice had used almost the exact same words when she'd called it quits. He clutched Anna against his chest. They were a family and they were going to remain a family. The vulnerability was the part of loving someone that got to him, that and the painful scenarios that zapped his brain when he thought of losing Christine. "Just tell me, straight out."

Her voice cracked. "Can we go inside?"

No, damn it, he did not want to go inside. He wanted to hear whatever pain she planned to dole out right here, now, before another second passed. But he had to be patient and fight the ache in his chest that threatened to squeeze the life from him. So, he said, "Sure," and headed toward the house, side by side, with Anna in his arms—like a family. Nate opened the sliding door and waited for Christine to step inside. He followed her into the living room, placed Anna on the floor with Lola, her stuffed dog, and said, "Okay, we're inside. What's going on?"

"Don't be angry."

"I'm not angry." He wasn't angry; he was scared.

She moved toward him, clasped his hands, and looked up at him, those blue eyes bright and tear-filled. She was beautiful and perfect, and he had known from the very beginning that she was too good for him, had known in his gut that one day she might figure that out, too. He'd never much believed in luck or good fortune, had counted on will and hard work to earn him scraps of peace, and maybe even a little happiness. Then Christine had come along and turned the unfortunate circumstances of their meeting into good fortune, and how could he consider that anything but luck?

And now he was a few sentences away from losing it all.

Anna squealed and said, "Da Da, Da Da." Christine scooped her up and kissed her cheek.

"Just tell me." He braced himself for the blow.

She licked her lips, lips he'd tasted so many times, and said, "Uncle Harry might be my father."

Nate had been prepared for words that might threaten their marriage, the same words that had ended his first marriage. He had not been prepared to hear Harry might be her father. "Come again?"

"Uncle Harry might be my father."

As bizarre as that sounded, it was a relief, a gigantic, incomprehensible relief. The ache in his chest cased and he blew out a long breath. And then he laughed.

"Nate? Why are you laughing?" Confusion and spurts of anger filtered her words. "This is not funny, not at all."

He smiled and clasped her face between his hands, placed a soft kiss on her mouth. "I'm not laughing about that. I'm laughing because for the last ten minutes my brain has been conjuring up horrible scenarios, and compared to those, this is nothing."

She pulled back, looked into his eyes. He was no good at hiding things from his wife, even ridiculous thoughts that had no basis. "Exactly what sort of horrible scenarios are we talking about?"

He shrugged, ignoring the heat creeping from his neck to his cheeks. They'd been through this a time or two before, and while he'd gotten better, the occasional insecurity crept in and threatened to smother his logic. The "Oh, Nate, I don't even know where to begin" might have been the same words Patrice used to signal the end of their marriage, but Christine was *not* Patrice. Not even close.

"Nate?"

The tone of her voice said *ticked off* and he knew why. "Okay, maybe my brain was having those thoughts it's not supposed to have." He stroked her cheek. "You know, the ones where I think I'm not good enough to change the oil in your car."

Her lips twitched. "So, you've graduated to changing the oil in my car? Wow. Last time it was taking out my garbage."

"You know what I mean." He brushed his thumb over her lips, pulled her closer. "I'm sorry for doubting you, and I'm sorry for making this about me, when it's not." He paused, let Anna grab his thumb, and said, "I'll always be here for you. Now why don't we sit down and you can tell me why you think Harry might be your father?"

Christine relayed the whole sordid tale, starting and ending with her mother and the accusations of seduction. Right. Nate didn't believe that any more than he believed Gloria Blacksworth was a helpless victim. That woman was like the cancer that eventually took her life, spilling into people's lives, destroying their dreams—destroying them. He actually felt sorry for Charles Blacksworth, an emotion he never expected to feel toward a man who had caused him years of resentment and anger. But there it was, lodged in his gut, maybe because Nate had a child and couldn't imagine her belonging to anyone else. At least Charles never knew. And Harry? Damn, but that was a rough one to accept. How had he sat at his brother's table, year in, year out, and not self-destructed from guilt and remorse? Was that why he'd been so reckless? Maybe he *had* been trying to self-destruct with the booze and the women. And maybe Greta had saved him. Well, Nate was not going to let Gloria Blacksworth destroy Harry's second chance.

"We'll get it sorted out." Nate stroked her back, kissed the top of her head, and sighed. "I'll talk to Harry."

Christine lifted her head from his chest and looked at him. "You will? What will you say?"

"I'll tell him I'm not going to let one miserable woman ruin a whole family." His voice hardened. "She tried that one already, remember?"

"I know. I thought maybe she'd changed." She paused, glanced at their daughter who'd crawled off the couch and was busy with a plastic cup and spoon. "She had to have known that hurting Uncle Harry would hurt me, and maybe even hurt us. I'm sorry I didn't tell you about this before, but honestly, I don't like to think about it, and I don't like to think about the possibility of the man who raised me not being my biological father."

Nate tucked a few strands of hair behind her ear. "Then don't think about it. You had a father and you have an uncle, and nobody needs to know any different."

"What about your mother? Should we tell her?"

"No." He didn't even hesitate on that one. "We're not going to do that to your dad, or Harry. My mother is a very forgiving woman, but I don't want her looking at Harry differently." He pulled her closer. "The guy's paid enough for his past." He thought of the notebook Gloria had sent after her death. He'd hidden it in the closet to protect Christine from whatever venom might be inside. Now he wondered if there were other accusations involving people who had no idea she wanted to destroy them. Well, it wasn't going to happen, not if he could help it. He'd read the damn notebook and if Gloria Blacksworth incriminated anyone on those pages, he'd burn the blasted thing.

"Nate? What about Greta? She's the innocent one in this whole mess. Do you think I should go talk to her?"

"No. I'll do it. She needs to know just how vicious your mother can be, even from the grave."

***

Harry wandered around for the next two days, trying to give Greta the space she claimed to need. He'd taken Pop's advice, headed straight to the florist and walked in the house carrying two dozen long-stemmed red roses. He even bought a card filled with words like *regret, starting over*, and *love of my life*. Nope. Didn't do the trick. As a matter of fact, they didn't do anything but make Greta's pink lips pull into the ugliest scowl Harry had ever witnessed—and it had been directed at him.

Turned out his wife didn't want things, she wanted *details*. Intimate details about his relationship—she refused to say the word *affair*—with Gloria. When she stated her request in a quiet voice, her gaze fixed on the corner of the kitchen table, Harry had struggled to formulate a response. She was serious. Greta wanted to know all about the affair—yes, damn it, call it what it was—from the first time the idea entered his brain to the second he slipped out of Gloria's bed for the last time. He'd tried to tell her that answering those questions wouldn't help them. In fact, it could only cause more damage, more hurt, some of it possibly irreparable. Didn't matter. Greta said she needed to picture it in her head so she could move past it. According to her, if she didn't know the details, the imagining would be so much worse.

Now how the hell did she know that? Maybe the details would prove much worse than her imaginings, and once he'd puked out the sordid truth, she'd look at him with disgust and say "I'm sorry, but this is so much worse than I thought it would be. It's over. I want a divorce." He couldn't risk that. Greta and the kids were all that mattered to him and he couldn't lose them. But if he refused to give her what she wanted, he might as well kiss life as he knew it good-bye.

The indecision is what brought him to O'Reilly's bar tonight. It was easy to drink among people he didn't know or care about, people who had their own problems and weren't interested in his. He finished his second scotch and contemplated a third when a woman climbed on the barstool next to him and slid a smile his way.

"Hello."

He nodded. She had a sultry voice and a body to match. Long hair, dark eyes, breasts that strained against the fabric of her low-cut blouse in a plea for attention. And curves, lots of curves.

"I'm Natalie." She extended a tanned arm. "Natalie

Servetti."

"Harry." He shook her hand; her skin was soft, warm.

"I know who you are." The smile spread. "Everyone does."

Harry liked the sound of that. At least *everyone* didn't think he was a degenerate. "I guess people talk in small towns."

"Oh, they do, but can you blame them?" She toyed with the pendant nestled at the top of her cleavage. "You're a very handsome man, Harry Blacksworth. Who wouldn't notice you?"

He grinned. Damn straight on that one. His pulse kicked in double time. "Keep talking like that and this head will swell so much it won't fit through the door."

"I like the sound of that." Her gaze slid to his crotch, settled there, moved back to his face. "A lot."

Hell, he'd been talking about the head between his shoulders, not the other one. But it was the other one that responded. He cleared his throat and looked away, pushed the sexy voice and vanilla scent from his brain. "I'm sure people are more interested in my swimming pool than me." He was a married man who loved his wife, and even though said wife thought he was a worthless piece of crap right now, he would remain true to her. He *would not* betray her.

"I'm interested in your swimming pool, Harry." She rolled his name around on her tongue like she was savoring a special treat. Sexy as hell. That other head perked up, waited. "I'm interested in everything about you. Will you invite me to swim in your pool? I prefer swimming in the nude, with the water lapping over every inch of me." She laid a hand on his arm, whispered in his ear, "Will you swim with me, Harry?"

Good Lord! He shifted in his seat, tried to still the

erection in his trousers, but the woman knew how to get a man going without even touching him. He bet she could rival Bridgett in the bedroom. And the hot tub. And hell yes, the damn pool.

"Why don't we find a booth and talk about how much fun we could have in your pool?" Her tongue flicked his ear, traced his earlobe. "Or we could go to your car and I can give you a sample." Her hand found his crotch, cupped him. Her laughter spilled over him, made him harder. "Oh, I see you like the sound of that. Come on, Harry, let's have some fun." She took his hand, placed it high on her thigh, and whispered, "I'm not wearing any panties."

He could have her in less than ten minutes, five if he slapped a twenty on the counter and didn't wait for change. This woman didn't know him, didn't know anything about him other than what she'd heard or maybe read in the newspaper. She was looking for a good time and someone to pay for it. There'd been too many Natalie types in his day: beautiful, sexy, ready and willing to do anything his imagination might require.

But they were nothing like Greta.

Natalie Servetti began to massage his erection, right there on the barstool, with the bartender three feet away, Bob Seger crooning in the background and the Yankees playing on the television.

"Stop." Harry jerked his hand from her thigh, grabbed her wrist, and stilled her hand. "I can't."

"Why?" She nipped his ear. "I know you want to."

"I'm married," he blurted out.

"I know." Another nip and an attempt to continue the massage.

"And I love my wife."

"Good for you." She slipped off the stool, pressed her

breasts against his side, and stroked his back. "Now why don't we take a bottle of wine and have our own little party in the back seat of your car? Or, you could come back to my place, stretch out on the bed, and we can really have some fun. Hmm. You look like a man who knows his way around a woman's body." She rubbed those breasts against his shoulder, moaned. "And I can guarantee I know my way around a man's. With my hands, my tongue…" Another moan. "I'll pleasure you so well you won't want to get out of bed for a week. Of course—" she kissed the back of his neck, trailed her lips to his cheek "—you shouldn't take my word for it. If I were you, I'd demand a lick-by-lick demonstration."

Harry clenched his jaw, tried to erase the words and the vision of this woman's supple body doing all sorts of crazy things to him. She knew exactly what to say, how to say it, and even what parts to leave out. Sex with her would blast him off the barstool, several times. But when it was over and the brain between his shoulders started working again, what then? He'd be no different than he was before Greta changed his life. In fact, he'd be far worse because he'd have to live with the knowledge that he'd held heaven in his hand and had thrown it away.

"Natalie." He turned in his seat and eased away from her. "Sit down. I want to talk to you."

She tilted her head to the side, folded her arms over her chest, no doubt to pump up the cleavage, and frowned. "Talk?"

"Sure. You know, one party communicating with the other, having a conversation involving words." He smiled at her as the head between his shoulders beat down the one between his legs, forcing that one into hiding.

Natalie Servetti inched onto the stool, crossed one

glistening, tanned leg over the other, and said in a tone Harry recognized as pissed, "Most of the men I've met say I have a very distinct method of communicating that they've rarely encountered before."

No doubt. Bullshit for good sex and a great tongue. He'd heard it all, done it all, too, or damn near close, and now that his thought processes were clicking again, he pegged the woman for what she was—a manipulative user who didn't care who she hurt in her pursuit of pleasure. "Do they tell you that before or after you've had sex with them?"

Oh, she didn't like that. People hiding from the truth usually didn't like to see their scars ripped open and left to bleed, especially when those scars were big and ugly. She pinched her lips together and narrowed her gaze on him, like a she-cat about to pounce. "Sex is sex and I'm very good at it." The nostrils flared, the left side of her jaw twitched. "Nobody's ever been disappointed."

Harry nodded. He didn't doubt her claim. "But do they stay? That's what I'm asking you." Now that his brain was working again, he knew he'd heard about this woman before. But where and from whom?

Her full lips pulled into a tight smile. "Let's just say they always come back."

"Ah." That meant she was a rebounder and had probably been passed around a time or twenty. "But don't you want your own man? Wouldn't it be more satisfying than stealing someone else's?"

She tossed a hunk of hair behind her shoulder and stared him down. "I have a voracious appetite. One man would be boring."

He actually laughed at that one. "That's code for 'I'm petrified of commitment and showing my true self to another person.' I know because that used to be me, until I met my wife." Harry rubbed his jaw, confident in his words and his commitment to the woman who owned his heart. "My wife and kids are my world, and while it might be exciting for a span of three seconds to consider, other, ah, diversions with a younger, uninhibited partner, it would only be about the sex. And honey, the sex isn't going to carry you very far. Once the excitement dies down, the sameness settles in, and guess what? You actually have to have a conversation with the other person. Not body language but real words, real thoughts." He paused, added, "Real feelings. That's when you know what you've got. If you can't string three sentences together without struggling, then you've got a problem."

"Maybe. Or maybe not."

She toyed with the pendant tucked in her cleavage again, plumping up her breasts, but this time the head between Harry's shoulders spotted the action for the game it was and ignored the ploy. He shrugged and said, "Let's just agree to disagree, okay? One day, you might change your mind like I did. You'll find that special someone, and then you won't need to sample every dessert within a ten-mile radius. You'll have your own special dessert tray, party of two." He kind of liked that analogy, wondered if Greta might like it—when she was actually talking to him again.

"I did find my special someone." Her voice thinned. "You even know him. It's Nate. Nate Desantro."

Chapter 8

Bree almost didn't make it to her own intervention. Of course, Gina didn't come straight out and tell Bree that's what it was; instead, she said Christine was on her way to Tess's with a batch of still-warm, double fudge brownies, the ones Bree loved, and wanted them to meet her there. Gina pretended it was a last-minute decision, influenced by Nate's double fudge brownies, when in truth, the get-together had been well planned. When Gina told her friends about Bree's near meltdown and how Ben Reed calmed her, they knew it was time to have an honest conversation with their friend. So, Christine asked Nate to make Bree's favorite dessert, Tess offered her home as the meeting spot, and Gina planned to swing by and pick up Bree. It should have been easy; Brody never worked Wednesday nights, and tonight was Wednesday, except on this particular night, he decided to head to Willowick to look at a new truck with his buddy, which meant no babysitter and no intervention.

And that's where Tess got very creative and asked her mother and Will Carrick if they could babysit for an hour or two. Olivia and Will Carrick married three months ago, and if ever there was a testimony to twilight love after loss, theirs was one. They'd just returned from a trip to the Grand Canyon and next February they were headed on a cruise. Olivia smiled more and Will seemed content to do anything he could to keep those smiles coming. All they wanted now were grandchildren, but both knew that might not happen. Unless you considered Henry, the rescue Lab mix who thought he was a child but didn't quite fill in for the two-legged variety. When Tess asked if they'd babysit

Bree's children, they agreed, packed up the truck, and headed into town before the offer disappeared.

"This is the most divine brownie I have ever tasted," Bree said, scooping up a hunk of double fudge brownie and ice cream. "D-i-v-i-n-e." For just a second, she sounded more like the old Bree, looked more like her, too: eyes bright, face flushed, smile wide. And then the voice and the look slipped away, disintegrating with the next bite.

"We thought you'd like it," Gina said, nibbling on a graham cracker. Of course, she'd rather eat a scoop of vanilla ice cream smothered with double fudge chocolate brownie, but the calorie difference was too big to ignore. Besides, she'd never be able to stop at one serving. She'd eye that dessert and dig through it until she'd finished off a good half of the brownies, and maybe an equal amount of ice cream, too. It was all about self-control; isn't that what her mother told her the first time she discovered Gina in a closet eating peanut butter out of the jar? And hadn't those comments continued, grown harsher as Gina's middle expanded? There'd been no forgiveness for larger pants sizes or shirts that could have fit her mother *and* her cousin Natalie. Years of careful restraint, exercise, and planning each bite had rewarded her with an almost average figure and a number on the scale she could almost accept.

"Nate said he'll share the recipe if you like, but I told him you prefer them this way." Christine lifted a forkful of brownie. "Baked and delivered."

Bree offered a half smile and shrugged. "That is so very true."

Gina couldn't wait any longer. "Ben Reed said you visited my house the other day."

Bree's head shot up, her eyes wide. "Yes, I did visit." Her voice softened, "He's such a gentleman. Did he tell you he took care of me? Washed my feet, cleaned up my scrapes—"

"What?" The man had mentioned nothing about feet or scrapes. Had he cleaned Bree's feet using Gina's pasta pot? And the dish towels? *Had he dried her feet with them?* "He didn't say anything about it. Why don't you tell us?"

Bree pushed her plate aside and looked at her friends. "I think he's very handsome, don't you? I mean, I know we thought he was a bit of a bully when he came to town last year with—oops—" she darted a gaze at Tess "—I'm so sorry to bring that up. I didn't mean anything by it. It's just that he did seem different from the first time we met him, and even at the wedding."

"What about washing your feet?" Gina asked, trying to picture him performing the task, with the help of her pasta pot *and* dish towels.

"Oh, well, when I started walking, I didn't know where I'd end up. Brody's Mom had the kids and I thought I'd take a stroll around the neighborhood, so why wear shoes, right? Before I knew it, I was at Gina's."

That could not have been exactly accurate, seeing as Bree and Gina lived on opposite sides of town. But if Bree wanted to remember it that way, they'd let it go. For now. "And your feet got scraped and dirty and then what?"

A tiny smile slipped over Bree's tired face. "He talked to me, all nice and soft, made me kind of sleepy." She eyed Gina. "Don't you think he has the kind of voice that makes you want to tell him anything?"

"No." Why was Bree looking at her that way?

"Listen next time; he definitely does." She sighed, toyed with a strand of strawberry-blond hair. "You are one lucky woman."

"What? Why would you say that?" They were supposed

to be talking about Bree and whatever was going on in her head, not Gina and Ben Reed's "I can get you to tell me anything" voice. She glanced at Christine and Tess, hoping for help, but their curious expressions told her they were as interested in her answers as Bree was. "Oh, for heaven's sake, will you stop? We're all worried about you and all you can do is go on and on about some man who washed your feet and has a soft voice?" Speaking of the man, she couldn't wait to ask him if he'd ever heard of washing a person's feet in the bathtub, or even a bucket, like the one in the garage.

Bree paled, picked at a fingernail. "Why are you worried about me? I'm fine."

"Right. Nobody who walks across town in her bare feet and doesn't even know she's doing it is fine. What's Brody done this time? Is he still on the I-want-another-baby routine?"

Bree's lips quivered and she looked away.

"Oh, Bree." Christine touched her arm. "Will you let us talk to him? Please? You need time to grieve the loss of your baby. It's only been a few months."

"I know, but Brody says the shelf life of my eggs is dwindling, seeing as I'm over thirty and all."

Damn that man and his insensitivity. Gina clenched her jaw and said, "Shelf life has nothing to do with it when you aren't mentally ready or recovered."

"These things take time." Tess weighed in, her voice soft, sorrowful. She might not even have a shelf life to dwindle. Their friend had one ovary and a questionable reproductive system that might not give her a baby. And yet, she and Cash were dealing with this sadness, accepting it as best they could, planning for contingencies like adoption and fostering if they couldn't have children of their own.

Bree's eyes glistened with tears. "What happens if I can't have any more children? How will Brody ever handle that?"

She meant because the brute didn't have a boy. Gina snatched a hunk of brownie, stuffed it in her mouth, and chewed. Why did Bree insist on selling out her own sex? Women were strong, powerful, capable. They were not inferior or weaklings. Why couldn't Bree understand that? Gina grabbed another hunk of brownie, lifted it to her mouth…and caught her friends staring at her. She set the brownie on the napkin beside her and shrugged. "Emotional trigger, I guess."

"I'm sorry, Gina." Bree reached over and patted her hand. "Please do not let my turmoil send you over the edge and back to the way you used to be." She sniffed. "I couldn't stand to think I was the cause of that. I truly couldn't."

"I know. I'm fine." Despite her pain and sorrow, Bree remained the eternal drama queen.

"Are you worried Brody won't love you as much if you can't have more children?" Tess asked.

"Sort of." Bree sniffed again. "We had a deal. I owe him babies, at least three more." She paused, swiped at her eyes. "And a boy."

"Bree, are you for real?" Gina tried to keep her voice even, but the irritation spilled over into her words.

"What's wrong with a plan?"

"Nothing's wrong with a plan," Tess said, quietly. "But you can't always control the plan. Sometimes things happen, bad things, and you have to make the decision to adjust and adapt, or give up and wither inside."

"Tess is right," Christine said. "We all have choices, not

someone else's, but ours. Do you agree, Bree?"

"Uh-huh."

"Okay." Christine gentled her voice. "I have a question for you. Do you want more children? I don't want to know if Brody does, because the whole town knows that answer. What I want to know is if you, Bree Kinkaid, want more children."

The truth filtered through the room long before Bree spoke, seeping from the slump of her shoulders, to the tears rimming her eyes, to the tremble of her lips, and finally, to the catch in her breath. "No," she whispered. "I don't want more children."

***

When Ben arrived at work the next morning, the police chief handed him a stack of fliers and said, "School starts next week and every year we send reminders out about crosswalks and pedestrian and vehicle rules. I want you to head downtown and hand these out to the storeowners. Ask them to post them in their windows and at the register." He made a sound with his tongue that sounded like a cluck and said, "New-guy duties." Then he walked away, whistling, leaving Ben with the fliers and an attitude.

Hand out fliers? The chief had been delegating crap jobs to him all week. Visit Lottie Germaine, a senior with a bad hip, and check the contents of her fridge. Make sure she has eggs, milk, cheese, one head of broccoli, and bananas. Play parking meter cop and hand out tickets to offenders whose meter time had expired. Check park benches for vagrants. What vagrants? In a town like this, someone would open their door and give the person a meal and a bed before letting them get picked up on a hacked-up charge like that. Ben wouldn't be surprised if he got toilet-paper pickup duty when the next third Monday rolled around. These were definitely not sergeant duties, but according to Rudy Dean, a sergeant's duties were what the police chief said they were. *Jerk.*

Jeremy didn't like his father's antics and neither did the rest of the staff, if the scowls and comments they made behind the police chief's back were an indication. Still, no one dared confront the man. He sat behind his big desk and barked out assignments and criticism without regard to personal situations, abilities, or effort. Jeremy said his father was in the army back in the day, had wanted Jeremy to enlist, too, but the boy's mother pitched a fit, said her son didn't possess the constitution to battle a fly, and the old man backed down. How the boy became a police officer was an interesting question and one Ben intended to ask. Maybe the parents reached a compromise: swap out the service for a police job with the father as watchdog.

Didn't either one of them know the boy didn't belong anywhere near a gun or a potentially dangerous situation? Apparently not.

Ben tossed the fliers onto the front seat of the cruiser and made his way downtown. It was still T-shirt and shorts weather and the street was cluttered with women and children doing last-minute "before school" shopping. He'd been hearing about it from Mimi these past few days as she told him of the sidewalk sales merchants had on Main Street, and the discounts on shoes, hair cutting, school supplies, and just about anything else you needed to get ready for that first day of school.

Great. Now the whole town could watch him look like an idiot as he passed out fliers for crosswalk etiquette. He'd called Cash and casually asked why his buddy had neglected to mention the police chief's pain-in-the-ass disposition. There'd been a long pause and then the truth.

Magdalena needed a human being in the police chief role, not a bully with a crew cut, and Cash hoped Ben would fit that role. In time.

What could he say to that? *I won't be around long enough to even think about it?* No, of course not, so he clamped his mouth shut and said nothing.

"Wow. I think you've found your calling."

Only one person possessed that special blend of sarcasm and dry humor. He turned and there she was, Gina Servetti staring up at him dressed in navy scrubs and navy clogs. "Hey. Impressive, huh?"

"Oh, yes. Magdalena's finest fighting crime and criminals—" she glanced at the front of a flier "—one crosswalk at a time."

The humor snuffed out the sarcasm, and her dark eyes lit up. She was very pretty when she smiled and the tension eased from her face. *Very* pretty. And that thought had absolutely nothing to do with fliers. He cleared his throat and said, "I can't say I've ever been so *entrenched* in the educational process of the community."

Her lips twitched. "I'll bet."

He grinned. "You could have warned me about Police Chief Rudy Dean."

"I could have, but it's a lot more fun to watch you squirming with those fliers, not your usual tough-guy assignment."

Damn, but this woman had a mouth. He certainly couldn't accuse her of trying to sweet-talk him. Most women buried the sarcasm when he was around, keeping it hidden until they thought they'd snared him with their bodies, as in sex. He'd bet Gina would keep that mouth going even in bed. No doubt about that. He blinked. Where the hell had *that* come from and how did he stop it from showing up again? Ben reached for the first thing that sifted through his brain and said, "Nice outfit."

She glanced at the navy scrubs and scowled. "Not every woman is obsessed with looking like she's just stepped out of a fashion magazine." The scowl deepened. "Some women even opt for comfort."

He laughed. "Yeah, yeah. I hear you."

Ben was planning his next response when a woman rushed up to him, placed a hand on his arm, and said in a sultry voice, "Are you the new police sergeant?" The woman squeezed his arm, her small, designer-clad frame inching closer, her large breasts a step away from his forearm. "I am absolutely delighted to meet you. I'm Cynthia Carlisle." She paused, added, "My father owns the car dealership in this town and four others." When she tilted her head, waves of black curls brushed her shoulders, slithered along her back, and swirled her perfume up Ben's nose in a mix of vanilla and musk. "Everyone's been talking about you, but nobody's really seen you, though one of my friends spotted you running the other day." Her voice dipped, purred. "Honest sweat and a shirtless man get me every time."

"Really." This from Gina. "No thoughts of handing over a bar of soap?"

The woman turned to Gina, her red-lipped smile slipping for a half second, before she recovered, pasted it back in place, and said, "Hello, Gina. My father's walking without a cane. Nice job." She turned back to Ben, her hand still clutching his arm. "Anyway, I'm having a get-together at the house tonight. Just a few friends." She eyed him with a look he recognized as "hunting mode" and added, "And a few people we'd like to consider friends." Long pause, too much eyelash batting. "Like you."

"Well, thank you. It's nice to know this town is interested in making friends with strangers." He spotted Gina's narrowed gaze and pinched lips. Any second now, she'd strike. Maybe Jeremy had been right; Gina was a viper. That thought made him smile.

"Let me give you the address and my phone number." She released his arm and stepped back to open the flap on her purse. "Any time after 8:00 P.M. is fine. What do you like to drink?"

Wow, this woman could give *him* "pick up" lessons. "As much as I appreciate the offer, I've already got plans."

Cynthia Carlisle's head shot up, her green eyes a mix of confusion and disbelief. "Can't you change them?"

Ben shook his head and slid a glance at Gina. "Sorry, can't do that. Gina's not big on change and I promised her dinner tonight."

Gina waited until Cynthia Carlisle stomped away on her three-inch heels before she turned to him and hissed, "What are you doing? Do you know she's the biggest gossip in town? She'll tell everybody what you said."

"So?" Why did she care what some high-society type said about her? He could tell the woman had an agenda and a daddy who never told her no.

Gina shook her head and sighed. "She's got a wicked tongue."

He raised a brow. "*She's* got a wicked tongue? Interesting, coming from you."

"I use mine for protection; she uses hers for destruction. There's a big difference."

He had to say he agreed with her. Ben had known a lot of Cynthia Carlisle types, and most of them had no remorse about scratching their way to the prize—usually, a man. He'd been that man a time or two. "If she starts talking

trash about you, I'll take care of it."

"You?" Those dark eyes sparked. "What are you going to do?"

"Shut her down." He shrugged. "Make her wish she'd kept her mouth shut and stayed in her big fancy house, using her daddy's charge card."

"That's pretty accurate."

"Right." There'd been too many Cynthias before and after Melissa. They were the real vipers, not Gina. "Now about that dinner? What time should I pick you up?"

***

When Ben asked if he could borrow the Heart Sent's kitchen to fix Gina Servetti dinner, Mimi hid a smile and said, "Absolutely," followed by, "Lovely girl," and then, "Need help?"

She'd taught Paul how to make macaroni and cheese, and he grew so skilled at the dish that she served his version to guests. He said white sharp cheddar was the trick and bits of pepper jack gave it a zing. Oh, but that boy had lots of ideas and so much energy; always moving and talking and making plans for his life. He wanted to move out West, live near the ocean, climb a mountain, see a volcano. But he'd done none of those. His life had been ripped away, his hopes splattered on a slick road one night. He'd just turned seventeen.

If he'd lived, she thought he might resemble Ben Reed, if only in the eyes and shape of the mouth. But she pictured her son tall and strong, too, confident and unafraid. Like Ben. Mimi pictured a lot of things for her dead son and found comfort in her mind's ability to re-create a world where her son still lived. Sometimes that was the only way to get through the day, breathing in, breathing out, waiting for the night to come so you could rejoin the person who

owned your heart.

Mimi had loved her husband, too. He was a good man, a hard worker with quiet dreams and a bad heart. Losing him was painful, but expected, and though she grieved the man she'd slept beside for more than thirty years, she did not lose her ability to breathe, as she had when she lost Paul. Losing a child stripped the color straight out of a person's life, leaving the world bleached out and brittle.

And now Ben Reed was here, and if Mimi looked at him long enough, her vision would blur and she could almost pretend he was Paul. Her heart thanked the good Lord for this small joy, and her soul joined in.

"I want to bake the chicken. No frying, no breading." Ben pulled two breasts from the package, placed them on a cutting board. "I think I'll sauté the asparagus with a little olive oil, no butter."

Mimi adjusted her reading glasses and glanced up from the recipe for mashed cauliflower. Her friend Wanda Cummings swore it was just as good as mashed potatoes and a whole lot less calories. Hmph. How could cauliflower taste as good as creamy mashed potatoes? She guessed if you wanted to take the pounds off bad enough and keep them off, you could convince yourself of anything.

Speaking of convincing, how on earth had Ben Reed talked Gina Servetti into dinner? He'd mentioned bumping into Cynthia Carlisle, "Miss I'm Rich and Make My Own Rules," but he'd been vague on the dinner invitation with Gina. Well, there was more than one way to ask a question. "I've known Gina since she was a little girl and she's very private about the company she keeps."

"Uh-huh." He grabbed a few asparagus, cut away the woody parts, and placed them on a platter. "I can tell."

"I'm a bit surprised she accepted your dinner

invitation."

He slid her a smile that was so like her son's, she had to look away. "Me, too."

She turned back, placed a hand on his arm. "Don't hurt her."

Ben set down his knife and met her gaze, his expression serious. "I wouldn't hurt her." Pause. "We're friends."

Had his voice tripped over the word *friend* just now? "Does she know that?"

His sigh meant one of two things. Either he was losing patience with her questions, or Gina's behavior toward him was causing serious aggravation. "What? That we're friends or that I wouldn't hurt her?"

"Both," Mimi said, her voice soft, encouraging.

"Gina's not like most women. You don't exactly have a conversation with her about emotions and what things mean."

"No, I don't imagine you do. But then, with a family like hers, she's got reason to keep her true feelings buried so deep inside, she'll never unearth them."

***

She should never have agreed to have dinner with him. Why had she done it? Why hadn't she simply forced a smile and told him "No thank you"? How hard would that have been? With a person like Ben Reed, he probably would have persisted and demanded to know why she turned him down. So, had she come to dinner because he'd coerced her? Of course not. She did want to ask him why he'd conveniently neglected to tell her he'd taken care of Bree, clean feet and all. Why hadn't he told her? She had a right to know. After all, it happened in her home with her pasta pot and dish towels.

But curiosity about the details of his time with Bree

wasn't the only reason she found herself sitting across from him, eating the chicken he'd prepared, savoring each bite. Ben Reed was a puzzle, a complicated one with missing pieces she hadn't quite figured out yet. He wasn't exactly as he appeared, though she wished he were. It would make it so much easier to study his traits and compartmentalize the man. He was arrogant and yet he'd taken care of Bree and somehow kept news of her barefoot travels out of the *Magdalena Press.* She was sure foot washing wasn't in the police handbook. Ben Reed was too good-looking and darn it, too well dressed, and yet he'd pushed aside "gorgeous and don't I know it" Cynthia Carlisle, an almost impossible feat. And what about—

"More wine?"

"No. Thank you." Gina stared at her empty wine glass. Mindful eating. Mindful drinking. Isn't that what she'd practiced these last five years, analyzing what went in her mouth, how large the bite, how long she chewed, what state of mind she was in when she sat down to eat? The setting mattered, too. No more on-the-run, multitasking dinner and snack time where she synchronized her book reading to the amount of food on her plate, so engrossed with the story, she could easily triple the serving size she ate by the time she finished a chapter. That all ended the morning she woke up and said, "Enough." She'd never said anything to her family about her decision to work on her weight and hadn't dared mention it to Tess and Bree until she'd had bits of success. With time, patience, and more willpower than she thought she possessed, the transformation began. Slowly at first, a quarter inch more room in a shirt, a less uncomfortable pair of jeans, an extra hole in the belt, leading to the need for a better-fitting bra and underwear, and finally, the ultimate reward: buying clothes from the

same racks Tess and Bree did. Maybe not the same size, okay, obviously not the same size, but at least in the same section of the store or catalog.

Ben Reed had distracted her and she'd polished off a glass of wine she couldn't recall drinking and *gasp*, eating three quarters of her meal. She'd tasted the chicken and the asparagus, commented on the tenderness and flavor, but when had she scarfed it all down? A queasiness grabbed her stomach, threatened to eject the food she'd just eaten. Gina sucked in a deep breath, blew it out through her nose. She could not regress to those earlier days of mindless eating and misery, she simply could not.

"Gina? What's the matter?"

She glanced up and there he was, looking down at her, studying her face with what looked an awful lot like real concern. "Nothing." She shook her head, rubbed her left temple. "I'm fine. Really."

He touched her shoulder and when she tensed, he removed his hand and stepped back. "Can I get you a glass of water? Fresh air?"

"No. Just go sit down, and give me a minute." *Calm, must remain calm.* She inched her gaze to the remaining food on her plate. *Mindful eating...mindful eating.*

"You know, I think you're fine just the way you are."

Gina's head shot up. *"What?"*

He pulled out his chair, sat down, his eyes on her. "You." His gaze slid from her face to her neck, skittered past her breasts, and stopped where the tablecloth hid the rest of her body. "You don't need to lose any more weight. You're fine." That gaze slid back up, slow, slower. "Really."

What on earth did a woman say to a man after an inappropriate and embarrassing comment like *that?* Gina

opened her mouth to blast him out of his chair, but she couldn't quite get the words out. While the comment had been inappropriate and definitely embarrassing, it had also been a compliment of sorts. Hadn't it? She wished Tess or Christine were here to correctly interpret for her. Bree would take anything as a compliment, at least the old Bree would. Who knew what the new one would think.

"Gina?" A dull red crept from his neck to his cheeks. "I'm sorry, that was out of line." He shrugged and threw her a smile that made her insides twitch. "For a guy whose never bungled conversations with the opposite sex, I'm crashing and burning when I'm around you."

So, he was uncomfortable, too. The acknowledgment relaxed her. She settled back in her chair and cleared her throat. "Thank you for admitting you've been less than chivalrous."

The smile slipped. "I didn't say that. I said I bungled my lines."

"Same thing." It was her turn to shrug, her turn to smile.

He crossed his arms over his chest. "Yeah, okay, you win. But I meant what I said about you being fine just the way you are."

"I know that." *Would he just stop?*

"Good." He rubbed his jaw and picked up his glass of wine. "Now your attitude and that mouth of yours? That's where you might need a little improvement."

Gina stared him down. "Should I toss the mashed cauliflower at you now, or wait for the next insult, so I can dump the asparagus on your head?"

"See what I mean?" He pointed a finger at her. "You don't have to get all huffy. I was simply trying to have a conversation and make a suggestion or two."

"Well, don't." Maybe she should toss her water at him,

too.

"Not even if it makes you more approachable?"

"I'm as approachable as I want to be." He really thought he was doing her a favor.

"You don't have a boyfriend."

"Is that a question or a statement?"

"Both."

"None of your business." And then because he'd annoyed her, she countered with, "Do *you* have a girlfriend?"

He grinned and studied her. "No. Are you applying for the position?"

"You really are a jerk, you know that? I don't know how you could be so kind to Bree, which reminds me, you had no business using my pot and dish towels for bathing purposes. Did you not hear of a bathtub?"

"Did you want me in your bathroom, invading that privacy of yours you work so hard to protect?"

He had a point. "No, but I didn't want you in my house either, and that didn't stop you."

"Damn but you are tiring." He sighed. "Does that sniping never stop?" He uncorked the wine, filled his glass, and took a sip. "No wonder you don't have a boyfriend."

"Of course, it couldn't be because I have no interest in a boyfriend, right? We all know women live and breathe for a man." *I had a boyfriend and he betrayed me.*

"Do you really dislike me that much, or is it men in general that you dislike?" he asked, his voice quiet, his expression serious.

She opened her mouth to spit out another biting remark, but the look on his face stopped her. He really did want to know. She should tell him it wasn't his business because it wasn't, but when the words slipped out, they were more truth than she'd intended. "I don't dislike you, but I have a lot of trust issues."

"Ah." He nodded, his gaze intense. "Me, too."

Chapter 9

"When are you coming back?"

Ben sat on the bed and pulled on a shoe. "Why do you want to know, little cousin? So you can clean up my place before I get back?"

"No. Because I miss you."

"Uh-huh." Paige either needed money or a favor. Or she was bored. He laced up his shoe, reached for the other one. "Why are you calling me so early?"

"I couldn't sleep. I can't believe you haven't reported those people next door. Their dogs barked all night."

Jed and Clara, a Golden and a Lab. He thought the owner's names were Mark and Jennifer, but he couldn't be sure. "I like those dogs; besides, they're good deterrents from break-ins."

"Right. And your high-tech security system isn't?"

He smiled. Once in a while, his cousin actually saw through his bullshit. "Extra layer of security."

"Uh-huh. I'm stuck in Philly for the next four weeks." Her voice dipped into pitiful mode. "I sprained my ankle and they bumped me from the L.A. trip."

"Damn, I'm sorry." Ben fastened his utility belt and grabbed his keys. He had three minutes to get out of here or he'd be late for work. "Can't you just relax?"

"Do you know how hard it is to relax when everybody tells you to relax?" She sighed. "It's impossible. All you can think about is the reason you aren't relaxing." Pause. "Are you sure you can't get away from that super-secret operation you're involved with to come home for the weekend?"

Poor Paige, she really thought he was doing undercover. Better she thought that than knowing he was in the same town as Cash Casherdon. That would not sit well. "Sorry, kid. I can't."

"You must be in deep."

If the town ever found out why he'd come here and how he had no intention of staying, he'd be in deep all right, real deep, as in quicksand-sinking deep, with Cash and Gina Servetti at the head of the line to push him in. "Yeah, you could say that."

"Well, be careful."

"I always am."

"And, Ben?"

He paused, hand on the knob. "Yeah?"

"Melissa's getting married next week."

Paige's revelation lodged in his gut, made him queasy with thoughts of Melissa's future husband next to her in bed, his baby filling her belly. If he thought that jerk really loved her, maybe he could let her go, but how could an arrogant sonofabitch like that love Melissa? Worse, how could she love him? Was Kenneth Stone, Assistant District Attorney, another emotional fixer-upper, like Ben had been? And did she think if she nurtured him with love, kindness, *and* a baby, then he'd shower her with the one thing she truly wanted—real commitment? Maybe that was it. Maybe Melissa needed to be needed and damn, maybe Kenneth realized that, something Ben hadn't considered until a few seconds ago. He was still thinking about Melissa and her new family when Jeremy Ross Dean sauntered in with a brown lunch bag and a big grin.

"Hey, Ben, I brought you something." He dropped the bag on Ben's desk and pulled up a chair. His blue eyes honed in on the bag as Ben opened it and removed a sandwich.

"Thanks, but you didn't have to do that."

"I was getting tired of seeing you eating Lina's chili." He lowered his voice and said, "She should use black beans *and* kidney beans. Mixes things up a bit."

"Huh." Who would have thought the kid knew the difference between a black bean and a kidney bean?

"Sorry the chief's been riding you so much. It wasn't right that he made you hand out those crosswalk fliers, and when he sent you to Mrs. Tessler, he knew dang well she'd be waiting on you, in that forty-year-old red negligee and nothing underneath."

That had been a sight. When Rudy sent him to handle Paulette Tessler's call that she'd seen a man running from her house with a bag, Ben hadn't expected the front door to be ajar, or the woman to call him from upstairs. When he entered the bedroom, he'd gotten an eyeful all right; he'd never seen a seventy-two-year-old woman in a negligee, see-through, no less, and he hoped he'd never have to see one again. He'd covered her with a bathrobe and taken her report on the intruder, even though they both knew there'd been no intruder. "I can't say I've ever encountered that situation before."

Jeremy grinned and shook his head. "She does that a couple of times a year. Some say she used to be movie-star beautiful, but kind of lost it when her husband up and took off with their cleaning lady." He shrugged and added, "That's why the chief goes easy on her; says the husband was her life, seeing as they couldn't have kids and all."

Ben had never gotten this much detail on a call before and he wasn't sure he liked it. *Taking off with the cleaning lady? Couldn't have kids?* That should be cataloged under Too Much Information.

"My mother says people go a little nutso sometimes as a way to deal with a pain that's too deep. That's what she said happened to Mrs. Tessler." He paused, his voice turning solemn. "She gave him everything, even gave up having kids because he didn't want them. Mom says she gave up so much of herself, there was nothing left." He looked at Ben, his expression puzzled. "You think that a person can do that?"

"Give up so much there's nothing left of that person? Yes, I do." He thought of Bree Kinkaid and how she was headed down that path if she didn't start sticking up for herself.

"I guess. I don't think my mom and the chief have to worry about that."

Ben wanted to ask Jeremy what he meant, but before he could ease into the question, the boy slid him a grin and said, "Heard you made dinner for Gina Servetti the other night."

"How'd you hear that?" Ben kept his expression blank, his voice casual. How the hell did this town find out about other people's business? He hadn't said anything and he doubted Gina had. Actually, he'd lay money down that Gina hadn't said a word to anyone.

"Cynthia Carlisle. She was at Kit's Primp and Polish getting her nails done when my mom was having her hair cut. Mom said Cynthia was going on and on about how you turned down her invitation to a party to make dinner for Gina Servetti."

"Even if I didn't have another commitment, I wouldn't have gone across the street with that woman. I've known my share of Cynthia Carlisles and every one of them is spoiled and self-centered."

Jeremy grinned. "Ah, so you prefer the viper types. Or

is it the jalapeño pepper types?"

He'd called Gina both. "I prefer either to a woman like Cynthia Carlisle."

"Okay, I'll remind you of that when you get bit. Or get too close to the pepper and can't breathe." He laughed and pointed to the brown bag on Ben's desk. "Now how about you take a look inside? I had a hard time deciding between the pastrami and the turkey breast, so I used both. And there's provolone, cherry tomatoes, avocado spread, leaf lettuce, and a few basil leaves to make the blend pop."

Ben lifted the sandwich from the bag, unwrapped it, and took a bite. "This is delicious." He took another bite, chewed. "Thank you."

"No problem. I grew the tomatoes, basil, and lettuce. I've got a big garden in my backyard. You should see the zucchini I picked last night." He held out his large hands. "Six of them, long and tender. You don't want the big, fat ones, because they're too tough and loaded with seeds."

"Yeah?" Ben continued to demolish his sandwich while Jeremy relayed information about when to harvest garlic, the best soil for spinach, how the absence of sun factored in zucchini production, and even what variety of green bean grows best in a cooler climate. "So, you're into gardening?"

A strip of red slashed the boy's neck, spread to his cheeks. "I'm into food, especially cooking it."

"Really? Like what?" Ben liked to play around in the kitchen, concocting marinades and dressings, mixing herbs and vinegars, adding them to chicken, steak, or vegetables, but growing the ingredients? If he couldn't find them in the produce section of the supermarket, then he chose a different menu.

"Name it, I'll cook it." Jeremy leaned forward, his gaze intense, his voice soft. "What I like to do best is take a familiar recipe, maybe one my mom cooked when I was growing up, and improve on it. Macaroni and cheese, lasagna, chili, chicken parmesan, beef burgundy, pancakes, stuffed pork chops." He grinned. "Everything."

Ben popped the last piece of sandwich in his mouth and when he finished chewing, he laced his hands behind his head and said, "Why am I just hearing about these culinary skills now?" He'd meant to humor the boy, maybe antagonize him for not offering a gourmet sandwich before now. But the look on Jeremy's face made Ben hold back.

The boy looked away, cleared his throat, and shrugged. "Chief's not big on it."

"I see." So, Rudy Dean wasn't "big" on it. What exactly did that mean? Did the old man hide Jeremy's mixing bowls? Threaten to dig up the garden? Or did he do something worse, more unforgivable? Did he demean Jeremy, tell him his interest in cooking was ridiculous? Possibly even forbid him to visit the kitchen? Did he try to take away something the boy loved? Ben could picture the guy doing any or all of those things. "Does anybody else know about your cooking skills?"

"Sure." Jeremy nodded and his face lit up like Main Street after dark. "The whole town knows." His voice slid several decibels and the light on his face fizzled. "All except for the chief."

***

From the time Bree Kinkaid was a teenager, she'd believed in love at first sight, destiny, and Brody Kinkaid. She'd also believed in frosted-pink nail polish, Kegel exercises, and blue Jordan almonds, though not with the same conviction as the first three.

But the Bree Kinkaid curled up on the king-sized bed in the honeymoon suite of the Heart Sent didn't look like a woman who believed in much of anything, certainly not love, destiny, or nail polish. When Gina got the phone call from Mimi a half hour ago, she'd been harvesting more zinnias and cosmos for pressing. She'd tossed the blooms in an old catalog, rushed to the car, and drove to the Heart Sent where she found Mimi trying to console an inconsolable Bree in the honeymoon suite. Gina had only seen the suite once, after Bree insisted: *You won't believe the magic of the place. It's pure love, and so romantic. Just take a peek at all those rose petals, all that love.*

"I found her here a little while ago," Mimi whispered, glancing up at Gina. "Crying her heart out, like she was about to burst from the pain of it."

"Help me." Bree's body trembled, her words spilled out with uneven breaths. "Help me." Fresh tears, more trembling. "Please, help me."

"We're here, Bree," Gina said. "Talk to us. Tell us how we can help you." In Bree's world, husbands and wives joined together in perfect union, had children, date nights, and honeymoons in the suite at the Heaven Sent. Husbands protected their wives and kept them safe, from money and other worries; they paid the bills, decided when the roof needed repair and which tire was best for the car. Wives tended the children, nurtured their brains and bodies, took them to the doctor's, grew their own vegetables, and groomed the dog themselves. Bree and Brody had figured it all out before their first anniversary and the birth of their first child.

But after the loss of their baby four months ago, the rules changed. Or maybe Bree and Brody did. The absent touching, long looks, suggestive smiles—all of the intimate gestures that had always made Gina uncomfortable to witness—dwindled. At least on Bree's part. Brody continued treating his "honeybee" as he always had, with kisses, bear hugs, and gusto. But it didn't take a relationship expert to recognize withdrawal when she saw it. The more Brody tried to squeeze his honeybee and jabber on about babies, the quieter she became, until the quietness erupted and she ended up barefoot at Gina's, then crying at Tess's with the truth: she didn't want more children.

And now, here she was one week later, curled up and crying again, on the very bed where she most likely conceived Ella Blue, her oldest daughter.

"What can we do for you, honey?" Mimi rubbed Bree's back and spoke in a soothing tone.

"I'm so tired." Bree sniffed, squeezed her eyes closed to keep the tears in. "I'm trying, but I can't get through the day." Her voice wobbled. "What's wrong with me? Why can't I be like I was before? I'm not the only woman who has three children." Her sigh pulled them in, told them she was indeed tired, but the tiredness came from living, not the children.

"Have you thought about seeing Doc Needstrom?" This from Mimi.

"Uh-uh. Mama said I should see him, but Daddy would have a fit and call me puny. I know Brody's mother would cause a stink because she'd fret her friends at bingo might hear about it. And, well, you all know Brody. He would not take kindly to me seeing a doctor about our personal issues and, heavens, he'd never let me take any medications."

Mimi's voice shifted and filled with a pain Gina knew had to do with losing her son. "Not even if you needed them for a time?"

"I'd never be able to convince him I needed them." She opened her eyes, tried to smile. "He says one of the things he loves most about me is how I just keep doing, no matter what." Tears streaked her face as she whispered, "No matter what."

"No matter what?"

Ben Reed stood in the doorway, taking in the scene. When he spotted Bree and her obvious distress, he moved toward her, knelt on the floor, and touched her arm. "Bree? What's going on?"

"Oh, Ben." Bree grabbed his arm, laid her head on it, and whimpered, "Oh, Ben."

He glanced up at Mimi, then Gina, his jaw set, his gaze dark. "Can someone tell me what's going on here?"

"Our girl's having a tough time," Mimi said.

"She needs help." His words sliced the air, grew cold. "Professional help. And medication."

"We were just talking about that," Gina said, uncomfortable with the way he stared at her, his expression a mix of anger and disbelief.

"Talking isn't going to help her. You need to take action. *Now.*"

"That's what we were trying to do, but it's a little more complicated than that; there are things to consider, people to work around—"

"People to work around? Are you serious? The only things to consider are Bree and the kids. That's it. Everybody else and their feelings are secondary." He smoothed a hunk of hair from her face, tucked it behind her ear.

"Ben." Mimi kept her voice low. "You don't know Brody or his family. They can be downright intimidating."

"Good," he said, "Because I can be intimidating, too." He turned to Gina, spat out, "You're supposed to be her friend; you're supposed to help her. She needs a doctor, and medication. And she needs to start talking to someone about whatever's eating away at her. If she wants to talk to you and your friends, great, but she needs a professional to help sort this out, someone who isn't going to sugarcoat her issues or make excuses for her."

"We were getting to that." What did he know about Bree's problems? He wasn't even from Magdalena, hadn't been friends with her for years. He should mind his own business and let her *friends* help. But even as she thought this, the truth seeped through: he was right. They'd ignored too many warning signs—she needed help. Now.

Ben stroked Bree's arm and spoke to her with a gentleness that made Gina wonder what it would feel like to have him talk to her that way. Thankfully, that thought only lasted a half second before she swept it away.

When Bree's whimpering settled, Ben stood and faced them. "What the hell's going on in this town? You're all supposed to be close-knit, right? Looking out for each other, helping, sharing, like an extended family. Isn't that what small towns are all about? Trust and community? But here's what I see: people keeping secrets, people afraid to stand up for themselves or those they care about. People lying about what they want out of life. That's big city stuff. We don't buy into sharing or opening up, but we don't pretend we're going to either. This place is worse, because you act like you care and damn it, you don't, not enough to take a risk and do something about it."

He narrowed his gaze on Gina in a way that told her those words were meant for her, then turned and left. Mimi made a quick sign of the cross and tsk-tsked. "Those are some mighty powerful words."

"That man is full of words. Ignore him."

Mimi sighed. "I can't. I fear he may be right. Do you

remember when Paul died? There were so many people lined up for the viewing, they said there was a two-hour wait to get in the funeral home. And the food? Ham and roast beef, and breads and pastas and coffee…so much we could have eaten for three years. And the cards filled with the kindest words and prayers for strength; beautiful words from people I would never have guessed possessed such a talent for the written word."

"Everyone liked Paul," Gina said. Ben Reed hadn't been here when they held a candlelight vigil for Mimi's seventeen-year-old son in the park. If he'd seen the outpouring of support, he might have different thoughts on this town and their sense of community.

Mimi's eyes grew bright. "Paul was so full of life you couldn't help but want to be near him." The pain in her words stretched, thinned, and burst. "But he was reckless, and everyone knew that, too. And yet, no one told us he'd been racing down Elderberry Road three days before the accident. We didn't hear about that until months after he died. Some days I still wonder if the knowing would have made a difference. Would we have grounded him and taken the keys to the car, or would we have convinced ourselves his recklessness was a stage that he'd outgrow soon enough." She cleared her throat and stared hard at the vase on the dresser. "That's what I don't know; that's what my husband died not knowing, and that, Gina, is exactly what Ben is talking about."

***

Ben tucked his T-shirt in his jeans and thought of ignoring the knock on his door. It was probably Mimi, come to give him her side of things and invite him to dinner. Well, he wasn't hungry, but he was damn tired of the people in this town dancing around the truth, himself excluded. After all, he'd never claimed to be a do-gooder, help-my-brother kind of guy like these people. First, there was Jeremy and the culinary expertise he kept from his father. And Bree, hiding her issues from her husband. Weren't husbands and wives supposed to share, as in tell all, support all, be all? Not Ben, of course, because he'd crashed and burned in that area...

And what about Gina? She had as many issues as he did, but she kept her feelings locked up so tight nobody would ever get to them, even somebody who might want to try. Her reticence annoyed him. A lot.

"Ben?"

Gina? What did she want now, an opportunity to defend her actions? She just hated to be on the short end of a losing conversation. Too bad, he wasn't interested. "I'm kind of busy." He sat on the bed and pulled on his shoes.

"I need to talk to you," she said from the other side of the door. "It'll only take a minute."

He sighed. In the short time he'd known the woman, he'd learned that Gina Servetti did not go away without making her opinion known. "Okay, okay." He eased off the bed, opened the door. "Yes?"

She glanced toward the bridal suite. "Can I come in?"

"Sure. Why not?" He stepped aside to let her enter. "What is it now, Gina?" She closed the door, turned to him, clasping her hands in front of her. Nervous? Gina Servetti? No way.

"Look, small towns can be just as intimidating and cold as cities. It still comes down to people." She cleared her throat and settled her gaze on his chin. "Some are cruel, thoughtless, only concerned with their own interests. Others are weak and easily hurt. You learn early on who you can trust, or think you can trust, and when one of them betrays you, that's devastating."

He knew betrayal. He'd had a mother who didn't love him enough to stay and a father he never knew about.

"Ben?" Her voice dipped with a softness that surprised him. "People get hurt no matter where they live."

He dragged a hand over his face and sighed "Do you know what it's like to not belong? I mean, really belong to the one thing you want more than anything?" The words spilled out before he had time to consider the consequences. Maybe Jeremy's confession and Bree's pain had jolted him to a new awareness, or maybe he was just too damned tired of hauling around the baggage of his youth. "And no matter what you do you're shut out?" To his surprise, she nodded. "After a while, you pretend you don't care, but you do. And it's the damn inability to *stop* caring that pushes you to lash out and keep others away."

"You can't trust them," she added, her eyes bright, a lock of hair falling over her left brow. "You can't trust anybody because you've been raised to believe you aren't quite good enough."

He nodded. She got it; he could tell from the way her expression pinched when she spoke with words coated in pain. Who had done her wrong? A guy? A best friend? Was that why she remained aloof with a kick-ass attitude? Maybe that was her wall. "Was it a guy?" He shouldn't ask, shouldn't even care, but for some crazy reason, he did.

She shut down right in front of him; lips flattened, eyes narrowed, shoulders squared. Yup, she was good and done with sharing stories. "Problems in life don't always start and end with a guy."

"But yours did, right?"

She looked away, reached for the doorknob. "I just came to tell you thanks for sticking up for Bree. She needs all the help she can get right now."

"Sure." He caught her wrist, eased her hand from the doorknob, and turned her to face him. "Not every guy is a jerk."

"I know that."

But the tremble in her voice told him she wasn't so sure. "Look at me." He cupped her chin with his thumb and forefinger. "Hey, don't cry."

"I'm not crying." Tears rimmed her eyes. "I never cry."

"I know. Nobody can make Gina Servetti cry."

She blinked hard. Twice. "And don't forget it."

"Never," he whispered, seconds before he leaned in and placed a soft kiss on her mouth. She flinched but didn't pull away. Her mouth tasted of honey and cherries, with a faint scent of mint. Tantalizing. Welcoming. Ben increased the pressure on her lips, slowly, gently.

It was the tiny moan that did him in, made him forget who he was kissing, why they should not be doing this, why they could never do more than this. Right now, it didn't matter. Right now, all he could think of were those lips and getting behind that tiny moan. After, he couldn't remember if he opened his mouth first or if it was Gina. And when the kiss deepened to include tongues, was it he or she who initiated it? Did he mold her body to his, or was it Gina who flung her arms around his neck, pressed herself against him?

His moans matched hers, soft at first and then louder, more needy. When his hand cupped her butt, she thrust her tongue into his mouth and slid both hands down his back, cupping *his* butt. *Damn!* Ben was hot, ready, and hell yes, in need. Deep need. Soulful need.

"Ben? Are you all right?"

Mimi's voice on the other side of the door busted them

Mary Campisi

apart, faster than a bullet. Ben cleared his throat and managed an "I'm fine." He shot a look at Gina: the swollen lips, messed-up hair, glassy-eyed stare that refused to look at him. She was regretting this already and she hadn't even left his room.

"Are you sure? You sound like you're in pain."

Oh, he was in pain all right. Physical pain, the kind that could do a man in. He stared at Gina and said, "Don't worry about me, Mimi. Nothing a night in bed won't cure." Gina's face turned to paste at the remark.

"You did look tired. I'm taking Bree home, but tomorrow, bright and early, we're calling the doctor." She paused. "I thought Gina might have a thing or two to say, but she up and disappeared. Do you know if she went home?"

Why don't I open the door so you can see for yourself? "I'm not sure. Probably."

"Such a sweet girl." And then, "Do you have any more dinners planned? Maybe you could cook for her at her place, you know, in a more intimate environment?"

Oh, he knew all right. Why didn't Mimi just say, "So you can be alone and maybe cook something up in the bedroom after you finish in the kitchen?"

"No more dinners planned." His gaze slid from Gina's face to her neck, lower still, in an attempt to get a reaction from her. It was useless; the woman had shut him out and there was no getting back in. Damn her. Not that he necessarily wanted to take whatever *this* was further, but she'd murdered the possibility with that cold stare and rigid stance. What pissed him was the way she fell into the kiss like she'd die if she didn't have it, and then pushed him away, like she'd *die* if she had to remember it. Or repeat it. Right. There'd been a helluva lot of emotion arcing

152

between them a few minutes ago and Ben wasn't the only one sending or receiving the signals. Let her pretend she didn't feel anything; let her try.

"I definitely think you should have a follow-up dinner." Mimi paused and a softness coated her words. "It's nice to see Gina with a young man. She has so much to give, but…well, she tends to give the wrong impression."

"No kidding?" When did someone people referred to as a jalapeño pepper with a viper tongue give the *right* impression?

"But it's not because she doesn't care," Mimi said. "It's because she cares too much."

Ben slid a look in Gina's direction. Bad idea. The face that a few sentences ago had been the color of paste had turned red, the kissable lips transformed to a thin line, the bright eyes downshifting to soot. Not happy.

"Okay, I'll keep that in mind." He needed to end this conversation now, before Mimi shared more personal information about Gina. "Have a good night. See you in the morning."

"Will do. And, Ben," her voice dipped, "Tell Gina she left her keys in the bridal suite."

Chapter 10

People might say Nate Desantro was a tough sonofabitch, but if Harry had to pick one person to stand by his side and do battle for him, it would be Nate. Once you had the guy's loyalty, you had it for life. Likewise, if you lost his trust, you were screwed. It didn't matter how wealthy you were, how much influence you had, or even if you were family, if you lost Nate's trust, you were done. No second chances on that one.

Nate was a man of few words, but when he did speak, people listened, and a short while ago, Greta had been on the listening end. Thank God. The plan had been for Harry to vacate the house early in the morning before anyone noticed. That hadn't been too hard, seeing as his wife barely spoke to him, and the kids still thought he had the flu and was off-limits. AJ was no fool, though: he'd been eyeing Harry these past few days as though he knew the flu story was buried three feet deep in bullshit.

When Harry walked into Lina's, she brought him his coffee and ordered up the special: two buttermilk pancakes, two sausage links, and two eggs, over easy. She brought him the paper, told him a few stories about the goings-on in town, and snapped her gum with each telling. There was something to be said for comfortable and easy-going that outweighed fancy silverware and waiters who scraped the crumbs from your tablecloth with a butter knife. He unfolded the *Magdalena Press,* spread it out on the Formica table, and perused the contents as he ate breakfast. *Jack and Dolly Finnegan donate new tree for the Magdalena Elementary School. Honor Cummings, granddaughter of Samuel and Wanda Cummings, traveled to London on a scholarship where she will study Economics. Community fresh market this Saturday at the town square. Rex and Kathleen MacGregor vacation in South Dakota, home of Mount Rushmore.*

He'd just started the story about Webster Donahue celebrating his 101st birthday and what the man had done for more than a century when Nate called to say it was time to head home and talk to Greta. "She misses you, you big oaf," he'd said. Those might have been some of the sweetest words he'd ever heard. Harry slapped a twenty on the table, waved to Lina, and was out the door before he remembered he still had his napkin tucked in his shirt like a damn bib. Pop Benito had got him doing that after the first time Harry spilled syrup on his silk shirt. He yanked it off and laughed. Life was good. Damn good.

How had he spent so many years fighting commitment and love, hell, fighting anything close to an emotion? None of that had made any sense until Greta. She'd changed everything, opened his heart, his soul, *his world* to what it could be like to love a person, the pure joy of it. Oh, there were times when it wasn't so joyful, but if you put the good and bad side by side, the good outweighed the bad every single time. It had to be with the right person, though, or you might as well forget it; the bad would smother you. That happened a lot; it had happened to poor Charlie. The man got sucked dry by a leech of a woman who wouldn't let go, long after the marriage was over. At least Charlie had found Miriam, and she'd given him moments of true happiness, even if only four days a month.

Harry pulled up the circular drive of his house, parked the car, and jumped out. The kids were inside with Mrs. Wright, the part-time sitter and cleaning woman. Greta said she didn't need a cleaning woman, that she was more than capable of scrubbing out a tub or two. But eight? That was a bit much. And getting the grit out of ten bathrooms, especially when Lizzie and AJ insisted on trying out a different one every day? Yeah, it hadn't taken much to convince Greta that she might need *two* cleaning women. He made his way to the sliding glass door and peered outside.

Greta was at the other end of the pool, picking up the kids' toys and beach towels. She wore a blue and white cover-up, her golden hair pulled back in a long braid, her feet in those ridiculous flip-flops she insisted on wearing. How could they be comfortable? Still, he must be the only person breathing air who felt this way because kids and adults wore them to his pool: pink, green striped, polka dot—even Pop had on a pair when he visited. Harry opened the sliding glass door and stepped onto the deck, shielding his eyes from the morning sun.

"Harry?" A smile burst onto Greta's face as she waved and ran toward him. "Harr—!" She tripped and fell, hard and fast, her head hitting the edge of the pool seconds before her body rolled into the water with a dull thunk. And then she disappeared under the water.

"Greta!" Harry tore down the steps, dove into the pool, fully clothed, shoes still on. *Dear God, please no*. He swam under the water, scooped her lifeless body into his arms, and carried her out of the pool. "Greta. Greta!" Her eyes were closed, her mouth open. Was she breathing? Harry eased her onto the cement, turned her head. *What to do, what to do? What the hell to do?* He laid a hand on her chest but, damn it, he couldn't tell if she was breathing. She must need CPR. *Oh, no*, he had no idea how to do it. He tried to mimic what he'd seen in the movies, fumbled with his hand placement, and managed a few awkward attempts. "Breathe, Greta. Dear God, breathe." The tears started then, his tears, scalding his face, falling onto his wife's soggy clothing.

He didn't know when the EMTs arrived or who had called them. Later, he would learn that AJ, his nine-year-old stepson, had been the one to maintain his wits and save his mother after Harry fell apart. The rest of what happened was a blur and again, it was AJ who remained calm, called Christine, and asked for a ride to the hospital. Harry hadn't considered that; he'd had his keys in his hand when AJ stopped him. If the boy hadn't, Harry might have ended up like Charlie.

The hospital wait was painful. Bells, buzzers, beeping. How did people work here every day amidst the chaos and adrenaline-fueled activities, and then take lunch breaks, read the newspaper, call their kids? How did they lead a *normal* life? How did they turn it all off? He and AJ sat side by side, silent, as the drama of the emergency room played out before them. If he weren't panicked before, the activity and worry had him on his way to a full-blown attack. It was coming. Soon.

"You okay, Harry?"

Harry slid his stepson a glance and managed a word. "Sure."

"Just take deep breaths, not real fast, though." AJ looked at him, his dark eyes bright. "You gotta be strong for Mom, okay?"

"Right." *I'm scared shitless.*

"It's going to be all right." AJ's smile wobbled. "You'll see."

Harry didn't see anything but Greta in the pool, and then lying on the cement, eyes closed, a blackish-purple swelling on her right temple. *Dear God*, help her, help all of them.

"Mr. Blacksworth?" A young doctor with wire-rimmed glasses and a shock of curly black hair and a beard nodded at him, maybe even smiled, hard to tell with the beard covering so much of his mouth. "I'm Dr. Whitlow."

Harry stood, held out his hand. Above all, even in the face of possible misery, he knew his manners. "Dr. Whitlow. How is she?"

The mouth moved, opened an inch. "Your wife suffered a concussion. She took a pretty nasty fall and we want to keep her tonight for observation."

"But she's okay?" He glued his eyes to the mouth, waited.

"The preliminary tests were fine, but we want to keep an eye on her. Of course, Mrs. Blacksworth will have a pretty big bump on her head and she'll be banged up from the fall, bruises on her side and hip, but if there are no issues tonight, we'll release her tomorrow."

He glanced at AJ. "Can we see her?"

Dr. Whitlow opened his mouth and this time, Harry spotted the smile. "She's been asking for you."

Harry followed the doctor to the fourth cubicle where Greta lay on the bed, IV in one arm, lump the size of a cherry tomato on her right temple. She tried to smile, but the effort proved difficult. "Harry," she breathed.

"I'm right here, Greta." He lifted her hand and kissed it. "Right where I belong."

"I'm sorry, Harry. So sorry." Pause. "Nate paid me a visit."

"I know."

"Mom?" AJ moved to the side of the bed so his mother could see him. "I came with Harry so he wouldn't be alone."

"Thank you."

"Your boy saved your life," Harry said. "If it hadn't been for him..." The words clogged his throat and he couldn't push them out. *If it hadn't been for him, you could have died.*

AJ shrugged. "All I did was call 9-1-1 like you taught us. You were unconscious. When the paramedics got there, they did the rest."

Harry had been so turned around and frantic he hadn't even thought about 9-1-1. No, AJ had saved his mother's life and Harry would never forget it. And tomorrow, he'd find a CPR class and sign up.

"I can't wait to come home." Greta squeezed his hand, smiled at him. "Back to our family."

"Damn straight." He leaned forward, placed a gentle kiss on her mouth and said, "Damn straight indeed."

Later that night, as Harry sat on the deck drinking bourbon and contemplating the events of the day, he wasn't so sure he could just move on and forget what happened. In fact, he was certain he couldn't do it. Greta was the heart and soul of this family and yet, he'd put her life in jeopardy today. Why the hell had he thought he needed a pool? He'd never stopped to consider the dangers, because that's not how he worked; if he wanted it, he got it. Bigger, better, faster. What else had he insisted on that might bring misery to this family? The sauna in the basement? One of the kids could turn it on and get trapped in there, die from the heat. He didn't know how, but it could happen. That's why they were called *accidents*. He could pick apart the whole house, starting with the ceramic tile—a good fall and a conk on the head could do you in—and ending with the fireplaces, five of them. Fire was always bad and what if the flue got clogged by a squirrel's nest and asphyxiated all of them? Mrs. Wright would find them dead in their beds and then she'd know Harry Blacksworth slept in the buff.

By the time Harry finished his third bourbon, he'd convinced himself they were all doomed and it was because of him.

"Don't you know it's unhealthy to drink alone?"

Harry swung around and spotted the man standing on the other side of the sliding glass door. "Nate?"

Nate Desantro stepped onto the deck and handed Harry a glass. "I'll have what you're having."

"You'll have to drink fast to catch up." He filled Nate's glass, then his own.

"To family," Nate said, holding up his glass.

"To family." Harry took a healthy swallow and enjoyed the burn. "I owe you another case of this stuff after what you did for me."

Nate shrugged. "Not necessary, but I won't turn it down. How's Greta?"

"Left her at the hospital a few hours ago. I would've stayed but she made me come home, said I had to get a good night's sleep." He dragged a hand over his face, sighed. "How am I supposed to sleep with her in the hospital and me responsible for it?"

"It wasn't your fault."

"Not true. I'm the cause of it, me and those damnable flip-flops. I was watching her before she saw me, thinking how beautiful she was and how I hated those flip-flops that half the world seemed to love. She looked up and saw me, called my name and started running…"

"Harry. Don't."

"I'm not good for her, Nate. I love her more than my own breath, but I don't deserve her. She's an angel, and I'm nothing but the devil."

"She loves you."

Harry shook his head. "Greta doesn't know any better; she's too kind, too naïve. Hell, I can't even work a damn riding lawn mower without putting it in a ditch. Not much with a screwdriver either, even a wireless one. Greta had to show me how to use it and then I stripped the screw." He wouldn't tell him about his second attempt, where he forgot to use a screwdriver bit. "What man can't work a wireless screwdriver?"

Nate cocked his head. "You mean a *cordless* screwdriver?"

"Huh? Oh, yeah, I knew that. What the hell, I can't even remember the name of the friggin' tool, let alone how to use it."

"You don't have to know how to do any of those things. You hire out, or at least you did, until you got it in that thick head of yours that you had to be Mr. Fix-it *and* Mr. Fashion. I bet Pop gave you his 'you can do it all speech,' didn't he? You should have asked him if the duct tape he uses to repair everything qualifies him as Mr. Fix-it, or if the fancy sweats and high-top sneakers make him Mr. Fashion."

"How did you know Pop was behind it?" He wouldn't tell him about the pizzelle maker the old man suggested.

Nate shook his head. "Pop's behind three quarters of what goes on in this town. I'll bet he didn't tell you Lucy was the one who did the repairs in that house, did he?"

"Hell no, he didn't. Not a peep." Wait until he saw Pop again; the man would need those high tops to get away from Harry.

"Didn't think so. And I doubt he mentioned the son in California who probably pays to have his toilet paper rolls changed."

"Nope." He'd give the old man a two-second start and then he was coming after him.

"Right." Nate folded his hands over his belly and leaned back in the chair. "The point is, we are who we are. You can put a tie on me, but I'm still the guy who's going to open his mouth at the wrong time and say what's on his mind. That doesn't fly in corporate circles. And don't ask me what gabardine is, or when to choose pleats versus plain-front slacks." He paused, scratched his jaw. "I didn't even realize it mattered until I met you."

"Don't be an asshole. This is serious."

Nate laughed. "You've got to go with who you are, Harry. That's who Greta fell in love with, not some hands-on craftsman like me." His lips twitched. "She prefers the 'smooth operator' in a suit."

Harry scowled. "Yeah, now you are an asshole. Greta deserves better than me, a helluva lot better, but damn it, I can't give her up."

"I know." Nate turned serious. "You think you're the only guy who believes the woman he loves is too good for him? You think I don't have those same thoughts about Christine?"

"Nobody's good enough for Christine, but she seems to want you around, so don't screw it up."

"Not planning on it."

"She's really happy here with you, Anna, this life. I never would've dreamed it, but I can see how this kind of place grows on you, and I can see why Charlie couldn't give it up."

"Yeah...well..." Nate finished his drink, set the glass on the table.

"He must've hated leaving here and having to go back

to Gloria every month. That woman's determined not to let us forget how powerful she can be, dead or alive."

Nate poured another bourbon for himself and Harry. "That ends now. We aren't going to let her try to destroy any more lives."

"How the hell are we going to do that when she's taking pot shots from the grave?" Harry sipped his bourbon, corrected, "Or should I say from the urn?"

"You know the letter Gloria sent notifying Christine of her death? Well, she sent a notebook, too, one that apparently would enlighten the world and explain life before she became the miserable person we remembered. I'm sure it was full of tortured soul-searching and he-done-me-wrong garbage."

"You don't know? Didn't you read it?"

Nate shook his head. "Nope. I hid it; figured that woman had just enough poison in her to try and kill us all with whatever was inside. You've seen her handiwork. A single sentence could take out a family."

"Don't I know it?" He considered the notebook, the destruction it could cause. Did this woman never stop? Was she that evil that she would ruin a whole family, then a town, to seek vindication? Or did she realize she was beyond vindication and simply wanted to spread lies and treachery so no one would have peace, not even her own daughter? "What did you do with the notebook?"

"Brought it to the office and stuck it in my desk drawer."

Harry sighed. "Don't read it. Pandora's box and all that. You should burn it."

"I know."

"So?" *Burn the mother.*

"It's not mine. She sent it to Christine."

"That thing's a grenade, ready to blow. You need to get rid of it."

"I can't do that without Christine's permission, and I don't want to bring it up because she hasn't mentioned it since I took it."

"Oh, the old she-forgot-about-it trick? Let me tell you, women don't forget anything, except when you tell them you're stopping for a drink or will be home late. *That*, they forget. The other stuff, the drama, oh no, that's just in a holding pattern. One night, you'll be lying in bed and two seconds before you drift off, she'll cuddle next to you and say, 'Where's that notebook my mother sent?' And then, you are so screwed. You won't be able to sleep and you'll be thinking about how you're going to handle the disaster that's going to land on your chest."

"How is destroying property that isn't mine any better?" Nate sighed and rubbed his jaw. "It's worse. It reeks of dishonesty."

"Why can't it reek of insecurity? You can say you were protecting her, didn't want to expose her 'tender sensibilities' to more of her mother's past. That would be the truth, wouldn't it?"

"Come on, Harry, I'm not doing that."

"You have no idea what's in that notebook. Look how she made up crap about me seducing her. So sincere, so traumatized, with enough misery to infect us all, and don't think she didn't know exactly what she was doing. You can't challenge a dead woman. Once her words get in your head, they burrow and eat away, making you question things you know are true. You want to deal with that, because I sure as hell don't."

***

Ben was into the second half of his run when a black

truck pulled off the side of the road, sending gravel and dust spewing a few feet from him. The door flung open and Brody Kinkaid hopped out and barreled toward him.

"Stay away from my wife."

The man had six inches and a solid fifty pounds on him, and he could probably hurl Ben into the brush with one hand, but he had to catch him first. Ben grabbed the towel from around his neck, wiped his face, and pretended nonchalance. "Calm down, Brody. Tell me what's going on."

"What's going on is you, sticking your nose where it's not your business, putting ideas into my wife's head. *My wife—*" he jabbed his chest with his finger "—not yours."

So Bree was standing up for herself and Mr. Muscle Head didn't like it. "Can you be more specific?"

Brody Kinkaid clenched and unclenched his fists as if he wanted to hit something—probably Ben. "You tell her she should see a doctor, that she needs a little help, maybe some pills." He took a step closer, his booted foot kicking up dirt. "My wife doesn't take pills, you got that?"

"Not even if she needs them?" He kept his voice even, his eyes on Brody.

"Bree doesn't need pills. Why would she need pills? She's got a good life, a family, a house." He paused, sputtered, "A front-loader washing machine."

Oh, that would make any woman happy. Was this guy for real? "She lost her baby."

"Hey." Brody's eyes narrowed, his neck turned red. "That's private."

"It's part of the reason she's depressed."

"Depressed? Who said she's depressed? No wife of mine's getting tagged as depressed. And don't think I was going to have her taking those pills either. No way. I got rid of them."

"Brody. Bree *is* depressed and part of it has to do with losing the baby."

"I said that's private, and besides, once she's pregnant again, she'll be fine."

"Once she's pregnant again?" *Somebody ought to neuter this guy.* "She needs time to heal and get back to where she was last year, at Tess and Cash's wedding. Remember how alive she was, how happy?"

Brody's mouth flattened, his voice switched to deadpan hostile. "Are you after my wife?"

"Of course not."

"You want her for yourself." His nostrils flared, the muscles in his jaw twitched. "That's what this is all about. Convince her she's unhappy, pump her with drugs, and try to talk her into leaving me."

"That's crazy." How was he supposed to reason with somebody like this? The man was not only on the lower rung of the IQ ladder; he was jealous and insecure.

"If you weren't a cop, I'd lay you out right here."

Ben stared right back at him. "If I weren't a cop, I'd welcome the challenge."

Brody spat on the ground, glared, and said, "Don't come near her again, or I'll file harassment charges."

That last comment stayed with Ben the rest of the night and into the morning. Bree was trapped and unless she could find a way to stand up to her husband and tell him "no more babies," she'd end up miserable *and* depressed. Why couldn't the guy be happy with the kids he had? So what if they weren't boys? Ben had never been a father and didn't know if he'd ever be one, but he did know he wouldn't be griping about the sex of the kid. How ungrateful was that? Nate Desantro hadn't seemed unhappy about his little girl, and he doubted Cash would care if he had a boy or girl. Speaking of, they'd probably start a family soon. Everybody was having kids or getting married. Even Melissa. The thought didn't ping his brain like it had when he first got here, maybe because he was getting used to the idea, or maybe because he didn't care so much anymore. He guessed people moved on with their lives and their mistakes, changing what they could, accepting what they couldn't and forgetting the rest.

When he reached work, Rudy Dean pounced on him before he could pour his first cup of coffee. "Got a live one for you," he said, his voice a mix of humor and sarcasm. "This is a show you won't want to miss." He handed Ben a piece of paper with an address on it. "Domestic disturbance. The husband and wife are at it again. Your turn."

"Thanks." Ben poured extra cream in his coffee, took three gulps, and set the mug on the counter. "I'll check it out."

Rudy Dean nodded, ran a hand over his crew cut. "Good luck. Hope you had your shots." His laugh followed Ben out the door, slithered to a stop at the car.

What the hell did that mean? He wished Jeremy had been in so he could ask him about the occupants at this address. The chief sure knew something about them and it didn't sound good, especially for Ben. He drove to the address that was located on the south side of town, not far from the railroad tracks. The shoebox-sized house sat on a lot cluttered with plaster creations of animals and flowers. Dogs, birds, owls, deer, roses, daffodils, lilies, and flowers Ben couldn't name sprawled over most of the front lawn and extended to the sides.

He made his way up the driveway and rang the doorbell,

Mary Campisi

curious about what constituted a domestic disturbance in Magdalena. In Philly, he knew, but here? It took three attempts and four minutes for a woman to answer the door.

"Oh. Hello, officer."

She was short and slender, black-haired with almond-shaped, amber eyes, heavy eyeliner, and red lipstick. Her earlobes dangled with gold hoops; her body squeezed into a black-lace top and pants. Some might call her attractive and maybe twenty years ago, she had been, but a woman in her early sixties trying to look like she was in her thirties was never a comforting sight. "Ma'am, I'm Sergeant Reed. Someone reported an issue."

"Hah!" She lifted her chin and pointed to the ranch house on the right. "Just because they never make a peep—" she lowered her voice and rolled her eyes "—probably not even in the bedroom, does not mean the rest of the world lives in a semicomatose state."

References to this woman making "peeps" in the bedroom was not the visual he cared to see. "May I come in?"

"Please do." She pulled her full lips into a smile and turned, the jingle of earrings matching the sway of her hips. "Would you care for a drink?" She slid onto a faded floral couch, lifted an opaque glass, and took a sip. "Or you could come back later if you'd prefer."

Or not. "Actually, Mrs...."

"Marie." The smile spread, followed by a tip of pink tongue, licking her upper lip.

"Marie."

"Yes?"

"I want to talk about a call we received. Is your husband here?"

She shrugged and crossed her legs, revealing an expanse

168

of tanned thigh. "Somewhere."

"I'd like to talk to him."

Big sigh. "Hold on." The woman stood and made her way across the room toward the steps that led to the second story. "Carmen! Come down here!" She turned and smiled at Ben. "Have a seat, get comfortable."

"I'm fine, thank you."

Ben glanced around the room, noted the heavy draperies, the matching couch and chairs in faded floral, worn at the arms, the couch skirt torn from its base. There were pictures on the wall, posed school photos of a young girl at various ages. He moved closer, studied the dark hair and eyes, pulled in by a familiarity he couldn't identify.

The footsteps jerked him back, followed by a man's voice. "I'm not changing my mind, Marie. No means no. What the…"

"Sergeant Reed," the woman said. "Domestic disturbance call." She pointed to the right. "I'm sure it's the Ketrowskis again. Damn busybodies."

The man combed a hand through his slicked-back hair and nodded at Ben. "Sergeant." He could pass for a male version of his wife: short, slender, black-haired, almond-shaped brown eyes, but with a pencil mustache. He also wore black, but instead of gold earrings, he'd chosen a gold chain and bracelet.

"Can you tell me what happened?"

The man shoved his hands in his pockets and shrugged. "The wife wants a new ring and I told her no."

"That is not what happened. You told me if I cleaned the house and cooked you dinner for a week, you'd buy me a new diamond. Look around, Sergeant Reed. Can't you see the fruits of my hard work? I did it all in good faith that this worthless piece of scum would honor his word and get me that ring."

Ben glanced at the stacks of magazines on the chair, the coupons and scissors next to the coffee table, the shoes lined up next to the television. And the small mound of jewelry on a corner of the end table. This woman had an odd definition of cleaning.

"Clean is clean, Marie. Like my mother used to do." His voice ratcheted up two notches. "That's clean and that's what I meant."

She crossed her arms over her middle, plumping her over-large breasts out. "You never specified."

"Because an idiot could figure it out!"

And they were off, squabbling about food and mothers and what constituted clean and who the real liar was.

Ben stepped between them and said, "Enough. Now settle down, both of you, or I'm taking you in."

Carmen sidled next to his wife and grasped her hand. "I did want to get you that ring, Sweet Pea. You deserve it, but I ran a little short on cash."

Sweet Pea patted her husband's hand and said, "You shouldn't have told me you'd buy it for me if you didn't have the money."

He frowned and muttered, "I thought I did. I thought I could get a loan from Gina."

Gina? Gina who?

"Huh. She'll give a dog a loan before she gives us a penny."

Carmen snorted. "Thinks she's too good for us."

"Is Gina a relative?" This could not be Gina Servetti's family.

Marie's lips pinched like she'd tasted an extra-sour lemon. "Not according to her. Does family ignore your phone calls? Does family refuse to help you out when you'd in a bind? Huh? And what kind of family doesn't even tell you when she gets a new car, like we're going to beg for the old one."

Carmen picked up right where his wife left off. "She thinks she's hot stuff because she went away to college and got some fancy degree. Who wants to touch arms and legs and body parts that don't work right, might never work right. Where's the glory in that?"

"And those scrubs she wears?" Marie laughed. "Not that she's got much to show off, but they make her look like a walking sheet." She shook her head and sighed. "See if she'll get a man in that get-up."

They *were* talking about Gina. Damn them.

"We heard she's pals with Nate Desantro's wife, the rich one," Carmen said. "Probably thinks she's too high and mighty for us."

Marie sipped her wine. "Don't mention that man's name in this room. He belonged with Natalie and if that woman hadn't come to town, our niece would be the one in that house, wearing his ring and carrying his babies."

Natalie Servetti, the woman who almost destroyed Nate and Christine Desantro's marriage.

"I'm not sure about that," Carmen said, stroking his thin mustache. "Natalie's getting a reputation around town and if she isn't careful, there won't be a man who'll have her."

Marie glared at her husband, pitched her voice three octaves higher than her last sentence. "How can you say such a thing about that lovely girl?"

Carmen shrugged. "Sorry, Sweet Pea, but no man wants what every other man in town has already had. Pure fact, no matter how sweet the honey is."

"Hmph. Well then we'll have to have a talk with her, tell her to get busy and find someone." She slid a long glance Ben's way, fingered a gold hoop. "How about you, Sergeant Reed? Would you like to meet our niece? Her name's Natalie, Natalie Servetti."

Chapter 11

Gina dumped the bucket of sudsy water into the utility tub. Kitchen floor, cleaned. One more chore to cross off the ever-growing list she'd created since the "incident" with Ben Reed. As soon as she finished one job, she added two more: organize linen closet, pay bills, vacuum car, clean basement, weed garden, steam-clean carpeting, tackle reading list. If she kept busy, the incident didn't seep into her subconscious and permeate her brain until it was saturated with that night.

How had it happened? Surely, she hadn't intended the kissing or the touching, hadn't wanted it. Had she? Why would she? Hadn't she vowed years ago to never let a man betray her again? The only way to do that was to shut down the possibility for man-woman emotions and physical need. And hadn't she succeeded all these years? Why now, with the one person who unsettled her, had she let her guard slip? She crossed off "wash kitchen floor" from the list and tossed in a load of laundry. *Stay busy, stay busy.* But even as she pushed Ben's Reed's face away, she felt his touch, the pressure of his lips, the sweetness of his tongue. She cursed and slammed the washing machine lid closed.

Next, she'd gather the art materials for tomorrow morning's pressed-flower session with Lily Desantro. They were making Christmas gifts for Lily's family that, according to her, had to be wrapped and hidden away before the first frost.

When the doorbell rang minutes later, she dropped the glue bottle and scissors on the floor and darted a gaze toward the door. Was it Ben? Would he come here after what happened two nights ago? Act like it was no big deal? Isn't that what he'd told her about the kiss at the wedding rehearsal? Or would he want to talk about it, dissect and discuss the kiss, the touch, the moans? Would he want to repeat it?

Would she?

The doorbell rang again, but this time a voice followed it. "Gina, open up. I have to talk to you." Yes, that voice was definitely male, definitely Ben Reed. She ran a hand through her hair, cleared her throat, and made her way to the front door. *Calm, stay calm.* She forced a blank expression on her face and pulled open the door.

He was just too darn good-looking and the heck of it was, the man knew it. Ben Reed stood there, tall, muscled, tanned. "Can I come in?"

She should tell him no, tell him Friday nights were cleaning nights and she didn't like distractions. Gina opened her mouth to shoo him away, but the wrong words fell out. "Sure." He nodded and stepped inside, his fresh scent swirling past her, sucking her in, filling her. Gina closed the door and turned toward him, planning her next words, but before she could say anything, he spoke.

"I met your parents today."

That was the last thing she'd expected. She'd rather he mention the other night and the kissing-touching frenzy. Anything but talk of Carmen and Marie Servetti. A sound fell from her lips—a moan perhaps, or a whimper. Maybe a cry. She couldn't tell as she pulled away, curled up, pretended she was invisible.

"I'm sorry."

She blinked hard, stared at the edge of the counter. He'd seen her family, spoken with them. Now he knew about them, knew there was no more hiding.

"Gina?" He touched her arm. "Talk to me."

There was concern in his voice, and sympathy, because of her sad excuses for parents? Had they talked about her, told him how disappointed they were that their only daughter could not follow the Servetti protocol and snag a man? Gina wouldn't go so far as to say *husband* because that prerequisite had faded long ago. The Servettis believed in security through coupledom and children, and while a formal license was preferred, it was not mandatory. No doubt, her parents had listed her education and profession as liabilities when compared to her cousin's beauty and sexuality. Of course, the subject of money probably surfaced as well, with snide comments on how Gina had more than enough and yet could not find it in her uncharitable soul to share any with her dear parents.

"Gina?"

"What?" She stared at him, blinked back tears she refused to shed. Years ago, she'd not been able to stop the tears; every unkind comment, every snub had pierced her heart and stolen a piece of her confidence until nothing was left but a shaky self-esteem that could only be soothed with carbs, sugars, and fats. Lots of them. She believed it would be different once she left for college and for a time, it was. Until the betrayal. That's when she shut down and barricaded her heart from ever getting hurt again.

Ben clasped her hand and said, "Let's sit down. We need to talk."

"I don't think so."

He touched her cheek, so tender, so caring. "Yeah, we do."

Darn it, the tears started and she couldn't stop them. He pulled her against his chest, held her. "Just give me a minute," she sniffed.

"Let it out. It's okay."

More tears, shoulder-shaking ones pouring from years of loneliness and hurt. Ben stroked her back, rested his chin on the top of her head, and murmured soft words she couldn't make out, but it didn't matter because the tone in them soothed her, made her feel not so alone. When the crying settled, she lifted her head and swiped her eyes. "I got your shirt all wet," she said, staring at the splotch of damp fabric near his heart.

He placed his thumb and forefinger under her chin. "I'd say it was worth it." There was humor in his voice, and tenderness.

She tried to smile but it wobbled and fell flat. "Thank you."

When he kissed her, she forgot to breathe. When he touched her neck and trailed his fingers along her collarbone, she clutched his shoulders so she wouldn't lose her balance. And when he molded her body to his, she wrapped her arms around his waist and deepened the kiss.

He was the one to pull away, his breathing hard, his gaze intense. "Let's talk." He grabbed her hand, led her to the couch, and sat down. She sat beside him, not touching, though part of her wanted to feel that closeness she had a few seconds ago. He rested his arm along the back of the couch and waited for her to speak.

"My parents wanted me to be more like my cousin Natalie, but I couldn't." She shrugged, picked at a thread on her shirt. "It wasn't in me to primp and play coy. And I sure didn't look like Natalie."

"I like the way you look."

She slid a glance at him. He seemed as if he meant it. Her heart skittered against her ribs, made her lightheaded. Gina swallowed twice, sucked in a breath, and mumbled,

"Thank you. My parents didn't like my looks or much about me. They said I ate too much, read too much, and didn't know how to walk across a room without tripping. Food became a good place to hide, that and books. My mother didn't talk to me for three days when I told her I wasn't going to have some man support me because I planned to support myself. She did not like that."

He rubbed his jaw and smiled. "Oh, I'm sure she definitely did not like that."

Gina's lips twitched. "I told them I was going to have options in life, lots of them, so I wouldn't be forced into marriage, but I might as well have spoken in Hungarian. They didn't even try to understand." Her lips flattened, her voice dipped. "And when I said I was going to college, they called me uppity and asked if I thought I was too good for them." She swiped her cheeks and cleared her throat. "I just wanted to get away and have a different life. Was that so wrong?"

"Absolutely not." He grabbed her hand, laced his fingers with hers. "They had no right to crush your dreams."

"I know they believed what they were doing was right, but it hurt." She'd never admitted that to anyone else; she'd barely admitted it to herself, and yet she'd just told Ben.

"I never knew my father," he said. "And my mother took off when I was five. My grandmother raised me, and I loved her, but I envied kids who had a mother and father. To me, that meant family, and if I didn't have one, I must not be good enough."

She'd known years of believing she wasn't good enough. "Blood doesn't always make a family."

Those eyes dug into her soul. "I'm learning that." He tucked a lock of hair behind her ear. "I'm also learning that first impressions aren't always the right ones."

Maybe they'd both been wrong about each other. Gina tilted her head and said in a soft voice, "I'm learning that, too."

He eased her toward him until their lips touched, gently at first and then with more force. It was difficult to think when he kissed her. Actually, it was impossible to think, and Gina gave up as the last shreds of logic suffocated with his kiss.

"Gina," he breathed as he lifted her onto his lap, coaxed her mouth open, tasting, sharing.

Oh, but he was delicious and tempting, and it had been so very long. "Ben." The need in her voice surprised her. She wanted him. All of him. His fingers made tiny circles along her collarbone, traced the opening of her shirt. She strained toward him, waiting for him to unbutton her shirt, dip his hand inside her bra...touch her nipples...

"I want you," he said. "But what happens next is up to you." His gaze turned darker, burrowed deeper into her soul. "If you want me to leave, I—"

Gina threw her arms around his neck, straddled him, and kissed him long and slow, letting him know exactly what she wanted. She rubbed her breasts along his chest, made him moan and grab her butt. He pulled her closer and she didn't think about tomorrow or next week, or next month. Not rules, or must-dos and should-nots. Right now, all she did was *feel*, for the first time in years, maybe ever. And the feeling brought passion and need and a boldness that stripped them of their clothes and Ben Reed of his control. *She* was the aggressor, *she* was the one who rode him, head flung back, eyes closed, moans escaping her lips. And she was the one who climaxed first, convulsing with pulses of white-light intensity, carrying Ben to his own, equally forceful, equally pleasurable climax.

They slept, snuggled on the beige carpet with Gina on top of Ben. Naked. Her head on his chest, his arm slung across her back. She woke hours later, curled at his side, his arm still around her. Gray light poked through the slats of the living room blinds, signs that morning would be here soon. What time was it? *Oh, no.* Ben's car was in the driveway, had been there all night. People would see.

Panic slithered through her, settled in her gut, making her queasy. People would think he'd spent the night. Maybe there was still time to get him out of here before anyone noticed. If he hurried…Gina unwound his arm and eased away. For just a second, she missed the warmth of his body, the smell of him. She grabbed her shirt, stuffed her arms in the sleeves, and pulled on her panties.

"Going somewhere?"

She jerked and glanced up. Ben was awake, his blue eyes fixed on her.

"It's late." She paused, stumbled on. "Or early. What time is it, anyway?"

He glanced at his watch and said, "Five."

"Oh." She stepped into her jeans, zipped them. Her gaze skittered to her bra, which lay near his left hand. "I think you should leave."

"Huh." Those eyes narrowed. "This is a first for me."

"What?"

"I've never had a woman ask me to leave her bed before." He crossed his arms behind his head as though he were in no hurry to go anywhere.

"Technically, we weren't in bed." She ran a hand through her hair, trying to smooth the tangled mess.

"No, *technically*, we were right here, on the floor." Sleep had turned his voice into a velvet rumble that teased her belly. "But we could try the bed if you like."

She shook her head. "No. I don't want people to see your car here."

"Ah." And then, "Why?"

"Why?" How could he ask her that? The answer was beyond obvious. "Because then they'll know you stayed here last night."

"Uh-huh. And?"

She ignored the tenseness in his voice, the tightness in his jaw. What did he want her to say? That they should stroll outside, hand in hand, and collect the morning paper? "And I don't want them to know."

"Right. Of course not."

He snatched his shirt, pulled it over his head, grabbed his boxers and jeans. Gina looked away while he dressed, the silence sucking the oxygen from the room, making her wish she'd been more careful with her words. She'd hurt him and that surprised her because she'd thought he'd welcome an easy way out. What if she ignored the time and the gossip his car would create and asked him to stay? Was it too late? Would he do it? Come back to bed with her, a real bed this time, and make her feel like he had last night? Like she was the most beautiful woman in the world? The *only* woman in his world?

"If anybody asks, you can tell them someone was lurking around the house and I wanted to make sure you were okay. Say I slept on the couch." He grabbed the keys from his pocket and shrugged. "Hell, say whatever you want."

"Ben?"

He looked at her, waited. She tried to push the words out, but they wouldn't come.

"Good-bye, Gina."

Then he was out the door, his car rumbling down the driveway. Not until the sound faded did Gina put sound to words. "Stay. Please, stay."

By the time Lily arrived at 10:00 A.M., Gina had showered, cleaned up the living room, and removed all signs of the night before. Not exactly true. Ben Reed had stamped her heart and touched her soul, and no amount of disinfectant would remove that.

"Hey, Gina, are you ready to make presents?" Lily carried a box of ribbons and a plastic container. "Ribbons for the decorations and a fruit salad from Mom."

"Thank you. How very kind of your mother." For too many years, she'd judged Miriam Desantro and Charlie Blacksworth, not considering circumstances that might have made what society judged as wrong seem almost right. Her attitude had changed when she met Christine, saw how much she loved Lily and the town. And when she learned of Christine's mother's attempts to break up her marriage, well, that was unforgivable.

"What do I smell?" Lily stood in doorway, sniffed her way into the living room.

"I don't know. What does it smell like?"

The child sniff-sniffed her way to the kitchen. "A man." She turned and stared at Gina, her dark brows pinched together. "Was Uncle Harry here?"

"No."

"Cash?"

"Uh-uh."

"Well, I smell a man's cologne." She scratched her chin. "Nate smells like woods and fresh air, so it's not him. And if it's not Uncle Harry or Cash, who is it?"

Gina inhaled, detected the faint scent of Ben's cologne. She shrugged. "I don't know."

Lily's smile stretched across her face. "It's Ben Reed, isn't it?" she asked, her voice a singsong whisper.

"Why do you say that?" Why *would* she say that? Had someone spotted his car last night and already started the gossip?

"'Cause he's cute and you danced with him at the wedding." She tilted her head, her eyes bright beneath the thick glasses. "And when I say his name your face gets all pink, *and*, because if you married him, your name would be Gina Reed. Isn't that a cool name?"

***

Ben wouldn't say Mimi was actually waiting for him when he got home from Gina's a little before 6:00 A.M., but she sure pounced on him the second he stepped out of the car. He spotted her on the front porch, sipping coffee and reading the paper. When he pulled in, she pushed her reading glasses on top of her head and stared. Then she smiled. Neither of which was a good sign for a person hoping to avoid conversation and discussion. He trudged up the front steps and waved. "Morning, Mimi."

"Good morning, Ben." The smile faded, replaced with a knowing look as she took in his tousled hair and wrinkled clothing. "You look like you could use a strong cup of coffee. Have a seat while I get it for you."

If he'd thought there was a way out of answering Mimi's questions, he'd have declined the coffee and headed to bed. But what he'd learned about Mimi Pendergrass was that she was a straight shooter who didn't like to hide behind politeness if it hid the truth. So, he sank into a chair and said, "Sure. Thanks."

She disappeared into the Heart Sent, leaving him with the crisp morning air on his skin and thoughts of Gina in his brain. How had last night's intense lovemaking translated into this morning's "get out of my house and get out now"? Gina had burned him with her passion in ways he'd never known before. When they touched last night, she'd exploded in a frenzy of need, pulling sensation and desire from him with her kisses, her hands, her... *Damn.* Where had she been hiding all that passion? He hadn't been the only one to feel something special last night; she felt it, too, even if she refused to admit it. And then, to push him out the door like she didn't want to remember what they'd done and damn sure didn't want anyone else to know.

"Here you go." Mimi handed him the steaming cup of coffee and sank into the rocker beside him. "Late night, huh?"

He sipped his coffee, considered his answer, and settled on, "Yup."

"Hmm."

That word packed some serious punch. "Yup."

"I don't suppose you care to talk about it?"

"Nope." What man wanted to admit the woman he'd made love to had turned down his offer for a repeat and tossed him out when he was still half-asleep? Not only that, she'd been hell bent on keeping their "tryst" a secret? It wasn't that he wanted to advertise it in the *Magdalena Press*, but a little more finesse on Gina's part would have gone a long way. And then there was the possibility of regret. Is that what this morning had really been about? Get him out of the house so she could start purging herself of the memories, starting with a hot shower?

Mimi laid a firm hand on his arm. "You're saying more by not saying anything. And heavens, that look on your face is pure pitiful, which tells me you've got it bad. I don't imagine you've felt this way more than a time or two, and it's got you perplexed as all get-out." She grinned and patted his hand. "How am I doing so far?"

Oh, what the hell. His lips twitched. "I'd say you're dead-on."

"Gina's a good girl, but she's not one to trust easily. She'll be scared. You'll have to go slow." She paused and added, "That is, if you want this to go anywhere, which from the sad-sack look on your face, I'd say you do. But if I'm wrong and you're just looking for a way to pass time, please leave her alone." When he didn't answer, she pressed, "Well? Does that girl mean more to you than a few hours of fun?"

He hadn't thought about it before last night, but he hadn't planned on sleeping with her either. When she'd cried in his arms and told him about her parents, he'd seen a part of her he hadn't seen before. Open. Honest. Vulnerable. He'd wanted to protect her, and when he'd kissed her, it hadn't been with thoughts of going any further than that kiss. But then she'd exploded and sizzled with a passion that made him burn for her, made him forget their differences, forget everything but the need to be with her, inside of her. It had never been that intense before—not even with Melissa.

"I want an answer, young man."

Young man? So Mimi was pulling her no-nonsense voice on him. Now she really reminded him of his grandmother. Ben turned to her and hid a smile. "Is that your mayor's voice, or is it your Bleeding Hearts Society voice?"

She cocked a brow. "Whichever works."

"She isn't just a few hours of fun." He rubbed his stubbled jaw, shrugged. "But she might think I am."

Mimi's laugh spilled from her pink lips to the porch and down the front steps. "Oh, but that is so precious." The laugh deepened, spread down the sidewalk, to the neighbors' front door. "Imagine that?"

"Yeah, I am, but I'm not laughing."

She tsk-tsked and patted his knee. "Don't worry, that's just fear getting in the way of common sense."

"Why do you say that?"

"Why, Ben Reed, no woman with a heartbeat would turn you away from her bed. Fear's got hold of her, but once she knows she can trust you, well, that's when the magic starts."

Mimi left Ben to ponder things like fear and magic while she whipped him up a batch of banana-walnut pancakes. He'd offered to help, but she'd smiled at him and told him to rest and contemplate. Yeah, he'd contemplate all right, contemplate the mess he was in with Gina. He shouldn't have had sex with her until she trusted him; then she would have invited him to her bed and been so pleased with the results, she'd have asked him for several repeat performances, and not once would she have thought about his damn car parked in her driveway. He was too busy waffling between the importance of trust and remembering Gina's soft skin that he didn't see Nate Desantro pull into the Heart Sent until the man was halfway up the porch steps.

"Do you have a second?"

No hello from Mr. Personality? Ben stood and said, "Sure. What's up?"

"What's going on between you and Gina?"

He'd never pegged Desantro for idle chit-chat but he'd at least thought the guy would warm up before he took a shot. "Gina?" What did he know?

Desantro tried to bury him with those dark eyes. "Yeah. Gina."

Ben squared his shoulders and sliced him with a look of his own. "Unless she's your sister, I don't think it's any of your concern."

He didn't like that. Those eyes narrowed, the jaw clenched, the lips flattened. Nate Desantro was big and broad and at the moment, pissed off, which made him even more intimidating, but Ben had never backed down from a standoff, even when he should have, like now.

"Leave her alone. She's a nice girl and she doesn't need someone like you sniffing around."

"Spoken from Mr. Pure himself?" Now the guy was pissing him off. Who was he to warn him off Gina when he'd been sleeping with Natalie Servetti before his wife hit town?

Desantro stepped forward until they were almost chest to chest. "You hurt her, you answer to me. You may have this town fooled with your smiles and your manners, but I've got my eye on you. I can spot a fake ten miles away and you're a fake."

***

After three days of being in charge of the Blacksworth household, Harry knew two things: he did not want to be in charge, and God knew what He was doing when He gave a woman the ability to carry a baby in her belly. Men wouldn't be able to do it. No friggin' way. And actually having the kid? Pushing it out or having it cut out? He had to stop the visuals or he'd be heaving. Women had the gene to handle it and the smarts to know men were better off with less detail on a whole lot of things. Take the cookout they were having today to celebrate Greta's homecoming. When he'd insisted on organizing the event, he thought he'd only have to point and pay. That's what he'd always done in the past, whether it was a vacation, a wardrobe, or a redesign of his condo. Easy. Uncomplicated. Fast. He didn't realize he had to be the middleman in the operation, too. Someone else had always taken care of that for him, though he had no idea who that person was. When the check was big enough, you didn't worry about those kinds of details. After he and Greta got married, she'd managed the middleman job with efficiency, fairness, and enthusiasm. The same could not be said for Harry's attempts.

And now, because he'd waited too long to book a caterer, Nate and Cash Casherdon had been drafted to grill the chicken, sausage with peppers and onions, and hot dogs. Christine and Tess Carrick had picked up the sides from Sal's, and Miriam, a.k.a. "Wonder Woman," made whatever else she deemed necessary for the gathering, which included but was not limited to cake, chocolate chip cookies, and a fruit salad. Nate promised his double fudge brownies, and Pop Benito planned to bring what he brought to every gathering: pizzelles.

"Harry? Relax." Greta smiled up at him from the lounge chair on the deck where she reclined in a flowing, pink and white dress. "It's family and friends."

"Yeah, and it's family and friends who are never going to let me forget I didn't order beer or wine." The fact that he'd actually forgotten the alcohol was a sign of his supreme domestication, according to Nate. Of course, the damn guy couldn't wait to tell Chrissie who told Miriam and he'd lay Vegas odds 500 to 1 that Lily overheard. The next thing Harry knew, Pop Benito had spread it all over town before dinnertime. Even Phyllis at Lina's commented on it this morning when he stopped in for his eggs and pancakes. Harry tried for a "save" by saying he'd been working on bringing in imported beer and wine as a surprise and, of course, he had to go to the city, because, hell, this town had never heard of some of the brands he planned to bring in. Phyllis let him go on for a solid two minutes before she'd nodded and said in the same matter-of-fact voice she used when one of the young waitresses mixed up the orders: "You forgot to order them, didn't you?" What could he say but admit the truth? Seemed like people in this town could see through bullshit a lot quicker than the ones in Chicago, an unsettling yet comforting thought.

"Why don't you let me help you? The doctor said I had to take it easy, not stop living." Greta sighed. "And I'm very good at organizing and making lists." She slid him a look, said, "I could make you a list or two." Pause. "If you like."

"Damn it, Greta, is this about AJ's school list? How the hell was I to know the difference between a two-pronged folder and a plain one? What difference does it make? They really give kids extra credit for bringing in the right folder? That's ridiculous."

"It's about following rules and making the classroom work."

"Right. It's about control and turning the kids into robots who can't think unless someone else spits it out or pastes it in their brain. Are you saying the presentation is more important than the content?" It shouldn't surprise him if that were the case. Hadn't he been "presenting" himself to the world for years in his fancy duds and designer lifestyle without a care to the "content" of his life? And hadn't most people simply accepted that from him, especially the ones grappling for his credit card *and* his lifestyle? Still, this was the educational system they were talking about; it affected his kids and all the kids out there.

It should be about more than a two-pronged folder.

"Of course I'm not saying that, but if the presentation isn't recognizable, or if it's too difficult to understand, it doesn't matter what the content is because no one will take the time to look at it."

Hmm. She might have a point, but only a minor one. He'd seen a lot of bullshit wrapped up in shiny packaging.

"If you're that concerned with the educational system of our children, why don't you get involved at school? You could volunteer."

"Huh?" Volunteer for what?

Greta smiled the way she did when she knew she'd trapped him with his own words. "Volunteer at school. Lizzie's class has Parent Read a Book Day and Parents and Professions Day. I'll bet the kids would love to hear you speak." Her smile spread. "You could even talk to them about What to Wear to Work Day. I'm sure Ms. Hanson would appreciate a lesson on combining patterns with a stripe."

He scowled and shoved his hands in his pockets. "Very funny."

"I'm serious, Harry. You're a very persuasive speaker." Her voice dipped, gentled. "You do have a way with words."

He liked when she talked to him that way, and when those big blue eyes gazed at him as if he were the only man walking the earth, how could he wish for anything more? "Volunteering," he murmured. Lizzie loved his stories, made him repeat them two and three times until she giggled so hard, tears sprouted in those baby blues. But he was not about to spread those in the school district. Dumping a riding lawnmower when making a turn because he drove it like a sports car? Uh, that would be a no. Installing a towel bar with a cordless screwdriver that had no screwdriver bit in it. Nope. Three attempts to grill a cheese sandwich that sounded the smoke alarm and ruined the pan? Don't think so.

"What would you tell them about, Harry?"

"I could tell them about Harry's Folly, the restaurant that grew out of a desire to get a good bowl of penne pasta with spinach and garbanzo beans."

She laughed. "Yes, I like that."

Harry liked the idea, too. Damn, but he missed the restaurant. Greta made him penne with spinach and garbanzos, but it wasn't the same as having a place where customers could come and share a meal and a glass of wine. Maybe someday he and Greta could start another restaurant, right here in Magdalena. Maybe…the possibility burst through him so fast he had to sit down.

"Harry?" Greta leaned forward, touched his hand. "Are you all right? Your face is flushed and you're breathing hard. What's the matter?"

"Nothing, I'm fine. Actually, I'm great." He clasped his wife's hand and looked into her eyes. "I'm going to volunteer in Lizzie's class. I'll tell them all about second chances and how I got about fifteen of them." He squeezed Greta's hand and laughed. "That'll make them wonder. And then I'll tell them about the new restaurant coming to town." He paused, grinned, and let the words fall out. "Harry's Folly."

"Harry, what are you talking about?"

His grin almost split open his face. "I miss it, Greta. Me, you, us; we were good at it, weren't we?"

Her eyes sparkled with tears. "Yes, Harry," she whispered. "We were very good." And then, "I miss it, too."

Chapter 12

Tuesday nights were half-price margarita and fajita nights, but that's not what brought Gina, Tess, and Christine to their favorite Mexican restaurant because Gina didn't eat fajitas and Christine was sticking to ice water tonight. The latter proved an interesting observation that might have nothing or everything to do with her menstrual cycle. Tess, however, had ordered a margarita *and* a fajita, double chicken.

"So, did you hear about Brody tracking down Ben Reed the other day?" Tess asked, piling guacamole inside her fajita.

"What?" Gina had a tortilla chip with salsa halfway to her mouth. "What happened?" And why hadn't Ben told her? It wasn't as if they'd actually spoken since the morning after the night she couldn't forget, but still she thought he might have told her. Or maybe not. She'd behaved poorly and by the time she'd analyzed what she'd done and why, it was too late. Ben was gone, and it didn't look like he was coming back. Her stomach burned in ways that had nothing to do with spicy salsa or the margarita.

"Nate said he heard something about it." This from Christine who slid Gina a look before continuing, "If Brody doesn't settle down soon, he could risk losing everything."

"Cash is about ready to pay him a visit." Tess bit into her fajita, chewed. "Not a good sign."

Why had Christine given her that look? Had Lily said something about smelling a man in Gina's house?

"I heard Brody took her pills," Tess said. "Ranting on and on about how no wife of his is going to take a pill."

Gina blew out a disgusted sigh. "Oh, I'm sure Testosterone Brody would take that as a personal sign that he wasn't keeping his woman happy."

They laughed at that, but then Tess said, "It's really tragic how they seem to be imploding. Can't somebody stop it?"

"Not until they both admit there's a problem." This from Christine. "Bree's got to grieve her baby, and Brody's got to admit the way to do that isn't to just have another one."

"She's too intelligent for him," Gina blurted out, then wished she could yank the words back. "I'm sorry; I know that's horrible to say, but it's the truth. Brody has a brain the size of a lentil, yet he insists on making the decisions in that household, down to the number of children they have and when." She should stop, but the words kept spilling out. "Like he's the one who has to carry the baby in his belly, or gain the weight, or suffer the heartburn, or all the rest that goes with it. And darn it, but Bree always let him do it; she thought it was cute that he loved his Honeybee so much he wanted to manage every part of her life."

Tess nodded. "I know. Sad. Remember when she wanted to get her degree?"

"And Brody got her pregnant instead?" Gina scowled and scooped a hunk of salsa on her chip. "Yeah, I remember."

"Uhh…ladies, change the conversation fast," Christine said, then smiled and waved at someone. "Hi, how are you? Care to join us?"

"Sure. Thanks."

Gina had just stuffed a chip in her mouth when she recognized Ben Reed's voice. She glanced up as his smile circled the table, flattening a half second when it touched her before it corrected and continued.

"Sit down," Tess said, motioning to the empty spot next to Gina. "There's lots of room."

Ben slid into the booth, his scent smothering Gina with remembering. "Thanks."

There was a stiffness in his words, barely noticeable, but Gina heard it. When had she become an expert on Ben Reed's voice? He placed his hands on his thighs, within touching distance, and said, "Half-price margaritas and fajitas, huh?"

"And I'm the only one taking advantage of both," Tess said, scooping another tortilla chip with salsa. "How about you, Ben? Are you a margarita drinker?"

He laughed. "Can't say as I am. I prefer a Mexican beer myself."

The chatter went on, mindless, surface talk about beer and fajitas, homemade salsa, and when the first frost might hit. Gina sipped her margarita and provided an occasional word when solicited, but mostly she tried to blend in and act as though Ben Reed's presence didn't steal her breath and her senses.

When the talk slowed, Tess cleared her throat, pushed her almost-empty plate aside, and said, "We heard Brody Kinkaid threatened you the other day."

Ben took so long to respond that Gina thought he might not answer. But then he shrugged and said, "He and I have different viewpoints on how to treat a woman, especially a wife who's lost a baby."

Tess nodded, her eyes bright, her smile fragile. Gina bet she was thinking about the baby she and Cash lost and the ones they might never have. So tragic, and yet they were determined to get through the sadness by opening their hearts and their home to those in need. There was Henry, the rescue dog who thought he was their baby, and the camp they ran for youths in trouble, and maybe down the road, they'd adopt or foster. Cash had been raised by an aunt after his nomadic parents took off because "a child was too restrictive." Gina knew all about parents who thought of their children as nuisances. And with a father he never knew and a mother who took off, she'd bet Ben knew all about it, too. She settled her gaze on his hands: strong, tanned, so very capable.

"…anyway, I'd better get going. Morning gets here way too fast." He pulled out his wallet, laid three twenty-dollar bills on the table, and said, "My treat."

He waved and slid out of the booth before they finished thanking him. Gina watched him leave, his lean body reaching the door seconds before she realized she had to go after him. "I've got to talk to Ben." She scooted out of the booth and rushed past the hanging piñatas and potted palm trees to the large wooden doors. Gina pushed them open and stepped outside. "Ben! Wait!"

He was several steps away, heading toward his car, but he stopped and turned, his jaw set, his expression unreadable. "What do you want, Gina?"

Correction. His expression wasn't unreadable; in fact, it was downright angry. "I…wanted to talk to you." He shoved his hands in his pockets, waited. The man was not going to make this easy for her. "Thanks for helping Bree."

He shrugged. "I don't like to see people get bullied, especially women."

"Still, it was very kind and you didn't have to do it."

His gaze narrowed on her. "You mean because I'm a stranger and don't really fit in here, right?"

"No, of course not." Though that was exactly what she'd meant.

"Doesn't matter. I didn't do it for brownie points or any other reason." He paused, added, "I did it to help Bree."

"Right." He meant he didn't do it for her. "Well." She fiddled with the tassels on her purse, tried to push past the awkwardness. *I'm sorry I kicked you out of my house the other night and acted like I didn't want you to be there, like I was ashamed to be with you. I'm not ashamed...in fact...*

"I've got to go. Good-bye, Gina." And then he was gone, leaving her with a heart filled with apologies and regret.

***

Gina had never been one to take risks, not without analyzing the data and calculating the chance of a successful outcome based on statistics and past experience. Since the latter provided a relatively small sample, she usually decided against *any* risk, claiming she didn't like surprises. As she grew older, the chance for surprises dwindled, until her life settled into what many considered mundane, practical, and safe. Gina knew what people thought, knew what they said, but it didn't bother her because she'd erected a wall so strong and impenetrable, not even the cruelest comment could harm her.

And then she met Ben Reed. He'd found a way to barrel through her defenses and make her wish she weren't so mundane and practical. He'd made her wish she hadn't played it so safe, which was why she now stood outside the door to his room at the Heart Sent. She wanted to knock, wanted to tell him there'd been so many feelings surging through her the night they made love that she couldn't process them all and did what she always did in situations that scared her: she pushed him away. He might tell her it was too late, or that he wasn't interested, or that she was too much trouble with too much baggage. But he might not, and it was that small percentage she hoped for as she curled her hand into a fist and knocked on his door.

"Mimi?"

She sucked in a breath, blew it out. "It's Gina."

The door flew open and he stood there, looking fierce and untouchable, his chest bare, his jeans riding low on his hips.

"Ben, I..." The small percentage of hope in her heart shrank by half. Still, if this was her last opportunity with him, she might as well blurt it out. If it exploded in her face, she'd just avoid him for the rest of her life. "Is this a bad time?"

He crossed his arms over his chest, which probably meant "Any time with you is a bad time," and said, "Did you park your car three streets away so nobody knows you're here?"

The man was not going to let her forget that comment. "No, I'm right out front."

"Ah. Feeling brave, are we?"

"Will you stop? I came to apologize for what I said that night." She paused. "And how I acted. I'm sorry."

He rubbed his jaw and said, "As I recall, you didn't say much that night." His voice dipped, turned rough. "What you did that night, well. That was perfect, until morning came. That's when it all went to hell and you turned into a viper."

"A viper?" *Charming.*

He shrugged. "Or a jalapeño pepper, take your choice."

What on earth to say to that? She licked her lips, caught him watching her with those blue eyes. "I really am sorry, Ben. I...I was scared, but that's no excuse." Okay, she was done, now it was time to get out of here. She closed the distance between them and thrust out her hand.

He stared at her outstretched hand. "You're kidding, right?"

"Actually—"

He pulled her to him, devouring her mouth with passion and need. Oh, but he tasted wonderful, and the feel of his hard body pressed against hers was pure bliss. She would wish for this to go on and on...Seconds later, he broke the kiss, and said in a rough voice, "No man makes love to a woman and then resorts to hand-shaking."

Gina stared at his lips. "I'll remember that," she whispered.

Ben eased the door closed, backed her against it, and clasped her face between his hands. "If you're not staying until morning, then leave now."

She grabbed his shoulders, tried to bring him closer. "I'll stay."

The talking stalled after that as they touched and tasted, moans of pleasure swirling between them. Ben undressed her, one delicious touch at a time, and when her clothes lay in a heap at her feet, he stepped back and said, "You're beautiful."

Beautiful? No, she'd never been that. "Please don't say that."

"Because it's true?" He cupped her right breast, planted a kiss on her nipple. "When I look at you, I see a beautiful woman, all curves and softness. And when I taste you—" he licked the peak of her nipple "—that's pure honey."

His words smothered her and when he used that tongue, she absolutely could not think. Did he not see the extra belly flesh or the thick waist? And her butt? There was more than a handful there, no doubt about that. But he really didn't seem to care. That thought along with what he was doing with his tongue made her bold, made her want to show him how much she enjoyed *his* beautiful body. She unzipped his jeans, dipped her fingers inside his boxers, and cupped his sex.

"You're the beautiful one," she whispered.

He groaned, pushed her hands away, and yanked off his jeans and boxers, seconds before he pinned her to the door and entered her, hard, fast, completely. And then he proceeded to show her exactly how beautiful he thought she was.

After, they worked their way to the bed and made love again, this time as needy and desperate as the last. Who would have thought when Ben walked into Lina's Café a year ago, filled with arrogance and the need to protect his cousin, that Gina would end up in his bed, naked, satisfied, covered with his scent? And who would have thought she'd enjoy it?

"Gina, you awake?"

She lay with her head on his chest, his arm slung around her waist, holding her against his side. "Uh-huh."

"Tell me about the guy."

His words snuffed the oxygen from the room, circled her brain, made her dizzy. "Ben." She could not talk about the betrayal that almost ruined her life.

"Whatever he did to you, he was a jerk." He stroked her back, his voice soft, soothing.

She couldn't tell him. Could she?

"And you shouldn't have to carry that around with you for the next forty years." He paused, his words filled with force and conviction. "You should let me carry it for you because I'll toss that sucker to the ground and smash it until there's nothing left."

Ben wanted to help her. All she had to do was trust him with the worst secret of her life. Trust. It didn't come easily. "You have no idea…"

"No, I don't, but I want to. Tell me; let me help you."

She breathed in his scent, touched the springy hairs by his right nipple, and began to speak. "I never had a boyfriend until my sophomore year. His name was Jason; he was a pre-med student, so you can imagine some of our conversations. We talked about genetics, anatomy, physiology…" She paused, cleared her throat. "…and getting married. We planned to get engaged when he started med school and marry during his residency. I'd be finished with school and getting a job would be easy."

"Sounds like the perfect match," Ben said, his voice tight.

"We were." Long pause. "And then my cousin came to visit. Natalie didn't go to college but that didn't stop her from wanting what she called the college experience, which meant she wanted to hang out with guys, get drunk, and hook up. She kept bugging me to let her visit for a weekend. I didn't want to do it. We didn't even get along, but my parents insisted and finally, I gave in. It was late October and Jason and I had both been studying for exams. The fridge was empty, and we needed food. Jason suggested a pizza, but I'd been trying so hard to eat healthier, so I offered to make a food run. I often wonder what might have happened if I'd just eaten the darn pizza. When I got back to the dorm, I opened the door and found them…" She pushed back memories of Natalie's tanned legs gripping Jason's naked back, their moans filling the air, oblivious to anything but their own pleasure.

Ben cursed, pulled her closer. "I'm really sorry."

"Jason was, too. Begged me to forgive him, said he didn't know what came over him, claimed it was the result of exhaustion from studying so much. The thing is, Natalie had no idea he was my boyfriend, still doesn't know. I guess she figured when she was in the room, no guy could possibly want anybody else."

"Yeah, well, from what I've heard about her, she's a nice toy, but not one you'd want to keep."

"Actually, that's pretty accurate."

"And Jason? What happened to him?"

"I heard he's an anesthesiologist in California. Married, one child. I found a write-up about him in a medical journal. Imagine that."

Ben stroked her back, kissed the top of her head. "Guess you don't believe in second chances, huh?"

"With a guy who cheats?"

"With a guy who realizes he's made a mistake," he corrected.

Why such an edge in his voice? Gina lifted her head so she could see his face. "A mistake that involves hooking up with my cousin?"

"What he did was worse than wrong, no doubt about it. Still, people make mistakes and sometimes they hurt the people they love the most."

"People have choices. Jason had his and he made it, and whether or not he regretted that choice is really not the point. I knew I couldn't live my life with a man I didn't trust. If he came home ten minutes late, I'd wonder where he'd been and who he'd been with, and aside from zapping him like Pavlov's dogs when he veered in the wrong direction, I would never take a fresh breath again."

Those blue eyes turned opaque. "That's a pretty brutal statement."

"It's how I feel, and why I have such a trust issue. Once it's gone, it's gone." When he didn't respond, she prodded, "Haven't you ever been hurt by someone you trusted?"

"You mean like the mother who left me when I was a kid?"

He tried to hide the pain but she saw it in the tightness of his jaw, the flat line of his lips. "Or someone else."

He shrugged. "I never let anyone get close enough to do that." Pause. "Not even my ex-wife."

Gina stared at him, trying to comprehend what he'd just said. "You...had a wife?"

"I did."

"What happened?" A woman had shared his bed every night, not just at random hours, in strange beds. And she'd shared his name.

"It didn't work out."

Tell me more, she wanted to say. *Tell me all of it. What was her name? Did you love her more than your own breath? Where is she now? Do you ever think of her?* And the thought that made her queasy. *Do you ever think of her when you're with me?* Of course she would never ask those questions. All she could slip through her mouth was a simple, "I see."

"Gina, let it go."

She nodded, laid her head on his chest and tried to forget how much she didn't know about Ben Reed. He had an ex-wife, a past that didn't include her, and most likely secrets he didn't want to divulge. She'd opened up to him and confessed her darkest betrayal and while he'd comforted her, he'd shared nothing.

***

The pounding woke Ben seconds before Brody Kinkaid's voice boomed from the other side of the door. "Open this door right now, you bastard, or I swear I'll break it down."

"Hold on." Ben turned to Gina and whispered, "Go,

wait in the bathroom until I get rid of him." For once she didn't argue, but scooted out of bed, snatched up her clothes, and disappeared into the bathroom.

"You've got exactly three seconds before I come in."

"Then you can explain the broken door to Mimi. Give me a second, I'm getting dressed." Ben pulled on his jeans and T-shirt and padded to the door. He flung it open and there stood the angry Giant Kinkaid, fists clenched, face red, neck bulging.

"Is she inside?"

"Who?"

"My wife."

Ben sighed. "Are you still jagging on about that? I have no idea where your wife is, but she's not here." And then, because he was tired of the way the big oaf tried to intimidate everybody, added, "If you don't know your wife's whereabouts, I'd say that's a sign of marital discord."

"What do you mean by that?"

Right; he should have known the idiot didn't know what *discord* meant. "Problems," he corrected. "Marital problems."

Brody Kinkaid's eyes narrowed on him like a bull preparing to charge. "Step aside. I want to see for myself."

"Hey, get out of here. Now." Ben might end up with a broken bone or two, but he wasn't going without a few punches of his own. Gina was in here and he had to protect her.

"Whose bra is that? Is that my wife's?"

Damn. Ben followed the man's gaze and spotted the black lace bra on the hardwood floor near the bed. "Of course not." He picked up the bra, held it behind his back.

"And those panties?" Brody Kinkaid roared. "You

gonna tell me they aren't Bree's?" He charged Ben, knocked him on the bed, lifted a fist to pummel his jaw.

"Stop! Stop!"

Brody paused with his fist half-cocked, turned to his right. "Gina? What are you doing here?"

"Please don't hurt him, Brody. Please." She moved toward him, smiled. "Those are my things."

"Yours?" He stared at her, then at Ben. "You and this asshole? Why?"

"Brody, leave him be. Come on. Tell me why you're here." She took his hand and he heaved himself off the bed and Ben's chest.

"She's gone." His voice cracked and wobbled, "Took the kids, too."

Ben advanced on him. "And you thought I was hiding your whole family here? Where? Under the bed?" Now he was pissed. Bad enough the guy accused him of cheating with Bree, but he'd dragged Gina into it, and for what? Jealous stupidity?

"Ben," Gina shook her head at him, "Brody's upset. We're going to help him find Bree and the kids."

"Oh, for the love of—"

"You will?"

The guy had gone from Mr. Fierce to Mr. Wimp. "Sure. Why not?" Ben glanced at his watch. "It's only 1:45 A.M. We don't have anything better to do than to help you because you're such a great guy." Actually, he and Gina had a lot to talk about. He'd recognized the look on her face when he refused to talk about Melissa. Pure hurt. Hell, she deserved better; she deserved somebody who could open up and share, but damn it, he just didn't know if he could do it.

Gina shot him a look. "Ben. Enough."

"Okay. One more question. When did you discover your

wife and kids had gone missing? It's late, so where were you?"

The guy's face burst with red. "Me and the guys had a few at O'Reilly's."

"Huh." Ben shoved his hands in his pockets and leaned against the foot of the bed.

"Sit over here," Gina said, pointing to a chair near the dresser. "Did you call your mother and Bree's parents?"

Brody rubbed a sausage-sized hand over his face. "I didn't call, but I drove by and didn't see her SUV at either place. I couldn't say I didn't know where my wife and kids were at 1:00 A.M. How would that look? And you know Bree's dad; he'd have half the town looking for her and then he'd skin me for worrying him."

"Where else could you look?" She touched Brody on the shoulder and said in a soft voice, "Why would you think she's left? Did you have a fight?"

He shook his head. "It hasn't been the same since…"

"Since she lost the baby?" Gina squeezed his shoulder. "Is that what you mean?"

Ben watched her comfort the big oaf with ease and not a care that she wasn't wearing panties or a bra. Of course, she might be too involved with the current drama to remember, and when she did…He hid a smile. That would be interesting.

"Yeah, since then," Brody said, hanging his head.

"Well, maybe that's because she's still sad and grieving."

"What?" He looked up, confused. "Doc gave her the okay to try again." His gaze shifted to Ben. "But some people filled her head and made her think she wasn't happy and needed pills."

"That's enough." Ben pushed away from the bed,

crossed his arms over his chest, and confronted Brody. "I'm going to tell you the way it is. Your wife is depressed, got it? She lost a baby and she's not ready for another one, not even a boy." He stepped closer, fixed him with a stare. "And here's another bit of information; she might never be ready. Understand? So deal with it and be happy with the ones you have before it's too late."

"You don't know what the hell you're talking about."

"Oh, but I do. You keep ignoring the signs; don't go to counseling, don't listen to what she's trying to tell you—" he slashed a hand in the air, slapped his thigh "—and one day, it'll be too late. She'll leave you and you can go to fifty counseling sessions and promise her anything, but it won't matter because she's gone and she's not coming back."

Brody Kinkaid's eyes grew large, his expression grim. "I can't lose her," he said, his voice a mix of misery and pain. "She's my world."

"Then let's find her, and you need to start fixing things before it doesn't matter."

"Okay." He stood, held out his hand. "Thank you. I'm sorry I was such a hard-ass, but I can't think straight when things are off between me and Bree."

"I know." Ben shook his hand, slid a glance at Gina who watched him, lips pulled into a thin line, brows pinched, like she was analyzing what he'd said, trying to dig around the meaning inside of them.

"Bet you do." Brody grinned. "I had no idea you and Gina were together. Huh, who would have guessed Gina has a boyfriend."

"Well, actually—"

Brody's laugh cut off the rest of her sentence, taking with it the words Ben would have paid a hundred bucks to hear. "Does anybody else know?"

"No." Gina said, a bit too quickly.

"I see. Top Secret. Don't worry, I won't say a word."

Now that Brody Kinkaid considered Ben his new best buddy, the guy was a real talker, going on and on about everything from the year he scored twenty-one touchdowns in high school to the night Bree's water broke when she was sitting on his lap. *Wet all over the place, like a leaky faucet. You would not believe it.* That was way too much information.

They'd dropped off Brody's truck and checked the outskirts of Magdalena twice. How many times were they going to cover the same area? If this kept up, Ben would have just enough time to get back to the Heart Sent, shower, and head to work—and while Gina might have spent the night with him, she'd not spent it in his bed, a thought that annoyed the crap out of him, probably more than it should.

"I think we should check Bree's parents' house again," Gina said. "Maybe she parked the SUV in the garage. You know Kathleen won't let Rex put his truck inside, but she'd let Bree, and if I were trying to hide from my husband, that's what I'd do."

"Dang, if that's the case, then Bree's parents will know we've been having problems."

Gina sighed. "Brody, really? One look at Bree's long face and anybody can tell something's wrong."

"Guess you're right, but I'm going to fix it. Damn right I will. You wait and see. Tomorrow's a new start."

Ben thought about telling the guy he'd have to do a helluva lot more than just say the words. He'd have to do things that were against his nature and uncomfortable if he wanted a shot at saving the relationship. Not that anybody had ever stepped up and told him that, but how could they when they hadn't even known there was a problem? And by the time they did, too much time and and too many bad intentions had passed. The marriage was over, even if Ben couldn't accept it. Hell, he'd *refused* to accept that he and Melissa were done despite the divorce, her pregnancy, and engagement to Assistant DA Jerk. But none of that mattered anymore, hadn't mattered since the night Gina cried in his arms when he told her he'd met her parents. She'd opened up, shared that pain, and it had erased the wall between them, brought them closer, before the kiss that led to one of the most explosive nights of lovemaking he'd ever known. He supposed he owed Brody an opportunity to set things straight, even though it would take more time away from getting Gina back in his bed. "Don't forget the counseling; you'll both need that. She might even want to go alone for a while. And no blame games. And help her with the kids. And make her feel special. You know, like you used to before you had kids."

Brody scratched his stubbled jaw, pondered Ben's words. "We had Ella Blue nine months after the wedding." He slid Ben a smile and flexed an arm. "Honeymoon baby. So, we've had kids forever, but that don't make no difference. I'll treat my Honeybee special; buy her a sexy nightie like she used to wear and some of those fancy cherry cordials. She likes those, don't she, Gina?"

"Sure, Brody."

Ben didn't miss the fizzle of disappointment in Gina's words. "Sounds like you've got a plan." *And it's headed in the toilet.* As his Grandma Naomi used to say about someone you couldn't help no matter how much you pointed them in the right direction, "This dog don't hunt."

"And maybe, just saying maybe, down the road, three or

four months, we can try for that boy."

Ben and Gina didn't say much after that. It was Brody who babbled on and on, especially when Gina's hunch proved correct, and she looked through the Kinkaids' garage door window and spotted Bree's silver SUV there, right next to her mother's Cadillac. They took Brody home then, gave him instructions to visit his wife first thing in the morning with an apology and a bouquet of daisies, her favorites, a request to begin counseling, and a gag order on the mention of babies or boys.

"Do you think they have a chance?" Gina asked as they headed back to the Heart Sent.

Ben didn't even hesitate. "Nope. It's already too late."

"Why do you say that?"

"Because he thinks flowers and a counseling session or two are going to save them." He didn't tell her the flowers would be a one-time thing, two tops, and the sessions would fade even faster, if they happened at all.

"How can you be so certain?"

There was a question inside the question and that's what she really wanted to know. He'd seen it when he told Brody if he didn't get his act together, he'd miss out and then Bree wouldn't care anymore. That's what had happened with Melissa, and *that's* what Gina wanted to know about. "I know because that's what happened to me."

Chapter 13

Naomi Reed always said that disasters happen in the night and by morning they've turned into a full-blown catastrophe. Ben never bothered to ask his grandmother to qualify the difference between the two because he got her point. Bad stuff happens when you're not paying attention and by the time you realize it, it's too late.

Four mornings after Brody Kinkaid stormed into the Heart Sent looking to smear Ben's face against the hardwood floor, Jeremy plopped down in the chair across from Ben's desk and placed a lunch bag in front of him. "Portobello mushroom wrap with red peppers, onions, and asparagus. I put a side of marinara in there, too. Gives it a nice pop."

"Thank you." Ben moved the bag to the edge of the desk. "I'm looking forward to it." He'd almost been late for work twice this week. Sharing a bed with Gina was a huge distraction, as in he wanted her—a lot and often. Even after she exhausted him with lovemaking and he drifted off to sleep, he'd wake to find her soft skin touching his and the need started all over again. In the morning, between the first alarm and the second, he had to have her. Yesterday, she'd followed him in the shower and, well, that had been the best wakeup call he'd ever had. She seemed to share his need though they didn't talk about it, not in words anyway, but he could feel their bond strengthening, and he knew she had to feel it, too.

And not just in bed. They cooked dinner together, took walks, talked about city life versus small-town life. Ben almost told her he wanted to take her to a place like

Chicago or New York, but he pulled back. She might ask about a trip to Philly, and there was no way to explain that one without a lie, and damn it, he did not want to lie to her. Actually, he wanted to tell her the truth about how he'd ended up in Magdalena, but not yet. Gina might consider his subterfuge a lie, brand him untrustworthy, and he couldn't risk that until they were tighter.

"So, I hear you and Gina Servetti got together, huh?"

That comment brought Ben back around fast. What to say to that? It's not like he and Gina had been hiding these past few days. They'd taken walks after dinner, not holding hands but close enough to touch. And he'd parked his car in her driveway, even though it wasn't exactly visible from the street since she had a long drive and lots of shrubbery to obscure it. Still, they weren't hiding, they just weren't advertising.

"Well?" Jeremy leaned forward, planted both elbows on his knees, like he was getting ready to watch a movie.

"Well what?"

"Did you turn the jalapeño pepper into a sweet red? Or take the venom out of the viper?"

Ben leaned back against his chair and crossed his arms over his chest. "Don't you have work to do? And where's your father?"

Jeremy pointed to the report in front of Ben. "Waiting on you, and the chief's at the dentist, getting a crown fixed. Remember he said he wouldn't be in?"

"Right." He didn't remember but the less he saw of Rudy Dean, the better.

"Just tell me, Ben. Did you and Gina hook up?"

Ben's eyes narrowed. "Gina's not the kind of girl who hooks up, you got that?"

"Oh. Uh, sure. Sorry." Red splotched the boy's face,

slithered to the tips of his ears.

"Do you have a girlfriend, Jeremy?"

"Huh? Not really."

That could mean anything from "I'm in love with someone and she doesn't know I exist" to "I'm with so many women, all of them are girlfriends" or "None of them are." Ben guessed with Jeremy it would be the first possibility. "You aren't going to have one either if you don't learn to respect them and their privacy."

"Look, I'm sorry about what I said. I didn't mean anything by it, it was just that Pop said—"

"Pop? Who the hell's Pop?"

The boy's face lit up. "He's the Godfather of Magdalena. He knows everything that goes on in this town, sometimes even before it happens. They say he talks to his dead wife, Lucy, and she sends him messages about the residents." He paused, rubbed his jaw. "Advice, too."

"Sure he does." The guy sounded like a nut case, or maybe he had dementia. Or maybe— "Wait a minute; are you talking about that skinny guy with the big glasses and pencil mustache who faked a broken ankle at Cash and Tess's wedding so I'd dance with Gina?"

Jeremy grinned and nodded. "That's the one."

"Why is this Pop guy talking about me?"

"He's got it in his head that you and Gina make a good match and once Pop gets something in his head, he gets real determined to see it happen."

Ben didn't like the idea of anybody trying to force a situation, especially if it involved him. He might just have to check out this Pop and have a conversation with him that started and ended with "Mind your own business."

"Would it be reasonable to ask why this man was talking about me and Gina at all? It started somewhere."

Pause. "Was it you?"

"No." He shook his head and his ears turned redder. "I wouldn't do that to you, Ben. Honest. I did hear Pop say something about Bree Kinkaid. You think it's her?"

So Brody couldn't keep his mouth shut after all. Ben guessed if he had to spill to someone, it might as well be his wife. Of course, there was the off chance, though unlikely, that Brody had kept quiet and the culprit was Bree. She'd insisted Ben and Gina were destined to be together, long before he saw past Gina's sharp tongue to the real woman. "I have no idea."

"Oh. Well, just so you know it's not me." He stood, cleared his throat. "And I'm sorry if I offended Gina."

Ben nodded. He really did not want to discuss this.

"And if you let me, I'd like to cook for both of you tomorrow night at Mimi's. Your choice: veal saltimbocca or chicken Cordon Bleu."

"Jeremy, that's not necessary." Though he hadn't had veal in a while...

"I know, but I want to do it. I'll plan it all out. How about 7:00?"

"Sure." When the boy talked about cooking or food, his excitement spilled into his words, spread across his face in ways it never did when he talked police work. Why wasn't he doing something he obviously loved instead of doing something he obviously didn't? "Why aren't you a chef instead of a policeman?"

"What? No." He shook his head, glanced toward his father's empty office, and mumbled, "It's just a hobby. I only do it to pass time."

"Really?" Ben doubted that. He'd listened to the kid describe the pairings he chose for the sandwiches he brought Ben, and this was no hobbyist. "So, you only cook once in a while?"

"No." He placed his hands on the desk and leaned forward, lowering his voice, "I cook every day." Pause. "For people in town."

"You do?"

He stifled a smile. "Remember the ravioli you told Mimi you loved? That was mine. And the pulled pork with slaw? Mine, too. She lets me use her kitchen and we cook together, though she's pretty much just the prep person."

"I'll be damned. And the desserts, the apple pie and cream puffs?"

"Yup." This time the smile slipped out, burst across his face. "Cream puffs are my specialty."

"Now I'm really impressed."

"And you know that mushroom barley soup you order at Lina's Café every Thursday?" He pointed to his chest. "I make that. My special recipe."

"Do you cook for the whole town?"

He shrugged. "Seems like it, at one time or another, but I don't mind. I love the challenge."

"What's the chief say about all this?"

Jeremy looked at him as though he'd just asked the kid to chop off his right hand. "He doesn't know."

"Doesn't know? Why? You've got talent, kid, and a passion. You should be in a kitchen, not behind a desk or in a patrol car."

"Police work is my job. Cooking is my hobby."

Ben blew out a disgusted sigh. "Who told you to say that? You sound like a canned advertisement. Was it your old man?"

Jeremy's gaze skittered across the desk, landed on the bagged lunch he brought Ben. "No."

Damn Rudy Dean for screwing with his own kid. "Of

course, it was. Listen, Jeremy, nobody's going to give you a playbook and tell you to go out and have a good life. It's up to you to fight for what you want and don't let anybody else tell you what that is. You got that? Everybody has their own agenda, and they might try to convince you it's yours, but don't be a fool. I think your dad expects you to be a cop and you don't have the guts to stand up to him and say, no, you have other plans."

"He'd be so disappointed in me." He ran both hands through his hair and blinked hard. "The whole town would know and I can't do that to him. I just can't."

"Then you're a fool. Keep living someone else's life and see how far it gets you. There comes a time when you have to man up, and this is yours." He opened his ledger and grabbed a pen. "Now I've got work to do, and so do you. Thanks for the sandwich."

***

"And Brody told me how very sorry he was for not understanding my needs at this difficult time, and he brought me a bouquet of daisies with pink and blue ribbons." She smiled and touched her hair. "He said they reminded him of our first date. Isn't that the sweetest thing?"

Not really. Gina wanted to ask about the counselor. Had they made an appointment yet? Had they talked about the child they lost? And what about Bree's need to have a choice whether there would be more babies? Or had Brody merely filled Bree's prescription, grabbed a bouquet of daisies, and spouted his apologies? Something was wrong. Gina sensed it. Bree was smiling too much, going on and on about Brody and his wonderfulness. Nobody smiled that much, not even Bree, and nobody was that wonderful, especially Brody Kinkaid.

Bree had invited them to Lina's Café for coffee and dessert, and as she put it, "To show them she was alive and back on track." Gina thought the last part was debatable, because while Bree might be on track, they couldn't tell where she was headed. When she excused herself to use the restroom, Gina waited until she was out of earshot before turning to Tess and Christine. "What's going on? Where's the Bree who moped around and could barely comb her hair. She's gone from a sad sack to a whirling dervish. She's laughing, wearing makeup, doing the laundry, and cleaning the house...And don't tell me it's all because of the medication she's taking, because I'm not buying it."

Christine bit her bottom lip, narrowed her gaze on the bathroom door of Lina's Café. "I agree. Something's off."

"Yeah, like a cheerleader's invaded Bree's body and won't let go," Tess said.

"But why?" Gina had checked in with Bree every day and while her friend sounded better, the transformation didn't take place until two nights ago.

"I think I might have an idea." Christine leaned forward, lowered her voice. "Nate said Bree's dad called him a few days ago. He wants to retire and asked Nate what he thought about bringing Bree into the business."

"Really?" This from Tess. "I thought Brody was taking over."

Christine shrugged. "Didn't sound like it."

"Huh." Tess forked a piece of coconut cream pie and said, "I know Bree's always wanted to get involved, but her dad didn't want her in the manufacturing business, protecting his daughter and all that."

Gina rolled her eyes. "Maybe after the recent developments, he's figured out that his son-in-law isn't the best choice." Did Brody know? She'd had hopes that he might turn things around, but she'd called twice to check in and he hadn't returned her calls. Not a good sign.

"That would account for her excitement, wouldn't it?" Tess asked. "I just hope Brody's bought in. She'll need help with the kids."

"Nate said Rex is thinking about hiring someone from the outside. Bree would work with him to get familiar with the business until the kids are older and she's able to become more involved." Christine sipped her water and glanced at the bathroom door. "But I'm not sure what that means for Brody."

"Maybe he doesn't know," Gina said, as Bree opened the bathroom door and walked toward them. "And maybe that's why Bree is on the 'Brody's wonderful' kick. It's called guilt. She's in the Big Boys Club and he's gotten the boot."

"Could that be true?" Tess turned to watch Bree.

"Very possible," Gina said. "Actually, highly probable."

Bree flashed them a smile and slid into the booth next to Tess. "It's so good to have a little alone time with my friends." Her smile spread. "Life is good." She popped a pecan from her pecan roll in her mouth and chewed. "Very good."

Gina was about to ask her to expand on that when Bree clutched her hand and said, "How much longer are you going to make us wait before you spill the beans?"

"Excuse me?" Why couldn't Bree ever just say what she meant? Why did her meaning always have to circle around and around until she made them all dizzy?

"You know." She tapped a finger on Gina's arm. "Now don't get all shy and pretend. I am so happy for you. I absolutely knew this would happen, just knew it! And now—"

"Bree," Tess cut her off. "What the heck are you talking about?"

"Gina and Mr. Handsome Hunk." Bree's eyes sparkled like they used to when she was dreaming of weddings and babies. "Also known as Ben Reed."

***

"What the hell happened to you?" Ben stared at Jeremy. A mix of black and purple circled the swollen flesh around the boy's left eye, seeped onto the bridge of his nose, and filtered to the nostril.

"I ran into the door."

"A door?" Ben had never seen a door causing this kind of damage unless said door was made of steel and the person had been tossed into it.

Jeremy turned toward the coffee pot, away from Ben. "I wasn't paying attention and ran into a door."

Even if Ben believed everything, which he didn't, this story would be a hard one to buy. Something had happened to the kid that he didn't want Ben to know about, and that meant it probably had to do with his old man. "Did your father do this to you?"

The boy flinched. "No. Leave it alone, Ben."

"Like hell. If you won't tell me, I'll get the truth from your old man."

Jeremy swung around, his good eye wide, fearful. "Don't. Why can't you just leave it alone, huh?" His voice hitched, broke open. "Why can't you just leave *me* alone?" He tossed the coffee spoon on the counter and left before Ben could say anything else.

What had Rudy Dean done to his son? Had Jeremy taken Ben's advice and told his dad he wanted to cook instead of do police work? Is that what the black eye was all about? Ben tore into the chief's office, arms crossed over his chest. "What the hell did you do to Jeremy?"

Rudy Dean glanced up from the papers on his desk and shoved his reading glasses on top of his crew-cut head. "What did you say?"

Ben closed the door behind him so Mrs. Olsteroff didn't try to take notes and said, "Did you give Jeremy that black eye?"

The man blanched and hesitated a half second too long before saying, "I don't know what you're talking about."

"Really? That black eye doesn't have anything to do with Jeremy telling you he's more interested in baking soufflés than collaring criminals?"

"The boy fell."

"Huh." *Damn Rudy Dean and his lying bullshit.* "He said he ran into a door."

The man's thin lips flattened, his nostrils flared. "What happened between me and my son is none of your damn business. You're just some city-boy hotshot trying to make a young kid feel inferior."

"I'm trying to show him he has options."

"Options." Rudy Dean balled his hands into fists, clenched and unclenched them. "The kid barely made it through high school. He almost didn't pass the police exam even though I spent hours going over the friggin' questions. We had to find a place for him, so don't tell me about options."

"The boy can cook; maybe that's what he should be doing."

"Where? In a greasy spoon, frying up chicken wings and French fries?" He blew out a breath, shook his head. "Jeremy's never been fifty miles outside of Magdalena and not because we didn't try."

That information surprised Ben. Maybe Rudy Dean

wasn't such a hard-ass after all when it came to his son. Maybe it was more about protection than control, but the boy had a gift in the kitchen and maybe the old man was so beaten up by the prospect of his son's limited possibilities that he couldn't see he was suffocating the kid. Ben took a deep breath and said, "Look, I'm not his father and I don't know his backstory, but what I do know is that boy can cook. I could tell he didn't want to do police work the first time I met him. It's either in your blood or it's not."

"He's young. It'll grow on him." The man didn't say it with much conviction.

"You really believe that?"

Rudy Dean shrugged. "Hell, I don't know what I believe anymore." He shook his head, stared at the papers on his desk. "I came home and Jeremy was in the kitchen making chicken piccata. I don't even know what that is. He started on about the ingredients and the savory taste and then he up and told me he was quitting the force to become a chef." He snapped his sausage-sized fingers. "Just like that. Quitting. Said there wasn't a damn thing I could do about it because he was an adult and it was his choice. Never mind that he still lives at home and doesn't pay a cent of rent. We got into it, and it was bad. He turned back to the stove like I wasn't even there and I lost it. That's when I threw the spatula." His voice cracked. "I didn't mean to hit him; hell, I still don't know how I hit him."

Ben sighed. He didn't know much about family dynamics and he sure as hell didn't know about father-son relationships, but this one needed mending. He guessed Rudy's strong-arm tactics were the result of equal parts personality and an attempt to get Jeremy to move his butt. As for Jeremy, he could just meander along, not happy with his circumstances, but not willing to take a leap that might require extra work.

"Do you know your son cooks for Mimi Pendergrass and Lina's Café?" He'd bet the man had no idea.

"Cooks what?" And then, "When?"

"Spaghetti and meatballs. Pork chops and stuffing. And have you had Lina's chicken pot pie lately?"

Rudy Dean hesitated. "New to the menu. Had it last Tuesday."

"That's Jeremy's recipe. Seems like the whole town knows what he's doing but you." He paused, debated whether he should voice his thoughts, decided on it. "Do you think his mother knows?" Ben would guess she did.

"Maybe." The word slipped out, soft, uncertain.

Ben nodded. "Yeah, maybe so."

"Can you call Jeremy in here? I need to talk to him."

"Sure." Ben opened the door and went to find him. If all went well, Jeremy would be looking for a new line of work very soon. "Jeremy?"

"He left ten minutes ago," Mrs. Olsteroff said, her thin face pulled into a frown. "That boy was in an awful hurry and upset. Said he was going someplace where nobody could bother him."

***

Jeremy Ross Dean had been missing for nine hours. News of his disappearance spread through Magdalena faster than Japanese beetles on a zinnia. Some blamed Rudy Dean for being too harsh with the boy, said there was no way he could live up to the old man's expectations, and sooner or later, the boy would crack. Some blamed Jeremy's mother, Sueanne, said she was too soft on her only son, protected him from anything the least bit uncomfortable. And then there were some who said everything was fine and would have continued on just fine if not for the interference of Ben Reed. An outsider. A stranger. A person who had no business interfering with the goings-on in the community.

Gina fit into the last category. From the second he'd opened his door at the Heart Sent, she'd lambasted him with comments about minding his own business and insinuating himself in family situations he didn't understand. Okay, he got it. He should have gone easier on Jeremy, given Rudy Dean a pass in the hard-ass department, but neither the boy or his father was very forthcoming with their motives, and Ben was a fixer, couldn't stand to sit around and watch someone swallowed up in their own misery. But Gina didn't see it that way—not at all.

The passion in her voice tore at his gut, but the anger and disappointment on her face flattened him. So what if he'd fallen short of her expectations? He tried to make her see he'd meant no harm to the boy. "I was trying to encourage him to stick up for himself and live his own life. Was that so wrong?"

"No, but the way you went about it was."

Ben sighed. "What's with this town? You're all supposed to be a community; big on family and support, but everybody's got a side deal going on. I'll bet everybody in this town knew Jeremy was cooking for Mimi and Lina's and who knows where else? I'll even bet his mother knew." When Gina blushed and looked away, Ben latched onto that. "See what I'm saying? The only one who didn't know was his old man. What kind of screwed-up loyalty is that?"

She shrugged. "I don't know. It makes sense when you're in the middle of it, but maybe all it does is prolong the inevitable of owning up to the truth."

Yeah, there was the truth. Ben had his own share of

truths to divulge and he had to do it soon, because the more time he spent with Gina, the more he hated that she didn't know the real reason he'd come to Magdalena. Once he told her, he'd also tell her of his decision to stay and that it had to do with her. He pulled her into his arms, held her. "Where would a kid go who's never been much farther than the outskirts of town?"

"I don't know. Anger makes people do crazy things."

He stroked her hair, wished he hadn't pushed Jeremy so hard. Where could the kid be? What if he'd driven out of town and panicked? He could be on the side of the road somewhere. "I think I'm going to head out of town, drive around a bit."

Gina eased away, looked into his face. "I'll come with you." She touched his cheek. "He'll be okay, Ben. You'll see."

Two and a half hours later, Ben knew why people chose not to have children. It was the damn worrying that did them in, creased their foreheads, and gave them indigestion and a permanent scowl. They'd driven ten miles outside of Magdalena, stopped and asked folks if they'd seen a young man of Jeremy's description or a late model Jeep Wrangler. Nothing. Not one bite. When Ben checked in with Rudy Dean to tell him what he and Gina had done, the man sounded drained and anxious, nothing like the hard-ass who'd been riding him since he joined the force.

And that's what having a kid did to a person. It stripped them of their identity, humbled them, maybe even humiliated them. Why the hell did people have kids anyway? There must be some redeeming factor; at least, that's what all new parents probably believed. Did Melissa believe that? She and Kenneth would find out soon enough. Ben rubbed his jaw and slid a glance at Gina, who rode beside him, eyes closed, her nearness filling his senses. Could he ever deal with that kind of uncertainty and continual worry? Maybe if he didn't have to go through it alone it would make a difference. Maybe…

Gina yawned and murmured in a sleepy voice, "Are we going home?"

Home. He liked the sound of that. "Yeah, we're going home."

At 8:37 the next morning, Jeremy walked into the Magdalena Police Department, looking disheveled and worn out, his left eye a deeper purple than yesterday. "Hi, Ben. Is the chief in?"

Ben jumped up from behind his desk and made his way to the boy. "Where the hell have you been? We've been looking all over for you."

"Huh?" He scratched his head, frowned. "I needed time to think. Why were you looking for me?"

Was he serious? He'd better not be or Ben would be pissed at the kid's ignorance as well as his lack of consideration for the people who cared about him. "We were looking for you because you had an argument with your father, got a black eye you refused to discuss, and when I confronted you about it, you stormed off."

Jeremy shrugged, shoved his hands in his pockets. "Yeah, I guess I was a little pissed."

"Go see your father right now. He's worried sick about you, and call your mother." Damn, but he sounded like a parent. When the boy hesitated, Ben sighed and said, "You're going to have to grow up, kid. Come on." He headed toward Rudy's office, popped his head in, and said, "Somebody wants to see you."

When Rudy spotted his son, he gave a shout and sprang out of his chair. "Thank God, thank God." He thrust his big arms around his son and murmured once again, "Thank God."

Jeremy clung to his father, his lanky body swallowed up by Rudy's sturdy one. "Dad?" Jeremy eased away, looked him straight in the eye, and said, "I'm sorry I worried you. I had some things to sort out."

"Where the hell have you been?" Rudy's gruffness took over, spilling into his words.

"Out past Will Carrick's place. I slept out there last night."

His father scratched his jaw and said, "You were in the woods?"

"Yeah. And I did a lot of thinking."

"You did, huh?"

Let him talk, Rudy. Don't screw this up. Ben cleared his throat and shot the older man a warning look.

Jeremy nodded and said in a quiet voice, "It's time I grew up and turned responsible."

Come on, Rudy, you can do this.

"And, how would you do that, son?"

The boy smiled. "By becoming good police." He paused, added, "The best."

Rudy cocked his head to the side, studied his son. "The best, huh?"

"Yes, sir." The boy squared his shoulders, puffed out his chest. "I'll do you proud."

Rudy sighed. "Well, that could be a problem."

"Sir?"

Don't do this, Rudy. Ben shook his head. *Don't turn into a hard-ass now. Don't do it.*

"You see, I don't think you could be the best. I think you'd try, but if you're gonna be the best at something, it's got to come from here—" he jabbed his chest "—deep inside, like a burning that won't let up." He shook his head, sighed again. "You don't have it, son. You never will."

Jeremy bit his bottom lip, glanced at Ben who was seconds away from shooting a string of curses at Rudy with enough heat to singe him. What the hell was the matter with the guy? No wonder he didn't have a relationship with his own kid. How could he when—

"You see, you've got other talents, ones I didn't understand until the other day." He paused, smiled. "Did you really make that chicken pot pie at Lina's?"

Jeremy blanched. "Sir?"

"And is it true you've been cooking for Mimi?"

The boy took a step back, hesitated. "Yes. Sir."

"You don't belong here, son. You belong in a kitchen, filling our bellies, making pot pies and fancy dishes I can't pronounce."

"But…what about this?" He waved a hand at the office.

"This is *my* dream," Rudy said. "Not yours. Now go call your mother and tell her you're okay. Then go home, take a shower, and get started on your lists."

"Lists?"

"Yeah, job lists. And once you get a job, it's time to start paying rent."

Chapter 14

Gina buried her face in the pillow and breathed in Ben's scent. Would she ever tire of waking up next to him? Of touching him? Last night, they'd made love with such urgency and need, she'd almost cried. When they weren't together, she thought of him; when they were together, she thought of him...he'd started to consume her, and while she didn't like to admit that, it was the truth. She'd caught him watching her, his gaze fierce and possessive, making her wonder if he didn't feel the same way.

Was this what happened when you opened up to someone, trusted him?

Loved him?

The last thought skittered across her brain. *Did she love Ben?* She knew the answer, didn't even need to dissect the question the way she analyzed 97 percent of her life. *Yes. Yes, she loved him.*

Oh, dear Lord, now what? Her stomach jumped and gurgled with anxiety and apprehension. She glanced at the door. He'd be back from Mimi's kitchen soon, carrying coffee and whatever breakfast goodies he'd concocted, and she doubted she'd be able to eat a crust of dry toast.

Ben's phone beeped, distracting her from her dilemma. They'd have to have a chat about "no cell phones" in the bedroom unless he was expecting a call from work. Other than that, when they were in the bedroom, he was hers and she wasn't going to share him. The phone beeped again, indicating a text message, and ten seconds later, yet again. Gina glanced at the phone on the nightstand. Was something wrong? Should she take a quick peek to make sure there wasn't? As she debated the wisdom of checking Ben's text messages, the phone beeped two more times. Gina snatched the phone and read the stream of messages on Ben's phone.

Melissa had a boy. I went to see her.

Think she really loves Kenneth. Sorry.

Don't think it's going to happen between you two.

When are you coming home? Miss you!

Gina still held the phone in her hand when Ben opened the door, carrying a tray full of coffee and food. "Hey, sleepyhead, hope you're hungry."

She took in the easy smile, the warm gaze covering her, the muscled body, all of it. Why did people always sound the most genuine seconds before they broke your heart? "Actually, I'm not." Gina slipped out of bed and snatched her clothes from the chair. She'd stopped feeling embarrassed about her nakedness, had believed his story that he loved her body just as it was. She stepped into her panties, then fastened her bra. Had that all been a lie, too?

"Hey, what are you doing?"

He looked confused and if she had to toss out another description, she'd say "nervous." But why? What could a man like Ben Reed have to be nervous about? Unless he weren't telling the truth and feared he'd be discovered. She ignored him, pulled on her jeans, eased into her shirt.

"Gina?" He set the tray on the bed and clasped her arms to stop her from buttoning her shirt. "What's going on? Talk to me."

She did not want to look into that face, see those blue eyes that would haunt her for too many nights to come. What was the point? Better to get it out and over with, but she hesitated. Once she spoke, everything would change. *It would be real*. Could she let it go and wait, see if he told her about this Melissa and the baby and the man named Kenneth? Of course not. She wanted to know Ben's part in all of this, and why his cousin still thought his home was in Philly.

She wanted the truth and she was going to get it. "Who's Melissa?"

"What?" His tanned face paled, his expression turned grim.

"Melissa. Who is she?" Gina shrugged out of his grip. "You got a text from your cousin, several in fact. I was worried it might be work, but...it wasn't." He reached for her but she stepped back. "Don't.

"Look, I can explain."

"Oh? Why do you feel the need to explain when you don't even know what your cousin wanted." Pause. "Or do you? Hmm. I'm guessing you do know or you wouldn't look like you were about to throw up. So, who's Melissa?"

The left side of his jaw twitched, three times, before he said, "My ex-wife."

Ex-wife. She recalled the other texts from Ben's cousin, the more incriminating ones. *Think she really loves Kenneth. Sorry. Don't think it's going to happen between you two.*

He glanced at the bed, spotted his cell phone, and grabbed it, then proceeded to read the messages. "Damn it. Gina—"

"Stop. I read them. It doesn't take a neurosurgeon to figure out your ex-wife is in love with Kenneth, and you're still in love with your ex-wife."

"No!" He shook his head, grasped her shoulders. "That's not true." He pierced her with those damn blue eyes and said, "I love you, you, Gina. Nobody else."

How tragically pathetic that she'd waited her whole life

to hear those words and when they finally came, they were riddled with lies. Again. "Why couldn't you have left me alone?" She pushed his hands away and stepped back. "I might not have been deliriously happy, but I was content. There's a lot to say for being content. I wish you'd just left me alone instead of pretending you cared."

"I do care." He held out his hands, palms up, eyes bright, voice hoarse. "I love you. Please believe that."

"Hah. Your cousin thinks you're going 'home' to Philly. Now why would she think that, Ben? Huh? Because that's what you told her, isn't it?" She slashed a hand in the air. "Were we all diversions until you figured out a plan to get your ex-wife back?"

"No." But the word faltered, slipped a notch or two.

"Right."

"Okay, at first I just wanted to find a place to hide out for a while until I got my head together and could figure out a way to get back to Philly."

This was not what she wanted to hear, and yet, it was exactly what she needed to hear if it were the truth, and Gina had a sick feeling these were some of the truest words Ben Reed had ever spoken. "What did you do, get kicked out of town?"

The scarlet creeping up his neck to his cheeks told the story before he did. "Pretty much. I got into it with Melissa's boyfriend and I ended up breaking his nose." He dragged a hand over his face, sighed. "I could either leave town or get charged with assault. So, I decided to leave town." He paused. "That's when I called Cash…"

Damn him. "You used all of us to suit your own needs. And everything you did while you were here was just a way to pass time, wasn't it?" *I was just a way to pass time. I didn't mean anything to you.*

"I told you that's not true. Maybe it was at first, but then things changed." He gentled his voice. "We happened."

Gina bit her lip, hissed, "There is no we; there was never a *we*, not when you're sleeping with one woman and wishing you were with another."

"I know I screwed up, no denial there, but do not try to tell me how I feel. I love you," he spat out as though he were annoyed to admit it. "You, Gina Servetti."

Years from now she would remember these words, pull them out and replay them, lingering on the inflection in his voice, the fierce expression on his face as he spoke. She would hang onto them because that was all she had left. "You had weeks to tell me the truth. I shared with you, opened up about my mother and father, even my old boyfriend, and what did you share with me? The fact that you didn't know your father and your mother left you? That's it. You didn't want to talk about your ex-wife, didn't even want to tell me you had one. The opportunities were there, Ben, but you shut them down. Had you told me the truth about why you were here, I wouldn't have liked it, but we would have gotten through it. Instead, I had to find out myself."

"I know. Damn it, I know." He dragged a hand over his face. "Ask me anything and I'll tell you. Okay? Give me another chance. Please."

Gina was certain this was as close to begging as he'd ever come, and yet, it didn't matter. Not now. It only mattered before. "I'm sorry. It's too late. Good-bye, Ben."

As she closed the door and left Ben Reed and the Heart Sent, there was no way she could know that in twelve days, two days after Ben left Magdalena, she would fail the biggest test of her life—a pregnancy test.

***

"Are you sure you don't want me to talk to her? I can be mighty persuasive when I set my mind to it."

Ben had heard stories about Mimi's persuasive abilities, especially when it came to convincing a would-be troublemaker to "straighten out or risk a long road of heartache at the hands of the law." Those were the words she used on them, and most of the time they worked. But Gina wasn't a would-be troublemaker, unless they were talking about the destruction she'd caused to his heart. "Thanks, Mimi, but she was pretty clear. It's over."

"When you're in love like you two are, it's never over, even when you say it is."

He sipped his beer, pondered her words. It had been three days since Gina walked out of his life. Ben had spent the first two in denial, but on the third day with Gina's scent fading from his pillow, he knew she wouldn't be back. That's when he'd done something the old Ben Reed never would have done; he spilled the whole story to Mimi, including why he'd really come to Magdalena and ending with Gina tossing his "I love you" back in his face.

"You could always talk to Cash. You're buddies, and he'll talk to Tess who'll talk to Gina, and make her see things in a different light. You know, they had their share of issues and they might just be the ones to make Gina see that every beautiful flower garden has a weed or two that needs plucked."

"Cash isn't going to be exactly thrilled with me when I tell him the truth."

"Oh. So you plan to tell him how you duped him?"

He slid her a look, spotted the smile on her face. "Yeah, I'm going to tell him. He'll probably take a swing at me, but it's the right thing to do."

Mimi nodded her salt-and-pepper head. "Yes, and I'm

proud you've realized that." She paused and her voice dipped. "You remind me so much of my son. Some of the things you say, your smile, the way your dark hair curls...well, I imagine Paul might have resembled you."

"I'm really sorry, Mimi." Jeremy had told him the boy died when he was a teenager. Car accident. Speeding.

"Thank you." Her lips turned into a faint smile. "I'm grateful to have had the opportunity to get to know you. You're a very special young man, Ben Reed, and it did my heart good to see you smiling and happy, so different from when you first came. Gina was the reason for it, but not the only reason. You changed when you started to care about people. Look how you helped Jeremy and Bree." Her smile spread. "Why, the whole town's talking about it. They're not calling you a stranger anymore. Even Pop's throwing compliments your way."

He guessed he should be impressed if the Godfather of Magdalena had taken notice. Ben cleared his throat, uncomfortable with the praise, and said, "I didn't do anything special."

"You *cared* and that's more than most do. And you took the time to listen and help them. Do you know Bree's working at her father's three half-days a week? Loves it, too. Christine's helping her with accounting and basic business skills."

"And Brody?" He wondered if the guy really bought into Bree's new job.

"Ah, Brody." She tsk-tsked. "That boy has everything and yet all he can see is what he doesn't have, and what he wants. I hear he's not happy that his wife is spending time at the office when he has to work in the shop and can't take lunch whenever he wants."

"That sounds like Brody."

She nodded. "Unfortunately, it does. Pop says there will be rough patches ahead and lots more crabgrass, enough to choke out the good."

Whatever that meant. "I hope Bree makes out okay."

"She's stronger than most people think, and I imagine she's tired of playing the nitwit wife who must defer to her husband at all times."

"Good for her."

"Did you hear Harry Blacksworth is planning to open a restaurant with his wife? Working on the renovation right now; wants to open it before Christmas."

"Huh." He'd only seen the guy once or twice, but he seemed decent enough and the town sure loved him.

"I called him the other day, asked if he was looking for a chef." She grinned. "Jeremy has an interview on Thursday."

"Well, I'll be damned." Ben turned to Mimi, squeezed her hand. "You take care of everybody, don't you, Mimi? You're a regular guardian angel."

She met his gaze, her eyes bright, and said, "I don't know about that, but there is one thing I do know. I'm sure gonna miss you."

When news of Ben's leaving spread through town, people begged him to stay.

Rudy Dean offered him a bump in salary and no more flyer handouts or low-rate jobs.

Lina's Café promised free chili for a year.

Bree hugged him tight and declared he and Gina were soulmates and *must* remain together.

Cash, while initially ticked, confessed his not-so-stellar reunion with Tess and tried to convince Ben to talk to Gina again.

Even Nate Desantro shook his hand and said, "Tough

luck."

Jeremy asked if he could keep in touch and said he was real sorry things didn't work out with Gina. Then he told him he'd just been hired as a chef at Harry's Folly, which was scheduled to open in early December.

Carmen and Marie Servetti sought him out and begged him to have dinner with their niece, Natalie. They assured him she would make him change his mind about leaving.

Tess Casherdon hugged him and told him not to give up. Christine Desantro did the same.

Of course, the one person he really wanted to see was noticeably absent.

And the whole town knew exactly who that was.

***

Philly looked the same as it had when he left—the history, the crowded streets, the Philly cheesesteaks—but the appeal was gone. He stopped at his condo, glad Paige was on the road again. One less excuse he'd have to fabricate as to why he was back, and why he wasn't staying. He'd give her a reason soon enough, maybe even the real one.

Right now he had a mission. He didn't want to do it, dreaded the prospect as he drove to the address, parked the car, and stood in front of the two-story colonial. Even when he rang the doorbell and waited, he swallowed back his dread. But it didn't matter if he heaved his whole breakfast, he was going to do it because he owed her that much.

The front door opened and his ex-wife stood before him, shock and dismay on her face. "Ben, what are you doing here?"

"Hi, Mel. Can I come in?" She'd always been beautiful, but the after-baby glow made her even more so. Or maybe it was marriage to the right man that gave her that special glow.

She clutched the door frame, her face pinching. "You shouldn't be here. Kenneth will be back any minute—"

"This won't take long." He worked up a smile. "Please?"

The familiar sigh came next and a curt, "A minute, that's all."

He entered her home, correction, *their* home, the place where she lived with her new husband and new baby. That thought didn't bother him, hadn't bothered him in a long time. Not since Gina. "Nice place. I'm happy for you."

She stood a few feet away, hands clasped against her middle, like she thought she needed to protect herself from him. "Thank you."

He nodded. "Congratulations—" he paused, met her gaze "—on the baby and getting married. You deserve this. I want to apologize for my behavior the last time I saw you. I guess I should even apologize for punching your husband. He goaded me, but I get why he did it, even though I didn't back then. It was the only way he could get rid of me; I wasn't a part of your life anymore but I wouldn't give it up. I would have done the same thing."

Melissa's eyes grew bright. "Thank you."

Ben cleared his throat and pushed on with the truth, even though it made him uncomfortable and he'd rather pull a double shift than spit out the confession. "And I'm sorry I was a horrible husband. I thought loving you was enough. I couldn't buy into the sharing end of it and showing parts of ourselves and our past we didn't particularly like. But I get it now." He paused, sighed. "I really get it."

When she spoke, her voice covered him with knowing and sympathy. "You met someone, didn't you?"

He wasn't going to lie to her, even though that would be more comfortable and much less invasive. "Yeah, I did."

Her full lips curved into the faintest of smiles. "And you love her, don't you?"

Another necessary truth. "I do.

"So why the long face?"

He forced a smile and tried for his old lighthearted response, but the attempt wobbled and fell flat. "You know me, Mel. Give me a relationship and I'll screw it up. I screwed this one up bad."

"Oh, Ben." She closed the distance between them, touched his arm. "I'm so sorry. Can't you try to make it work?"

He clasped her hand, did smile this time. "If I learned one thing from this whole mess with us, it's that when it's over, it's over."

"Where will you go? What will you do?" Her voice held a hint of worry. For him. "I could talk to Kenneth, convince him to let you stay in Philly." She paused, squeezed his arm. "Just say the word and I'll do it."

"No, Mel." Ben shook his head. "I'm not staying here." He didn't belong in Philly, not anymore.

"But where will you go?"

"I've kind of grown fond of small towns. I'm thinking of heading back to the place where my grandmother lived before she moved here." His voice dipped, softened. "There's something about a small town that pulls you in, makes you part of a family, cares about you."

She nodded. "Keep in touch? I want to know you're okay."

"Sure," he said. "Kenneth is one lucky guy; I hope he realizes that."

Her eyes sparkled. "He does."

"Good. Now, can I see this baby before I head out?"

***

Twenty days later

Nate studied the drawings in front of him and didn't hear Lily come into the workshop until Cash called to her.

"Hi, Cash. Hi, Nate."

Nate looked up and spotted his sister. "Hey, Lily. I thought you were going to help Tess bathe Henry."

She stopped at the workbench and smiled up at him. "I am. She's getting Henry's shampoo and his towel, the one with his name on it." She glanced at Cash and said, "I told her I had to make a phone call first. Cash, can I have Ben's number?"

"What?" Nate tossed his pencil aside and turned to Lily. "What do you think you're doing?"

Her smile wavered. "I never got to say good-bye to him. He just left."

"Honey, Ben disappointed a lot of people, and it's better to let it go."

"No." She shook her head and her eyes grew bright. "He's nice and I liked him. He and Gina love each other. Why can't they be together?"

Nate looked at Cash, who shrugged and shook his head. "Lily, this is adult talk."

"Can I please just call him? I'll be real quick."

"Here." Cash pulled out his phone and dialed a number.

Lily took the phone and started toward the door. "Be back in a minute. Thanks!"

***

Ben almost didn't answer the phone until he saw the call was from Cash. "Hello?"

"Ben? Ben Reed?"

"Yes. Who is this?"

"This is Lily. Lily Desantro."

Nate's sister. "Hi, Lily. How are you?"

"Fine. You didn't say good-bye before you left."

"I'm sorry."

"Yeah. It's okay." Pause. "Ben?"

"Yes?"

"Gina's sad."

"Lily—"

"I saw her cry. Nate told her she shouldn't waste her tears on you, but that only made her cry more."

Damn that Nate Desantro and his self-righteousness.

"Nate said you'd be a horrible father, but I think you'd be a great dad."

"Um, I don't know. Why are you talking about that?" Why *was* she talking about that?

"You just need practice, but how are you going to get practice if Gina and the baby are here and you're there?"

"Lily, what baby?"

"Gina's baby, silly. And yours."

Those words pounded his brain, squeezed his gut, and propelled him from Philly to Magdalena, stopping only twice; once for gas and once to grab a sandwich and a bathroom break. Gina was pregnant? *With his child?* When? How? Well, not how, but…there'd only been a few times when he hadn't used a condom and she'd told him it wasn't a problem. He'd never fallen for that line before and he'd heard it enough. Condom was king and his "get out of jail free" card as in years of child support, a never-ending connection to the mother, and the possibility of an STD. But he hadn't even thought about that with Gina. Had she played him? Had she only wanted a sperm donor? Was that why she'd pushed him out the door and refused to even try to work things out?

He'd told her he loved her.

She hadn't admitted the same.

Because maybe she didn't.

Maybe it was all about a kid.

What he knew about Gina said this was craziness; such chilly calculation wasn't in her nature. And yet, in a way, it was. He'd watched her embrace analysis over emotion on several occasions. She'd even confessed a greater comfort with the interpretation of a spreadsheet over a conversation.

But he wasn't a spreadsheet and neither was his kid. He smacked the steering wheel and cursed. *Damn her.* She was the only woman he'd ever met who could turn him upside down and make him doubt himself. When he pulled into Gina's at dusk, he had too many questions and no answers.

Ben knocked on the door and waited. He'd thought of calling before he arrived, but why give her an opportunity to avoid him? She'd never expect him, and that's exactly what he wanted. The element of surprise usually produced the most candid results and Gina didn't like surprises, which meant he'd catch her off guard.

When she opened the door, he forgot for a half second that he was saturated in anger and hurt, forgot everything but the darkness of her eyes, the pink fullness of her lips.

"What are you doing here?"

The question snapped him back to his mission, reminded him that she'd withheld valuable information and, at the moment, was an adversary, and a dangerous one. "Hello, Gina." His gaze flitted to her belly, then back to her eyes. Was that panic he'd just spotted? Good, let her panic.

"What are you doing here?" she asked again, hand on the door as if she might slam it in his face given half an opportunity.

"Are you pregnant with my baby?"

"What?" Her hand slid to her belly. "What are you talking about?"

At least she hadn't out and out lied to him. Yet. "I asked if you were pregnant with my baby."

She tried to laugh, but it fizzled into a muffled cough, ended with, "You're being ridiculous."

"And you're avoiding the question. Now, you can let me in, or we can have this discussion on your front doorstep." He forced a smile. "It'll be all over town by morning. Is that how you want to play it?"

"Fine."

Her sigh told him just how much she didn't want to have this conversation. Too bad. She opened the door and Ben stepped inside, memories of the days and nights they'd spent here smothering him with an ache that made his chest hurt. Would it ever go away? "Can you please just tell me the truth?"

She met his gaze, her eyes bright. "Why does it matter?"

"It does." *A helluva lot.*

"You're not the baby type."

Ben shrugged. "Not many guys are until the baby comes along."

She squared her shoulders and said, "Yes, I'm pregnant."

He nodded, tried to remain calm and unaffected when what he really wanted to do was pick her up, swing her around, and kiss her. Not happening. Ben shoved his hands in his pockets to keep from doing something stupid, like reach out and touch her. "How do you feel?"

She shrugged. "A little off. Morning's aren't so great."

"Bet not." He knew nothing about babies and less about pregnancy. Why would he know when he'd spent most of his adult life avoiding both? Until now. *Gina was having his baby.* He was going to be a father. He could learn whatever—

"I don't want anything from you." Pause. "I don't even know why you're here."

Her words smacked him in the face, stomped on his thoughts, and shredded them into tiny pieces of nothingness. When he could find his breath, he managed a weak "What?"

"I won't ask for child support or any help with the pregnancy. The last thing you want is to be tied to a baby and, by default, to me."

She spoke as though she were reading a medical journal and not talking about their lives and their baby. "You've got it all figured out, don't you? Gina Servetti, woman with all the answers." He eyed her, eyed her belly, and the nagging thought that she'd used him to get a baby took over. "Did you plan this pregnancy all along? Use me as a sperm donor?"

"A what?"

"A sperm donor; a way to get a baby without the encumbrances of a man."

"I know what a sperm donor is," she hissed.

"Well, did you?"

She crossed her arms over her middle, glared. "Of course not."

She did look horrified by the prospect.

"So, the pregnancy was an accident even though you told me not to worry about it? Guess I should have— worried about it, that is." He was glad she was pregnant. Was she?

"I told you it wasn't an issue because I haven't had regular periods in years. The doctor didn't even know if I'd be able to get pregnant."

Ben slid his gaze to her belly. "Now he knows you can."

"Yes," Gina said, her voice thin. "Now he knows."

"When I came to see you before I left, did you know you were pregnant then?" *When I told you I loved you? That I wanted a life with you?*

She shook her head. "No."

It was a small comfort, but at least she hadn't known about the baby when she sent him away. He wanted to ask if she would have, had she known, but the answer might be too brutal, so he left it alone. "Gina, you don't get to make this choice alone. I'm going to be part of this baby's life."

She pinned him with those sad, dark eyes. "Ben, be honest. You don't want a baby." Her voice dipped. "I'm giving you a way out. Take it."

It would be easier to hear those words if he didn't love her, but he'd never done easy. He touched her cheek, let his hand fall. "If you think I can just walk away, then you don't really know me at all."

***

News of Ben Reed's return spread through Magdalena faster than last month's grease fire in Lina's Café. Some said the boy had come back to do the right thing by Gina. Others said he was on the run and this was the best place to hide. Still others said he had a secret life like Charlie Blacksworth.

Mimi didn't believe the tales because she knew the truth. Ben was in love with Gina, and the boy was going to make them see that he wanted this baby. In fact, he wanted Gina, too, wedding ring and all. But convincing a girl whose parents had told her she was unlovable her whole life, not good enough, not pretty enough—*not enough*—well, that left wounds so deep the scabs opened at the first sign of trouble. And that was why Mimi took it upon herself to visit Gina.

"I've come to say what needs said, and I hope you'll listen." Mimi sipped her raspberry ice tea, glanced at the flowers in Gina's back yard. The girl had a way with her perennials and a gift of turning them into beautiful pictures by pressing them and creating unique designs. Word had it she was teaching Lily Desantro the art of it, was even helping the girl make Christmas gifts, though you'd never know from Gina. The girl didn't spread stories or puff herself up with tales of how she helped this person or that one like her cousin Natalie did, even though that girl never helped anyone but herself. Gina did what needed doing and kept quiet, unless someone ticked her off. Then watch out.

"Did someone send you to talk to me?"

Mimi slid her a look. "You mean Ben?" She smiled and shook her head. "Heavens, no. I'm sure he wouldn't like it if he knew I was here." Her voice faded, turned soft with memories and regret. "I've known you since you were a little girl, watched that family of yours treat you like you were never good enough, until you believed it. You carried that on your shoulders for too many years. That's why you were always alone, except for Tess and Bree, and no man." She waved a hand at Gina. "It wasn't about your looks or your weight. It was about you never thinking you were good enough. And then, in walked a fine male specimen named Ben Reed. You two were pushing and pulling like magnetic forces the first time I saw you together at Tess and Cash's wedding. Ben didn't know about your history, but I think he felt the loneliness in you, the same one he had inside himself. You were good together." She paused, settled her gaze on the pinkish-gray sky. "You could still be good together."

"He lied to me." The words tumbled out, coated in

misery and pain. "And now I can't trust him."

"But you want to, don't you?" Gina made a sound that could have been a yes if not for the sniffs smothering it. Encouraged, Mimi pushed on, "While Ben's reason for being here wasn't the truth, his feelings for you were honest and sincere. I think he found himself in a predicament of his own making and didn't know how to get out of it, especially because he didn't want to risk losing you. That boy never expected to meet someone like you, and I'm sure he never expected to fall in love. But he did. Now it's up to you. If you can picture him sharing a life with another woman, maybe even his name and a child or two—" she paused, gentled her voice "—and of course, his bed, and it doesn't bother you, then let him go. You'll still share a child, but nothing else, and the sooner you cut him loose, the better. However, if the thought of him touching someone else, loving her and saying the words he once said to you, drives you absolutely crazy with jealousy and desperation, then go to him as fast as you can and tell him."

Gina set down her glass and looked at Mimi, her voice a mix of confusion and wonder. "I love him, with my whole heart, so much it hurts."

Mimi nodded and hid a smile. "Then go to him. I'll clean up here, don't you worry." When Gina's car pulled out of the driveway, Mimi sat back, sipped her tea, and smiled. "There's going to be a wedding in Magdalena, and mark my words, it'll be soon."

Chapter 15

Gina knocked on the door of Ben's room at the Heart Sent. She'd practiced her speech on the drive over and if she didn't get it out the second he opened the door, she might not be able to do it. Fear would claim her. Or nerves. Or—

"Gina?"

She looked up and there he was, handsome, strong, guarded. *Say the words, say them now.* "I...I..."

"Yes?"

She opened her mouth and blurted out, "I love you, Ben Reed, so much I can hardly breathe. I'm sorry I hurt you, I love you, and I want a life with you and the baby." And yet again, in case he hadn't heard. "I love you." He didn't say anything. Not one word. His expression turned darker, his jaw clenching and unclenching as he watched her. Had he changed his mind in the last hour since he'd visited her? "Ben? Say something."

"Do you trust me?"

"I do."

The brackets around his mouth eased. "And you aren't going to change your mind if you wake up tomorrow and decide I don't deserve you?"

"If I do, that would be hormones speaking, so be forewarned."

His lips twitched, the tension on his face relaxed. "Noted."

Gina took a step closer. "You're really happy about the baby?"

"Yes." He pulled her into the room, closed the door, and

planted a soft kiss on her mouth. "I'm really happy about the baby."

"I'll gain weight."

He started unbuttoning her shirt. "No doubt."

"And ask you to make midnight runs for things like avocados and cream cheese?"

His hand stilled and he stared at her. "Avocados and cream cheese? What happened to pickles and ice cream?"

She shrugged and clasped her hands around his neck. "Too ordinary. Baby Reed is not going to be ordinary."

"He's not, huh?"

"No, *she's* not."

Ben eased her shirt from her jeans and kissed the flesh that peeked out of the top of her bra. "I've missed you so damn much. Too much." He unclasped her bra, buried his face between her breasts, and whispered, "I love you."

"Show me," she murmured. "With your hands, and your mouth, and your—Oh!" He carried her to the bed, laid down beside her, planting kisses on her bare skin as he removed her clothing.

"Show you?" He slid her panties off, stroked his hand along her thigh until her breath hitched and she sighed. "I will take great pleasure showing you—" he yanked off his jeans and boxers, entered her with one deep thrust "— as many times and as many ways as you desire."

"Oh, Ben..." Gina moaned as he moved inside her, creating exquisite pulses of sensation and need, capturing her body, her heart, her soul. "Oh, Ben!" And then the free fall began and didn't stop until Ben joined her.

After, as they lay spent and exhausted, he placed a hand on her belly and said, "Marry me. Make me the happiest man in the world."

"Yes." She touched his cheek, traced his lips with her

fingers. "Absolutely yes."

"As soon as possible."

She liked the sound of that. "Or sooner," she added.

"And I want Lily Desantro in the wedding."

"Lily?"

His smile covered her, filled her with delicious heat and promise. "She's the one who called me and in a roundabout way, told me you were pregnant. We owe *us* to Lily Desantro."

Twenty-six days later, the *Magdalena Press* printed the following article:

It was a perfect fall day for the union of Benjamin John Reed and Gina Rosa Servetti. The ceremony, officiated by Mimi Pendergrass, Magdalena's very own mayor and the proprietor of the Heart Sent, took place in the backyard gardens of the bed and breakfast. The couple was surrounded by friends, family, and clusters of lilies, cosmos, roses, hydrangeas, and the bride's favorite, hibiscus. The Heart Sent held special significance as it was here that Mr. Reed stayed when he first arrived in Magdalena, where he formed a friendship with Mimi Pendergrass, and later, where he proposed to his future bride.

The bride wore a tea-length fuchsia dress with tiny eyelets, a fuchsia ribbon in her hair, and a matching diamond bracelet and earrings—a wedding gift from the groom. The maid of honor, Ms. Lily Desantro, wore a green chiffon dress with a wide belt and carried a bouquet of lilies. Other bridesmaids included Tess Casherdon, Bree Kinkaid, and Christine Desantro, in matching chiffon dresses in the following fall colors; rust, brown, and orange, respectively. Ella Blue and Lindsey Kinkaid were flower girls.

The groom wore a black suit with a red rose on his lapel. Cash Casherdon served as the best man, also in a black suit, sporting a white rose on his lapel. Catering services were provided by Jeremy Dean Ross and included his signature lasagna, chicken piccata, rice pilaf, green bean almandine, salad, and homemade bread. Carrot cupcakes were served in lieu of a wedding cake.

The new Mrs. Reed is a physical therapist at Magdalena General Hospital, and Mr. Reed is a sergeant with the Magdalena Police Department. Following a honeymoon trip to Chicago, the couple will make their home in Magdalena.

Note: The couple's wedding night was spent in the honeymoon suite of the Heart Sent, where, as everyone knows, the bed is strewn with rose petals. The petals on Mr. and Mrs. Reed's bed held special significance: they were harvested from the bride's very own backyard!

If you see the new couple about town, make sure to extend them a warm welcome. Ben Reed might be new to Magdalena, but the town has embraced him as one of our own.

The following were comments made by friends and relatives at the wedding:

"We always knew our girl was special, and now she's found that special someone to brighten her days and warm her nights. We're proud to play a part in making her who she is today." Carmen and Marie Servetti

"Ben and Gina—forever. No more sad colors for Gina!" Lily Desantro

"Gina's a great girl and Ben Reed's lucky to have her. If he forgets, I'll remind him." Nate Desantro

"I'm gifting Gina a bag of Blue Jordan Almonds and from her wedding night on, she'll never smell a rose petal again and not think of that night." Bree Kinkaid

"I'm already working on a welcome home dinner." Jeremy Ross Dean

"The heart is a wondrous thing, filled with love and the capacity to forgive. May Ben and Gina enjoy many years together." Mimi Pendergrass

"Keep talking, no matter what." Pop Benito

"Forever and ever. And even after that." Tess Casherdon

Epilogue

Nate opened the screen door and stepped into his mother's kitchen. He'd promised to stop over and move Lily's bed and dresser. According to Lily, Lizzie had her bed next to a window and she could look at the moon and the stars before she went to bed—like Harry did. The damn man had given them some song and dance about how he used to stare at the stars and make up characters that lived there. Nate suggested the glow-in-the-dark stars that stuck to the ceiling, easier and less rearranging, but Lily had frowned and insisted she wanted the real thing. Damn Harry and his stories. They were probably a bunch of BS; you never knew with Harry.

The man was occupied with his latest venture, opening a Harry's Folly in Magdalena. Said he even found a chef, Rudy Dean's kid, Jeremy, the policeman-turned-chef who catered Gina and Ben's wedding. Okay, so maybe Harry had a chef, but he had a long way to go before he could open his doors and start serving that damn penne pasta with spinach and garbanzos he went on and on about. Nate bet Harry had the building inspector's phone number on speed dial. Why anybody would want to buy that piece of crap on the edge of town and try to turn it into something other than a pile of rubble was beyond Nate. But Harry saw potential, said Greta did, too, and with enough vision and cash, Nate supposed it could work out. Or not.

The whole town would be watching Harry to see if he could spin some magic into the old building, and more, if he could do it by his promised Christmas deadline. Nobody had the heart to tell him the sad story behind that place, not even Nate or his mother. He sighed; Harry would find out soon enough.

"Ma?" He headed toward the stove and the pot simmering on top. Vegetable beef soup, one of Christine's favorites. He bet his mother planned to give him a container to take home. "Ma?" Nate passed the tray of chocolate chip cookies, fresh from the oven, snatched two, popped one in his mouth. His eye caught the fancy envelope on the edge of the table, addressed to his mother with a return address of San Diego, California. He leaned closer. Anthony Benito. Why the heck would Pop's son be contacting her?

"There you are, Nate. I thought I heard you come in. I started moving a few of Lily's things." She wiped her forehead with the back of her hand and smiled. "I see you've found the cookies, and I'll send some soup home with you."

"Thanks." He gave her a hug and a kiss on the cheek. "I found the letter from Anthony Benito, too." He paused. "What's he want?"

When his mother looked away, he knew that meant she didn't want to discuss whatever he'd asked. She used to do that a lot when the subject of Charles Blacksworth came up, to the point Nate stopped asking, and that's when the real animosity started. That was long in the past, but he still remembered the behaviors that had caused him such grief.

"Ma? What's going on?"

She poured a glass of water, took a sip. "Anthony asked me to keep an eye on his father and let him know if there were any problems."

"Problems? Like what? Eating too many pizzelles? Walking four miles a day? Playing matchmaker for the whole town?" He could go on, but his mother got the point.

"He thinks someone's been in his house, stealing those

blasted pizzelles. He's become obsessed with it." She paused, said in a quiet voice, "I told Anthony his father should have a neurological exam."

"For what? Alzheimer's?"

She shrugged. "That or maybe dementia. I don't know; what I do know is he's been ranting about someone stealing his pizzelles and that's not normal."

Nate hated to ask, but he had to. "You don't think Lily's been helping herself to a few extra ones, do you?" The girl was almost as obsessed with them as Pop, but his sister wasn't a thief.

"I asked her, but I knew she didn't do it. If Lily wanted more, she'd pester him until he gave in, and with Pop, he and Lily are so tight, she'd never have to pester. He'd just hand them over."

"So, what's Mr. Hollywood plan to do? Swoop Pop to California and stick him in a home?" She shrugged but didn't answer. The idea of Pop in California with a son he'd only seen twice in ten years didn't sit well with Nate. "What's this guy know about Pop? Blood doesn't make a family; you should know that."

"I do know that, Nathan."

"This town's his family. We're the ones who were here for him when his wife died, not Anthony, who flew in with his glamour wife for what, forty-eight hours? They wouldn't even let their daughter take time off from school to attend her grandmother's funeral. Who does that?"

"I don't know. Anthony said it was finals week."

Was she serious? "Ma, listen to yourself. You sound like one of them, more interested in statistics and placement scores than people. Pop almost died out there the last time he went. We're not letting him get in that situation again."

She met his gaze, her eyes bright, face pink with

emotion. "But what if he does have the beginning signs of Alzheimer's or dementia? What then? We have to keep him safe."

Nate leaned against the counter, crossed his arms over his chest. "If I thought you had those same issues, would you want me to whisk you away, no choice, nothing?"

"Of course not, but his son has a right to know."

"Right. The son who's been back to Magdalena twice since he left twenty-some years ago."

She looked away. "He may have had his reasons."

"I'm sure. Don't they all? Starting and ending with dollar signs and ego."

"Nathan." She heaved a sigh. "Do you have to be so critical?"

"Some call that being honest." Why was his mother so jumpy about this? It wasn't like her to side with the likes of Pop's son. She was more of a champion for the underdog. Did she know something he didn't? "So, what's the plan?"

There was a long pause before she met his gaze and said, "Anthony's coming to Magdalena for Christmas, and he's taking Pop back home with him."

***

Nobody stole from Pop Benito, and if they thought they'd get away with it, they could think again. Pop rested the BB gun on his right knee. In his day, he could hit a tomato paste can at one hundred feet. Actually, he'd loaded up his rifle until Lucy made him promise to quit. That's when he'd pulled out the old BB gun, loaded it, too.

"They ain't going to get us, Lucy. I'll catch the thief and press charges, I can promise you that; I swear on our basil plants."

Stealing pizzelles from Pop was a declaration of war and everybody who knew him knew that. It was a pizzelle that got him his first date with Lucinda Vermici, and it was a pizzelle that had a part in making their son, Anthony, and later, it became the solace for the news of the cancer.

Dang it if anybody would dishonor his Lucy by stealing his pizzelles. He'd sat up a good part of the night, making a list of all the possible suspects and around 3:00 A.M., he'd narrowed the list to six, five kids and one adult. The adult was Joe Pescatori, because he'd always had an eye for Lucy, even though the man never stood a nickel of a chance. But Pop wouldn't count the old geezer out, even with a double-knee replacement and a pacemaker.

This afternoon, Pop ate two pizzelles with the lemonade Lily brought him this morning. There'd been nine left in the box. Now there were three. He kept an extra two dozen in the cupboard behind the cereal, and the thief should count himself lucky he didn't go for the mother lode because despite his promise to Lucy, Pop would have pulled out his rifle.

"Don't you worry, Lucy, I'll catch the bugger that stole from us." He dozed off in the living room chair, gun resting on his lap, flashlight on the table beside him. He slept until the car next door with the bad muffler pulled out of the drive. That would be Chet Carlson on his way to the box factory fifteen miles away. The guy could afford a six-pack of beer a night but not a new muffler.

Pop grumbled and thought about heading to the bathroom before he took up his post again when he heard a shuffling noise in the kitchen. He clutched the gun against his thighs and reached for the flashlight. Seconds later, more shuffling. Definitely in the kitchen. Dang, but the culprit was into his pizzelles! He eased out of the chair and moved toward the kitchen, gun in one hand, unlit flashlight in the other. There was a reason he'd never let Lucy move the furniture, and here it was—moving in the dark, quiet, steady, not stumbling over a misplaced end table.

The shuffling turned into the faint *click* of a cupboard opening and then the *clack* of a drawer. Now the robber was after the mother lode! Pop swung the BB gun in the air and took aim into the darkness a half second before he switched on the flashlight. "Hold it right there!" The circle of light illuminated the figure, cast a halo around the red curls, the white face.

"Lucy?" Good Lord in heaven, it *was* her! Oh, but his prayers had been answered. His very own Lucy stood before him, pizzelle in hand, as real as the last time he saw her. His gaze devoured her eyes, nose, mouth, traveled to her neck, landed on her protruding belly. He squinted, once, twice, zeroing in on that belly that wasn't the result of too many pizzelles. "Lucy?"

"Hi, Grampa." She inched toward him. "I've come to live with you."

The End

And that's it for now! Next up we'll head to Magdalena for *A Family Affair: Christmas, a novella.* The town is preparing to celebrate the holidays when a snowstorm hits and threatens to ruin the festivities. But that's not the only threat blowing into town...Pop's son is here from California to enjoy Christmas with his father, but when he leaves, he's taking Pop with him...or is he? Will the town give up the Godfather of Magdalena, or will they show Pop's son that when we open our hearts, anything is possible...even second chances? Stay tuned!

Many thanks for choosing to spend your time reading *A Family Affair: Fall*. I'm truly grateful. If you enjoyed it, please consider writing a review on the site where you purchased it. (Short ones are fine and equally welcome.) And now, I must head back to Magdalena and help these characters get in and out of trouble!

If you'd like to be notified of my new releases, please sign up at my website: *http://www.marycampisi.com*.

A Look Ahead:

I love creating secondary characters—they can be so complicated and yet so very intriguing. I've often wondered how they'd react if they were given the opportunity for their own story.

Well, the opportunity has arrived!

I plan to introduce people from That Second Chance Series to *A Family Affair*'s Magdalena, New York, starting with *Simple Riches*' "Bad Boy," Michael Androvich and "Good Girl," Elise Pentani. They'll both appear in *A Family Affair: Winter*, which is not going to make them one bit happy, seeing as they'd rather live in different universes than spend another minute in the same town. I guess that's what happens when a person gets left at the altar... (Not saying which one, but it's going to be brutal and humiliating.) I can't wait for the residents of Magdalena to meet these two and see if they can help heal two broken hearts. With Lily's curiosity and Pop's matchmaking endeavors, it will be quite interesting...

Note: The following characters from That Second Chance Series will appear in future *A Family Affair* books, though not necessarily in the order listed:

Grant Richot (*Pulling Home*, That Second Chance Series, Book One)

Angie Sorrento (*The Way They Were*, That Second Chance Series, Book Two)

Adam Brandon (*Paradise Found*, That Second Chance Series Book Four)

See you in Magdalena!

It's all about that second chance...
Simple Riches is Book Three of *That Second Chance Series*. (These are stand-alone books tied together by a common theme—belief in the beauty of that second chance.)

Alexandra "Alex" Chamberlain is a big city girl who knows nothing about close-knit families, sibling rivalry, or receiving an unsolicited opinion in the name of family. She's been raised by an aunt and uncle who've provided her with a wealthy lifestyle and a fancy education, but have withheld what she craved most—love and acceptance. Her uncle has taught her to disregard everything but the bottom line on a balance sheet and she'll do anything to earn his approval. She prides herself on excelling at her job which is selecting small towns to buy, flatten, and replace with luxury resorts. When Alex decides to investigate Restalline, Pennsylvania, as a potential site for the next resort, she enters the town under the guise of a researcher gathering information for a documentary. Her uncle wants this project badly, and she's not going to disappointment him.

This town should be like all the others. Only it isn't. This town has the Androviches, a family who values hard work, honesty, and doing the right thing. And this town has Nick Androvich, the town doctor with a battered heart who doesn't quite trust her, but can't deny the mutual attraction.

Oh, but it's going to get messy when the truth about Alex's real purpose for being in Restalline sneaks out...and the truth always does. But fear not, the town is not going to sit by quietly and watch this meant-to-be-together couple lose their happily ever after...

About the Author

Mary Campisi writes emotion-packed books about second chances. Whether contemporary romances, women's fiction, or Regency historicals, her books all center on belief in the beauty of that second chance.

Mary should have known she'd become a writer when at age thirteen she began changing the ending to all the books she read. It took several years and a number of jobs, including registered nurse, receptionist in a swanky hair salon, accounts payable clerk, and practice manager in an OB/GYN office, for her to rediscover writing. Enter a mouse-less computer, a floppy disk, and a dream large enough to fill a zip drive. The rest of the story lives on in every book she writes.

When she's not working on her craft or following the lives of five adult children, Mary's digging in the dirt with her flowers and herbs, cooking, reading, walking her rescue lab mix, Cooper, or on the perfect day, riding off into the sunset with her very own 'hero' husband on his Ultra Limited aka Harley.

Mary has published with Kensington, Carina Press, and The Wild Rose Press. She is currently working on her next A Family Affair book as the saga continues...

website: www.marycampisi.com
e-mail: mary@marycampisi.com
twitter: https://twitter.com/#!/MaryCampisi
blog: http://www.marycampisi.com/blog/
facebook: http://www.facebook.com/marycampisibooks

Other Books by Mary Campisi:

Contemporary Romance:

Truth in Lies Series
Book One: A Family Affair
Book Two: A Family Affair: Spring
Book Three: A Family Affair: Summer
Book Four: A Family Affair: Fall
Book Five: A Family Affair: Christmas – (2014)
Book Six: A Family Affair: Winter ¯ (2015)
Book Seven: A Family Affair...the saga continues (TBA)

That Second Chance Series
Book One: Pulling Home
Book Two: The Way They Were
Book Three: Simple Riches
Book Four: Paradise Found
Book Five: Not Your Everyday Housewife
Book Six: The Butterfly Garden

The Betrayed Trilogy
Book One: Pieces of You
Book Two: Secrets of You
Book Three: What's Left of Her: a novella
Boxed Set: The Betrayed Trilogy

Begin Again: Short stories from the heart
The Sweetest Deal

Regency Historical:

An Unlikely Husband Series

Book One - The Seduction of Sophie Seacrest
Book Two - A Taste of Seduction
Book Three - A Touch of Seduction, a novella – (2015)
Book Four - A Scent of Seduction – (2015)

The Model Wife Series
Book One: The Redemption of Madeline Munrove

Young Adult:

Pretending Normal